Alexandra Stepp
and the
Summer of Quiet Light

a novel by

Allen Fowler

Cover painting by Elizabeth O'Malley

Off the Common Books, Amherst, Massachusetts

Printed in the United States of America

ISBN 978-1-937146-59-7

for

Georgia

❧ 1 ❧

Tracking

Alexandra stayed on the path, following its large bend deeper up into the trees. Her lanky twelve-year-old frame picked its way along the path. Nearly a year since she had been in these woods, she moved gingerly as if her senses needed to reacclimatize to the forest. Something of the fawn about her movements, timid yet curious. Something of the mature deer as well in her desire to press on.

Certain that her wily older cousin Becca had not simply hidden behind the first convenient tree or boulder, Alexandra didn't waste time stopping to check every possible hiding place. She moved as quickly and quietly as she could. She enjoyed being drawn into the woods with its mix of sunlight, shadow, freedom and mystery. *Like swimming in the ocean*, she thought, all that water stretching out endlessly yet full of the unseen, your own body not much visible past your waist. Here it was much the same, trees in all directions, full of half-seen shapes and shadows, the occasional larger sounds without apparent source. And the different air. Again like the ocean with its clean salty smell, the woody air was an air all its own, moist and rich, full of the smell and release of both the rotting and the new.

She slowed to a stop at a familiar fork in the path and let the memories come. She gathered a handful of light brown hair off her neck and felt the cool air against her skin. She knew exactly where she was. The ground covered in these last few minutes used to take forever when she was a short-legged kid, and this fork represented the difference between being a little kid a or an older one. The path to the left looped back around and down the mountain near the where the Dwyer's drive began. As a child this was the path she chose because it got her into the woods and back to the house in less than an hour. For her first few summers visiting her aunt and uncle, it was the only path she and her dad took. It provided the right amount of adventure with the promise of being back to the safety of the house where Aunt Sue always seemed to have brownies or banana bread waiting on the kitchen counter. She remembered the first couple of times that her dad gave into her pestering calls to venture up the other path, the path that led into the *real* forest. She led the way but only as long as the main path stayed in view. Like going into a cave but only as far as the safety and escape of daylight remained visible. Before she ever lost sight of the promise of a safe return, she'd get hungry or have to pee and they would take the short loop as usual or simply head back out of the woods and through the field, glad for the sight of the farmhouse and the thought of sweet snacks.

Which path had Becca taken? Alexandra asked herself. For a moment, she imagined her cousin sitting on the porch back at the house visiting with her Uncle Cyrus having changed shirts and convinced the adults to play along as if she'd been inside from the start, as if that person on the hill had been a perfect stranger all along.

The shirt was essential to the ploy, Alexandra thought to herself remembering how this game of hide and seek had begun. Having driven up the drive, spilled out of the car, given and received greetings and hugs, Alexandra immediately asked for Becca. Her uncle had gestured up toward the woods, and there at the far end of the field stood a little figure waving a piece of red cloth.

"Where did she find a red flag?" he had asked to no one and to everyone.

"I think it's her shirt," replied her aunt in her most deadpan voice.

"It's going to be a long month, isn't it?" he moaned.

"You have no idea…" sighed Becca's mom then asked, "Alexandra, would you please go tell my fifteen year old daughter to put her clothes back on?".

The logic of the trick proved almost irresistible – make a big show of the red shirt, circle back, change, cajole the others to get on board for the prank – but Alexandra forced herself to move past this impulse to quit so easily. I'm not looking, she thought, I'm not tracking. She looked down both paths and then behind her down the main path that had led her to this choice.

She crouched down, closed her eyes, and slowed her breathing. *I need to see better. I need to be able to track*, she thought to herself and suddenly felt the onset of the shudder, the chill, the light rippling pressure, and when she opened her eyes, she saw the woods around her as she had never seen them. Her heart raced. The gift-vision had finally returned. Everything was doubly lit, once from without by the filtered sunlight and once from within by a light which she did not understand but which Alexandra accepted by the fact that she could see it. She pivoted slowly as if any sudden movement would rob her of this heightened sight, yet her new eyes held.

When she looked back down the path, she gasped. *I'm watching my own footprints disappear*, she thought. And for lack of a more sophisticated explanation, she was. She saw a subtle dulling at each place where she had stepped, a dulling not in terms of how each imprint was illuminated by the daylight but by how each imprint had lost something of the light within. As she watched, each dull impression was slowly reclaiming its interior glow so that the evidence of where she had been faded. She could also see movement as the dulling faded. Clumps of damp leaves were slowly filling back out to their original shape, twigs were unbending, even the bare soil was recovering from the brief impact of Alexandra's weight. To see this kind of detail, Alexandra's sight telescoped out and back in, further back down the path then back to where she had slowed her pace when approaching the fork. The girl's mind could not keep up with what she had to think in order to hold all these images and their consequences grounded in reality. She grew dizzy, brought one hand up to rub her eyes, and sank back off her crouch to sit crossed legged on the forest floor.

What is going on? she asked herself over and over like repeating a mantra. She wanted an explanation to come. She wanted to know why she could see this way. She wanted to know what it meant. She rocked herself gently back and forth, then heard an answer with the aggravating simplicity of some instructive paradox, *What is going on is what is going on.* Within this non-response came the full memory of that February night when she had stepped outside in search of her cat, a night when without a moon the world had suddenly been lit as if from within, a night when even in the dark her eyes found detail. Alexandra laughed to herself.

This soft but sudden sound sent an unwary chipmunk into conniptions and to chirping its alarm from beneath the fallen tree where it now hid. Alexandra drew herself back fully into the present. She rolled and readied herself to track her cousin. She stood up and still grinning whispered to the woods around her, "Nothing hides from me now."

The pulse of whatever it was that conferred this new sight upon Alexandra spread for miles upon miles. For most things living, it came like a flutter, a joyful quickening, like the giddy impulse that makes fawn or colt suddenly leap and skip. Down at the Dwyer's house, both Gruff and Muffin, the two farm dogs, perked their ears and wagged their tails. Soon, however, the joy passed. Like a pebble dropped in a pond, its rippling rings quickly getting lost among the chatter of other little waves and disturbances, the quickening with Alexandra at its center soon dissipated among the swirl of the thousands of other spirits and emotions coursing through the day and was lost – except to one thing.

At the bottom of a cold crater lake something else felt the pulse of gift vision descend. It had felt the same tickle back in February when Alexandra sought out her wayward cat. Now as then, it stirred but did not wake. In the folds of its mind, a mind that had been awake for ages and now had slept for the same, a mind for whom the seasons come and go as tides, it sensed that an old power was back in play. What was curious to the dreaming thing was not the feel of the gift-sight, it knew that feeling well, it knew the exact source of such gifts. What was curious to the dreaming thing was that the gift had found a host, that it had been caught at all, that something had somehow been attuned to catching it. Usually the pulse of such a gift merely coursed through all the little beings now, gave them a slight nudge or tickle and then was lost, but this time the pulse had taken root or was trying to take root. The thing that nestled in the numbing waters decided instead to dream on it, see where this little shudder led, see where this hint of a power past might wander, whether it be toward a fancy that could be forgotten or a concern that called to be answered. Before drifting back toward sleep, the thing rolled, and though nothing on the lake's surface hinted at the movement deep in its waters, two deer that had come to its shores to drink snapped their heads up in unison and, sensing an unseen predator, turned and crashed recklessly back into the woods.

Though her legs were aching to run again, Alexandra did not sprint. Turning, she dismissed the short looping path leading back to the driveway and farmhouse as a ploy that Becca would not have taken. *She'll want me further in, farther up, take me past my comfort zone*, Alexandra thought and in the same breath, *But I'll see you by where you've been long before you ever see me.*

As she moved through this new, strangely lit world, still intent on remaining as quiet as she could, Alexandra scanned the path and the first few feet of forest floor to either side for signs of Becca's passing. Suddenly a thought burst into her mind - *it's the tracking that triggers it.* At this juncture of transition, however, between the Alexandra seeing ordinary daylight as others do and the Alexandra that sees the light-print left by foot falls, the thought passed without much notice. Nevertheless, it had come and hopefully would get filed away in some corner of her mind where in time it might make all the difference.

As she continued farther up the path, she grew more accustomed to the play of light. Like stepping out into the day after being in a movie theater, the initial shock passes and the eyes adjust, so Alexandra's eyes adjusted now. She discovered that the living plants threw off a different quality of light than the fallen trees and rocks, nothing as dramatic as might be suggested by being animate or inanimate, alive or dead. Rather living and dead both shimmered with some similar quality, as if their animation was only a matter of degree. Alexandra couldn't name it. Her mind still raced with the newness of her increased sight, but she got the clear impression that if not alive in the usual sense, everything she laid her eyes on was active. Wrapped up in the chase, however, wanting desperately to uncover her cousin, Alexandra filed this impression away as well.

When the path turned more sharply uphill, she paused before committing to the ascent and took in her surroundings with more care. She watched a group of chickadees flitting down the path toward her. The light they emitted blended with the sunlight so that they appeared in such wondrous detail that Alexandra imagined she wouldn't mind being turned to stone if only she could see and watch such explicit wonder. As she marveled at these twittering little acrobats, Alexandra saw that these creatures imprinted the world in a different way than she did. The imprints of lessened light where they perched and skittered lasted only briefly and with less contrast to the brightened gray hues given off by the bit of branch or bark. *Well, they weigh a lot less*, she thought. But that answer did not satisfy. Alexandra bent for a dead branch and pushed its larger end into the ground by her feet. When she lifted it, the imprint it had made was clear but not because of any shift in how it was lit but because there was a depression now in the ground itself. The wood did not appear to impact the ground the way her footfalls did. *Perhaps weight has nothing to do with it*, she thought. The light said so. The absence of a noticeable shift in light, by the birds, by the branch, suggested that these things landed differently, that they compacted surfaces differently. Perhaps, the girl thought, it was that their touch was more of a kind, that their touch was less foreign than her footfalls.

If the chickadees offered a response, it was both gleeful and fleeting. They skipped over, about, and around Alexandra as she stood mesmerized by the exactness of each feather more fully on view with her new eyes. She watched them until their tiny bodies blended into the other small movements of leaf and breeze then turned to study the path leading up the mountain. Nothing suggested that Becca had stepped here, and she was about to reconsider the possibility that her cousin had doubled back and returned to the house when it occurred to her that she wasn't looking for full footprints but partial ones, small pressure points rebounding more slowly, trace evidence but patterned and equally spaced. As if on command, Alexandra's eyes adjusted in concert with her thinking and suddenly a series of small evenly spaced points of dull-colored grays made themselves plain. The girl's stomach tightened, the hunt was back on.

As she walked on she tried and match her stride to the dull imprints but found it difficult. They were spread quite far apart, and for a moment, she thought she might be following the trail of a much taller person until she realized that what she was doing in stretching her legs to reach each next mark was a kind of loping pantomime of someone who was running. Suddenly it became perfectly obvious, Becca had *run* up the path. Alexandra broke into a run, and as more of the path fell behind her, the evidence of her cousin's footprints became more and more clear. If she could have seen herself, Alexandra would have seen the largest grin ever spreading across her face. For once in her life, she was not to be bested. Becca, for all her woodcraft and forest savvy, left a trail that was getting clearer with every stride Alexandra took. The girl began to sense that she was closing in on her quarry.

Alexandra noticed the spacing between Becca's footprints was growing shorter and shorter. She slowed her pace and shortened her stride to match until she reached a point where she once again simply walked along the path. She consciously tried to catch her breath so that when she stepped up to call her cousin out her success would appear effortless, as if there had been no dash uphill, as if Becca's trail were almost too obvious, no challenge at all to follow.

The dullness of the footprints became more noticeable. Alexandra grew certain that Becca was near. She came to the point where the footprints left the trail and led up and around a large boulder. Alexandra paused and immediately noticed a smudge of dullness on the rock's surface about shoulder high – *a handprint*, she thought letting her eyes telescope in to see the fingers of it.

The only question now was what to say, how to creep up and steal the moment. Should it be casual or loud and bold? Alexandra was about to step off the path and let her victory play out as it would when she heard the snap of a branch on the path below her. Startled, her vision shifted back to its normal caliber. Disoriented she spun to meet the thing that had managed to track her.

ও 2 ৵

Catching Up

Startled by the sudden return of her regular sight, Alexandra froze. Frantically she scanned back down path cocking her head slightly in an attempt to get a better view of what was coming. Unexpected sounds often deceive, coming off as louder than they should, suggesting larger threats. In the woods, the scuffle of a squirrel rooting through leaves can come off like a coyote or even a deer. To Alexandra's mind, the snapping branch that she first heard suggested something of size, so in those first moments of panic when she looked back to the path, she looked higher than she should have. She looked for a human figure, for shoulders and a head, but what had been pursuing her as she pursued her cousin was moving much lower to the ground and with a good bit of speed. It closed within a few feet before Alexandra focused on it and immediately recognized the bounding lope and sloppy grin of Muffin, the younger of the two farm dogs.

Muffin greeted the girl as dogs will with noses to places where one would rather not have a dog's nose go. Alexandra barely had time to pet her before she shook her fur and was off around the rock where the girl knew her cousin was hiding. Indeed, before Alexandra could make any claim of discovery, she heard Becca's giggle in response to Muffin's appearance.

Muffin reappeared around the other side of the boulder followed by Becca in her bright red shirt. Two years older, Becca's face looked more adult. Where Alexandra's face still carried the look of a child, especially in her cheeks, Becca's face had thinned. She strode toward her cousin like a girl who spends a lot of time in the woods off the path. She didn't pick her way back, nor did she bully her way through the underbrush. She glided through fern and side-stepped the woodier growth. The same light brown hair as Alexandra's framed her face, but her eyes shone all their own. Alexandra was jealous of her cousin's hazel-green eyes whose color shifted any number of ways depending on the light. Alexandra shared her father's blue eyes. *Pretty enough*, she thought, *but not pretty like Becca's.* As the older girl cleared the last few feet of underbrush, Alexandra watched the sunlight catch, and Becca's eyes sparkled green like the forest around her.

"So you brought the dog to help you track?" she half-asked, half-stated in her familiar older cousin tone.

It was not a spiteful comment, but Alexandra struggled not to take it that way. She had been robbed of her victory. It was a bitter moment and might have spoiled the day if Alexandra hadn't turned to see the older dog, Gruff, climbing the last steep bit up the path to join them. A farm dog mix of collie and shepherd, her mottled coat of browns and on a field of shaggy white brought a smile to Alexandra's face. The old girl didn't even have the energy the make the last ten feet, and upon seeing her pup, Muffin, and the girl who fed her, and the familiar other girl who remembered to scratch her behind her ears, she figured she'd made it far enough and plopped herself down for a well-deserved rest. Alexandra chuckled to herself, and as she crossed over to say hello to the momma dog, Gruff looked up with her seen-it-all eyes as if to confirm what was already obvious – *When it gets to be too steep, have a sit down and catch your breath.* That's exactly what Alexandra did. She let Gruff sniff her hand then she joined her on the forest floor reaching over to scratch gently behind the old dog's ears. Gruff leaned into the caress while her tail beat a slow but strong rhythm on the ground. This moment of metered peace, however, was short lived. As Becca emerged onto the path brushing herself off, Muffin took advantage of Alexandra's sitting to give her another snuffly greeting, first by sniff-poke-licking nose to nose and then, when Alexandra sputtered and turned her face, sniff-poke-licking her ear.

"Down, you great beast," commanded Becca, and with much less grace than her mom, Muffin dropped to the ground and rolled onto her back nudging Alexandra's leg as if to say, *Get scratching while you have the chance.*

Both the girls laughed, but Alexandra didn't waste a moment giving Muffin just what she felt she deserved.

Alexandra looked up to find her cousin studying her. "What?'

"Did you bring the dogs with you?

"No, I think one of our dad's thought it'd be clever to have them chase us down. Why?" Alexandra asked starting to sense some suspicion on the part of her cousin.

"I don't know. I mean, you were right here," she said gesturing to indicate this stretch of the path. "I heard you coming up the path. Running then walking then stopping."

Alexandra didn't respond. In part she was being coy. She remembered how Becca had a habit of begging a question without actually asking the question. Becca's dad did the same. He would make statements that moved toward a question but would leave the question unstated. More often than not in the silence that followed, someone would look to identify what could have been asked and offer up some kind of response or answer. Such a silence followed now, but rather than suffer the awkwardness that usually led to blurting out some information or admission to fill the silence, Alexandra was able to burn off the little bit of nervousness she felt in petting the two dogs. Moreover, she was trying to decide how much, if any, to confide in her cousin.

This strange sight first came months before during a dark, new-moon night. Back in February, Alexandra Stepp stood by the back door of her father's house trying to coax her cat Boxy back inside. It wasn't yet spring. It wouldn't be spring for another six to eight weeks, but a sudden push of warm air from the south and had delivered a strange balmy day of rain, welcomed warmth, a comfortable quickening to the pulse, and the moist promise of new greens. The burst of thaw emboldened Boxy, and there were simply too many smells packed into the odd dense air for the cat to heed Alexandra's first several calls.

Currently invisible to the girl, Boxy lurked around a large maple sniffing at squirrel scent. Alexandra couldn't see much of any detail in the darkness, and Boxy's figure blended deftly into the already ambiguous shape of the maple's trunk. Once out in the oddly mild air, the initial urgency just to get the cat and get back inside disappeared, and Alexandra found herself in a kind of daze as she let her eyes adjust to the darkness. A breeze pushed through the trees, and looking up, she was greeted by the sky's full host of stars. With no moon they seemed to have multiplied. She spent the next few moments chasing down and identifying the few constellations she knew including Orion and both the Big and Little Dippers. She stood contemplating the stars, reminding herself that their pinpoints of light had traveled for longer periods of time than she had yet to study in any science class, longer than she could honestly begin to imagine, letting herself grow smaller and smaller beneath the great dome of stars.

At twelve these were both old and new thoughts. Alexandra often inclined toward the dramatic, toward this kind of telescoping of significance, the heroines in her early doll play covering the great arc from obscure orphan to world-saving savant. For the last few years many of the characters in her play died only to be resurrected as themselves with the same face and name but changed, new capabilities, new knowledge. She let herself sink inward, let herself grow incredibly, unimaginably small. *A wisp of thought on a mote of a planet*, she thought dramatically.

Such was her mindset when the wind picked up bringing a chilly reminder that winter was not yet done. Suddenly, even as she found herself grasping for a clearer sense of distance and proportion within the great expanse of the night sky, she also found herself simply wanting to pierce the darkness, find the cat, and get back inside to the warmth.

So it happened. With her mind suspended between the great and the small, and with a strong desire to simply see more clearly, Alexandra felt a pulse course through her. She felt herself wobble and struggled to regain her balance. Then as if the new moon had suddenly gone full, a soft light coursed through the world. Alexandra discovered she could see remarkably well. It was not that night had turned to day, nothing that shocking, yet she could see detail upon detail. Her mind expected the light to be projected, but its source remained ambiguous. After several moments of looking around, she focused on a cluster of iris stalks left over from the previous year and realized she could see at each one's tip the dried seed pods flared open. It made no sense to Alexandra's mind that she could see such detail in the dark of night. She pondered the ground where the plant's stems pierced the snow sensing that a secret was hiding in plain view. *There are no shadows*, she realized. She scanned her yard, at the base of bushes, trees, the rock wall, no shadows anywhere. She moved closer to the clump of iris and bent in to examine what she was seeing. Whatever illuminated the seed pods ever so slightly pulsed and wavered.

She stood up and stared around her, still trying to chase down the notion of how it might be that light could come out of things, when her eyes settled on her cat. Boxy still nestled up against the maple, and the cat was looking directly back at Alexandra. The girl found herself thinking, *I can see you and you know it.* Yet before she had time to examine this realization for any significance, Boxy bounded toward her, purring and purring, and the world forfeited its glow. With the cat snaking around her legs, Alexandra found herself immersed once again within an ordinary darkness.

Her second sight was gone. She looked to the irises only to find them flattened to blackness, their stems limited again to lines faintly drawn against the gray backdrop of snow. More than a little puzzled but even more chilly, Alexandra scooped up her cat and carried her into the well-lit warmth of the house.

Nothing had really changed. This vision-sight remained too integral, too subtle, too vague. Keep it close had been the conclusion back in February. Keeping it close was the pending conclusion now. She wasn't even considering talking to her dad about this strange shifting vision, not with him leaving in the morning. She wasn't even sure how exactly to explain what was going on. She might try and tell Audrey, but it would be another week before her dad returned to drop off her best friend, and this was not something she was going to attempt to explain over the phone. And again, what could she say to explain it in a believable way? Without realizing it, the few seconds it took Alexandra to mull this over made her appear resilient to the Dwyer habit of letting others respond to the unasked, so Becca decided to answer herself.

"You seemed to have tracked me pretty well. Either that or you just got lucky stopping where you did when you did and then having Muffin show up to finish the job," Becca offered up happily as she continued to study her cousin. She had learned to read kids her own age. Having grown up in a tight knit community where most parents gave her a pass because her mom taught at the local high school and where her dad, in spite of wanting to be a sculpture, worked as a plumber. So the one knew a lot of their kids and the other had been in most their houses. She felt that she had to work harder to earn a standing among her peers to avoid being dismissed as the golden child. She knew the sound of a half-truth when she heard it, and her cousin was holding something back.

"I think that was it. Me stopping and this clever girl showing up," agreed Alexandra giving Muffin an extra vigorous tickle-rub so that one of the dog's back legs frantically pawed the air.

"Hm."

Alexandra could see that her cousin was still not fully convinced, but she was thankful for a story that was reasonable enough to defend, one that would hold even more water because Becca had been the first to lay it out. If Alexandra had tried to play down the little bit of coincidence that led her and Becca and Muffin to the exact same spot on a very large mountainside, then it might appear that she was trying to concoct an excuse. Having Becca lay it out first gave Alexandra the chance merely to concede. With both her hands nestling warm fur, all of this settled well with Alexandra.

Keep the secret, she thought, *until it makes more sense to me, until it makes sense enough to tell. Maybe run it past Dad first,* and with the thought of that possible reality and her faith in that concrete relationship, she grew calm and resolute. She knew that there was this man back at the house just down this path who would be glad to see her reemerge safe from the forest, who would listen to her – who would listen to her even if she tried to explain what it was she just experienced, who would tease her about it if it didn't manifest itself ever again, but who would not dismiss her because he believed too much in the possible of the impossible. She pictured him reading all those adventure stories to her, his voice swelling with emotion when the action turned dramatic, with a lilt when it got romantic, and with glee when it went comic. With all this in her heart and mind, she realized that while she might find herself alone in this forest, she was not alone in the world. If she had seen footfalls in their fading dullness, then that is what she had seen.

Becca joined her cousin on the ground choosing to sit where she could stroke Gruff, and much to Alexandra's relief, she didn't voice any further doubts or leave any further questions unasked. Instead the girls spent the next half hour catching up on school and sports and the larger issues they expected to face. Like Becca, Alexandra was a strong student which, like her older cousin, was a reflection of her parents. Alexandra's mom and step dad both taught at local colleges, and her, more a journeyman teacher, drifted from high school to high school teaching English and Social Studies. They both grew up around books and teacher-talk of class prep, grading, reading lists, concern about this or that student, impatience with this or that colleague, and the expectation that school was to be both enjoyed and taken seriously from the start. If asked, they would each remember being read to early and often, everything from Dr. Seuss to J.R.R. Tolkien. But their bookish worlds were forgotten as soon as Becca brought up softball.

"Fast pitch?" asked Alexandra.

"Girl," cooed Becca dramatically, "this ain't rec league."

Alexandra rolled her eyes.

"I got better at hitting, but that's about it," admitted Becca.

"Did you ever get hit by a pitch?"

"Once," said Becca looking hard at her cousin, "and I thought I was going to cry."

"Did you?"

"You know how it is. With all those other people. No, I choked it down, but it hurt like hell."

15

Alexandra grimaced in empathy. "I want to play something next year, but I can't decide between softball or track."

"Definitely softball," declared Becca, wondering if her cousin had a similar community of kids to impress. She remembered how much the ball stung her back and how hard she tried to shake it off so that her team mates could see she was for real.

When the talk turned to what they heard on the radio driving with this or that parent to be dropped off at school, they both tried to sound a little more adult than they felt. It seemed to them both that bombs were going off every day but always overseas in places they knew very little about but where they both agreed they were glad not to be living.

Suddenly Becca announced, "I'm hungry."

"Me too," agreed Alexandra.

The talk of hunger with its suggestion of food got everyone moving. The dogs took to their feet and shook bits of forest off their fur, Muffin with a little more gusto than Gruff. Muffin circled around Becca looking up expectantly.

"I said I was hungry, dog, not that I had food," explained Becca with mock exasperation to which Muffin responded with her own dismissive combination of a whine, yawn, and snort before turning and trotting back down the path toward the farmhouse. Becca turned to see if Alexandra has seen this little bit of doggie drama only to find her cousin crouching down, hands on the ground for balance, and eyes closed. Gruff stood by her protectively, looking up to Becca.

"You okay?"

"Fine," answer Alexandra with more confidence that she felt. "I just got up too fast and got dizzy." In truth, she felt tired as if tapping into her sight for just those few minutes had taxed her.

"We need to get you back into mountain shape," asserted Becca, using the term Alexandra's dad had coined years ago to explain why each summer his first few forays into the woods and up the mountain always wore him out. *Not in mountain shape*, he would say, and then, after a couple of days of getting exercise, *Flatlander comin' through.*

Alexandra grinned and stood up with a clear head. "I guess so," she admitted.

"Crap."

"What?" asked Alexandra completely surprised by the sudden change in Becca's voice.

"You're as tall as I am."

"Sorry."

"Well, you ought to be. I'm three years older."

Too wrapped up in the aftermath of the game to notice the change, Alexandra found herself looking directly into her cousin's eyes. Becca shook her head and gave her cousin a more thorough once over.

"You're all leg," she said then added, "and lanky."

Alexandra knew it was true. She had grown a lot in the last few months, maybe as much as an inch, and when she caught a glimpse of herself in a shop window or department store mirror, she thought she looked stretched. *She's more proportioned,* thought Alexandra. *She looks like an athlete.*

Becca looked down at her chest and then over at her lanky cousin's. The younger girl saw the hint of a smirk and felt her face flush. Suddenly self-conscious and looking to turn the subject away from any further examination of her condition, physical or mental, Alexandra asked, "What goodies did your mom cook up this visit?"

"Biscuits, brownies, and banana bread."

Alexandra wanted to counter the smirk but didn't want to hear the comparison of cup size spoken out loud. Becca read the look of consternation on Alexandra's face as confusion about the snacks.

"It's no accident. She's teaching a poetry unit and now bakes with a-litter-something, you know, when all the words start with the same letter. Susie sells seashells."

"Biscuits, brownies, banana bread," repeated Alexandra, letting the awkwardness subside.

"Exactly."

"I got no problem with that."

"Me neither," agreed Becca before adding, "best thing about your visits."

"Thanks."

"No worries," laughed her cousin as she began to lope down the path. Muffin sensed the chance for a chase-race and bounded after her.

"I'll just keep this old girl company," called Alexandra, but Gruff seemed to take exception to being called and *old girl* and broke into a trot of her own.

Alexandra held her pace for a few moments but decided not to let herself play the caboose too willingly. She hadn't expected the need to measure up to Becca. *But who am I kidding,* she thought, *It's all one big measuring up march.* As she moved more quickly down the path, she let her mind empty. She focused on footholds and avoiding the buckle of tree stumps and the larger loose stones. She paused now and again to let Gruff catch up but also to give herself a chance to continue to gather herself. She was beat, her legs felt like lead, her head seemed to float on her shoulders, and she was desperately hungry. She felt a great relief when the path straightened and Becca and Muffin came back into view. Thankfully, they had slowed their pace, and Alexandra hoped to better hide her condition by not appearing to lag too far behind. Soon they all walked in a clump with Muffin breaking off now and again to investigate a particularly interesting scent left by some forest creature.

They chatted again, already comfortable with each other. They both appreciated this about the other, that even though their time together was an annual event defined by eleven months of separation, their friendship felt and therefore was continual. These next few minutes passed with talk of bands and boys, stretches of silence, and giggly bouts of trying to toss bits of sticks at each other undetected. As they approached the main fork in the path, Alexandra felt a small twig bounce off her head, and she turned to find her cousin consumed in the study of the pattern in a leaf she just happened to be carrying.

When entrance to the forest appeared, Muffin dashed off and Gruff picked up her pace to a full trot. With the light of the open field, like moving out of deeper water toward a shore, the pressure and pull of the ocean lessening until ankles could swing free again, Alexandra suddenly felt a lightening of her step but a thickness in her head. It was a sudden rush of mixed emotions and impulses – *Tell this friend about it, get it out there, protect it, keep it close, don't leave it behind, don't lose it, don't ask what it is* – it was a confusing soup of thoughts.

Then they broke into the full light. Alexandra stopped suddenly. Becca turned to look at her. Alexandra seemed near tears then smiled. She skipped up to her cousin, threw an arm around her neck, gave her a quick hug, then playfully pushed her away and dashed into the field toward the farmhouse.

❧ 3 ❧

Stepp 'n' Dwyer's Gentlemen's Kitchen

Once the girls started their race, the hill made it hard for them to do anything but increase their stride and speed which at first was grand until momentum seemed more in control of their bodies than their own legs. The field leveled out just shy of the yard, and both girls used that shift in terrain to slow themselves down and come to a stop. There was a lull in the gasping as the girls caught their breath, and the slight jingle of dog tags sounded off to their right. Gruff emerged from the field about ten yards away, barely acknowledged the coos and kisses from the girls, and simply trotted toward the back of the house where the doggie-door awaited.

"How rude," scoffed Becca.

"And I thought we had a special bond," lamented Alexandra.

"Maybe after the water bowl," added Becca.

"Not a bad idea," agreed Alexandra.

After a few more moments to calm their breathing, the girls circled around to the front of the house, climbed onto the porch and entered to find Alexandra's suitcase and other belongings piled on the first little landing of the staircase, Becca's mom sitting on the couch flipping through a magazine, Gruff settling in for a nap at her feet, and the not so distant sounds of clatter and glee coming from the kitchen.

Alexandra could see something of her dad in her Aunt Sue, particularly around the eyes, not just in terms of their similar blue but in how deep set they were. But Aunt Sue's hair was all her own. No brown curly mess like her dad's just straight strawberry blond pulled back in a ponytail just like Becca's. With her legs pulled up around her on the couch, Alexandra could see her aunt's calf muscles and saw something of Becca's proportions and where she might have come by her athleticism.

Looking up from her reading, Mrs. Dwyer met the girls' eyes with a hint of mischief and more than a dash of stoic patience.

"There are a number of fruit juices in the fridge, along with a pitcher of ice water, and the last of some iced tea. And the banana bread." Seeing the question in her daughter's eyes, she quickly added, "The biscuits are for dinner and the brownies for dessert."

"Not even one?" Becca whined.

Her mother lowered her magazine slightly but a metallic crash from the kitchen and the happy baying of Muffin interrupted her reply. Gruff snapped her head from the ground, assessed the situation, uttered a dismissive *harrumph*, and settled back to her snooze.

"Is it safe to go in?" asked Alexandra laughing.

"Dad started it, didn't he?" added Becca.

Raising her magazine and clearly fighting to control a grin, Alexandra's aunt added, "Apparently your father and brother have decided to treat your uncle's overnight as one long play date,… but since we girls are looking to get a dinner out of it, I figured we could let it ride."

"Who's cleaning up," Becca asked immediately, clearly concerned how the responsibilities might have been divided.

"Oh, I got that in writing before the negotiations even began. The boys make the mess, the boys clean it up."

"Nice, Mom."

"Well, dear, these are the just some of the skills I hope to pass along to you."

The girls laughed.

"Will it be edible?" asked Alexandra sounding genuinely worried.

Her aunt quickly consoled the fears, "Actually, it should all move outside pretty soon. They're barbequing chicken, and I think, boiling some early corn, and so I'm fairly certain we'll be able to eat it."

The girls turned to brave the kitchen, but before they even reached the dining room, the motherly voice called out, "Becca?"

The girls turned back to meet the slight glare of her mother's eyes.

"You look really nice... *in* the shirt."

The girls spun giggling and pushed through the swinging door but could not have predicted the sight that was to greet them upon entering. Alexandra's dad, her Uncle Bob, and his son, Josh, were all busy at various tasks, all engaged in some kind of grumbling, half-articulate speech with a distinct English accent, and all wearing floral patterned aprons.

Tallest by several inches, Alexandra's dad sported the least controllable hair, so no matter how serious he might try to be, it always looked like it had been styled by Dr. Seuss. Shorter, stockier, and with his thinning hair completely under control, Becca's dad might be overlooked but for his eyes. Alexandra loved her uncle's eyes, those translucent hazel, and both Becca and Josh shared something of their impact but watered down. Just as Becca favored her mom, Alexandra thought Josh already looked like he would be more compact like his dad. Though for now, both the girls saw him as all elbows and knees.

Upon seeing the girls, Mr. Stepp began what was clearly a practiced chant in which all three of them spoke in turn from Mr. Stepp to Josh to Mr. Dwyer, and over again.

"Welcome to Stepp 'n' Dwyer's Gentlemen's Kitchen"

"Where we were born to shuck corn."

"And speak like Dickens while butchering chickens."

"I wear the pattern of the lily to avoid appearing silly."

"I the mighty sunflower to... to..."

"As an emblem of my power," stage-whispered Mr. Stepp to his nephew.

"... as an emblem of my power."

"And I the mighty rose in which I blow my nose."

To make matters worse, as each spoke of the pattern on their apron, they turned and curtsied. All the while, Muffin pranced around them either in like-minded support or in the hope that they would drop some bit of food. The girls stood speechless, then as one they crossed quickly to the cabinets to get glasses then just as quickly to pour their drinks. Yet their silence only seemed to invite a spatter of commentary.

22

"Colonel Dwyer!"

"Yes, Major Stepp."

"Lieutenant Joshua," continued Alexandra's dad, pronouncing Joshua's rank with the strong *eff* sound as the British would, "Lieutenant Joshua, reports women in the kitchen!"

Spinning, Mr. Dwyer waved a chicken leg above his head for emphasis, his voice filled with indignation, "Women in the kitchen?! Women in the kitchen?!"

"Shocking, Sir, I agree!" bellowed Mr. Stepp.

"Bad form, bad form!" chimed in Josh.

"Well spoken, boy! Bad form, indeed."

But for giggling, the girls continued to get their drinks without comment, snatch a slice of banana bread, and exit as quickly as they could but not before having to suffer a barrage of *Bad forms!*, a few *God save the Queens!*, many overly-dramatic throat clearings, and one loud and rather random *Pass the marmalade!*

They escaped back into the living room to find Gruff sound asleep and Mrs. Dwyer still reading her magazine as if nothing odd could have possibly transpired. The girls quickly finished their snacks and set the empty glasses on the dining room table with the promise of moving them to the sink once the Gentlemen's Kitchen had taken its business out to the grill. They then gathered Alexandra's things to take up to Becca's room where she would be staying for the duration of her visit. Becca cleared one drawer in her dresser and now helped her cousin unpack her things while they continued to catch up. Alexandra scanned Becca's bookshelves for Manga she had not read and her CD collection for names she knew. Still half-complaining about their similar height, Becca tried on some of Alexandra's clothes. They paused in their talk of favorite movies and whether or not Becca was going to admit to having a boyfriend when they heard the back door open and close several times. They couldn't help but sneak out to the hall window to see if their fathers and brother still wore the aprons. They did.

After a surprisingly edible dinner with the shadows growing long and a cool breeze moving down off the mountain, it was agreed that everyone should take their evening walk along the short loop path. It was chance for everyone to catch up and speak with anyone they had not yet had a chance to talk to. For a time, Mr. Stepp and Mrs. Dwyer talked shop about teaching while Alexandra and her Uncle Bob listened to Josh's description of the latest additions to his collection of some anime inspired gaming cards. All the time Becca walked backwards in front of the group tossing bits of stick at anyone not keeping their eye on her. Then, as if in a game of musical chairs, Josh joined by Muffin dashed off ahead to hide and wait for the rest to catch up, her aunt and uncle snuggled up to each other, Becca recapped the softball season for her Uncle Cy, and Alexandra dropped back to keep the lagging Gruff company.

She also dropped back for the privacy and the chance so see if she could summon her new sight. She knelt down as if to tie a shoe and tried to collect the world around, to feel it compress and then expand, to rise and see those in front of her in shimmering detail. Nothing happened. She listened to their voices moving off, heard her breathing slow, felt an added chill in the breeze as the sun dropped. Still nothing. She opened her eyes to find Gruff only a few feet ahead of her waiting and snapping at a random bug that flew too near her face. Disappointed, Alexandra rose to continue before the group moved much further ahead. Gruff sniffed her hand as she passed and then lollopped in stride beside her. She was deep in thought, analyzing the why's and how's of this strange ability. It had come that afternoon very much at her beckoning, yet just now when tried there had been not so much as an inkling of change, as if in fact she had no control over it at all. Those in front of her were shapes she did not hold in focus as her thoughts turned further inward. Had she thought to count their number, she might have realized they were still short one boy, but she and Gruff were oblivious, comfortable in their slack pace. So Josh's sudden war cry and leaping appearance out from the taller grass of the field took both girl and dog by complete surprise. Gruff spun and sank to her haunches only to fire off a short scolding bark at the boy before ignoring him and trotting up the path. Alexandra jumped as well, then glared at Josh with gritted teeth and a teasing snarled lip.

"Uh-oh," he laughed and ran off.

"I'm here for weeks Joshua Dwyer, weeks!" shouted Alexandra, and for a split second the boy's figure glimmered but the girl fought an impulse to sprint after him, to catch him before he could reach the safety of the adults. Her stomach rolled with something like nerves, something almost like nausea. Then it was gone. He was just a kid running away from the aftermath of a prank, the late sunlight glowing golden on his bare arms. She was just a lanky almost-teen who had lingered too long with her own thoughts and found herself pulling up the rear, alone, the mountain's shadow creeping unobserved across where she had passed.

≫ 4 ≪

The Secret of Two Houses

Alexandra woke with the same thought nagging her mind as when she fell asleep – *Am I making the change happen or is it making me happen?* Ever since she failed to summon the shift in sight during the previous evening's walk, Alexandra's doubts about her role in controlling it ruled her thinking. It had been months since she wandered out into her backyard to find her cat and first experienced these other eyes. Then yesterday in the woods, her new eyes descended like a hammer. *But from where? And how? Maybe it'll be months*, she thought, *before it happens again.*

She had fallen asleep trying to compute the precise amount of time that had passed, at the same time wondering whether or not the moon was in the same phase, and also if she had done anything similar leading up to the shift. She woke to a strange room that quickly became familiar as she listened to Becca's even breathing and immediately found herself focused on the same three questions. Floating between consciousness and the draw of early morning half-sleep, she figured that around five months had passed, that she had no idea what phase the moon was in, and that she had done nothing the same before each event. She had been outside both times, but when she pursued the relevance of that, the extreme differences between time of day and location seemed to nullify any significance.

Her frustration at her situation further stirred her awake. She relived the variation of this same mental chess match back in February after her first encounter with this gift. The questions then came fast and furious as well. *Would it happen again? How does it relate to other changes? What else is going to follow now? What to share, who to tell.*

Now as then, the choices tore at her. Tell her dad, her mom, her best friend, her cousin. Back in February she remembered calling her mom and trying to dive right into the story, but her mother had her own concerns.

"Have you had dinner yet?"

"Not yet?"

"What are you going to have?"

"Pizza," she said and regretted it as soon as it was out of her mouth. She was terrible at the quick white lie, and as she spent the next moments of that conversation trying to counter with the fact that it was a veggie pizza, she decided to hold her tongue about the vision-shift. She let the rest of the conversation drift into small talk and guarded reporting of bed times and homework done, avoiding anything that might put her father or herself further in the doghouse.

The night before had been oddly similar, *the strange dub-looped life of Alexandra Stepp*, she thought to herself. When she finally remembered to call her mom to tell her that they had arrived safely, before she could even try to circle around toward the subject of her shift in sight, the question of the menu arrived.

"Barbeque chicken and corn, and Aunt Sue made a salad," she reported dutifully.

"It's amazing that once you're out of your dad's house vegetables appear."

"Mom!" Alexandra complained playing along.

"It's true," her mother laughed.

In that laugh, Alexandra remembered, came the decision once again to hold her tongue.

She recognized the familiar mix of gut and head, the point where her inarticulate sense, her intuition, mounted until her thinking-self kicked in and made a decision. Even as she let the conversation with her mother last night drift toward its close, relief crept into her chest. Maybe these calls to her mother were never about confiding what had happened – maybe that decision had been made each time once she kept it from her dad. Instead, the calls became about confirming how she had not changed, how she could still negotiate the kinds of conversations she had in either house, confirming how easily she now shifted without losing her sense of self, how well she had mastered the secret of two houses.

For as long as she could remember, Alexandra lived in a maybe-maybe not world. Her parents divorced when she was only three, and since then she had been shuttled between two houses, two bedrooms, two sets of furniture, different kinds of food, different kinds of talk, different kinds of time spent with the other parent and with her stepfather, different qualities of light, sound, and smell, a fundamentally different approach to each place. What does any child do so potentially divided? If she's bright, she learns how to be chameleon, learning what face to show where and when, what to hear and not repeat, what to repeat and not to hear. If she's particularly bright and gets enough love to establish a foothold on some sense of security, she turns inward to find a constancy within herself. And Alexandra was well loved by all the adults with any claim to parenting, so she found in herself a constant that looked to move with greater and greater confidence between her two houses. At first, as with any small child, it had been intuitive, even defensive, to secret this kernel of constancy away for her own best interest. But as she grew so had the complexity of her awareness of the unspoken expectations that were required from her. This was the secret of two houses, how to change to meet and match others' needs and yet remain true to herself, and the tightly linked inverse, how to change her true self so that meeting and matching others' needs required less and less effort and worry from her.

As she had done on that first night, she now sat in the morning's half-light willing her perception to change. As she had seen happen on that first night, she now wanted to see the grays of this room slide toward lit from within. She wanted to be able to manage this new ability toward a new skill. In much the same way as she had managed her two separated worlds – the houses, the bedrooms, the foods, the talk – she wanted to believe that she could and would do the same with this new wrinkle. She wanted to feel more in control, but no matter how hard she concentrated, nothing happened. Then as on that first night, sleep again had its way, and as she began dozing, a series of thoughts poured over her mind's eye, drifting both within reach and yet beyond her full grasp. Back in February no shadows came with the new light. Yesterday in the woods, the new light

28

cut through the sun-made shadows. *What was it with the light and the shadows? Maybe the light I saw was already there.* Had she been more fully awake she might have thought *sight cast no shadows*, but instead she slept and dreamed of other worlds, all full of well lit, predictable detail.

❧ 5 ❧

What Wakes in Dreamtime

She woke again still harassed and befuddled by doubts only to hear the sounds of movement in the kitchen and the smell of coffee. She roused her cousin and they headed down to join the others.

"I like this hotel," cooed Alexandra as she sat down. She looked over a table filled with dishes offering scrambled eggs, sausage, muffins, fruit salad, and yogurt. "How come you never put out a spread like this, Dad?" she asked sweetly.

"I do, dear… it's just that by the time you get to the table, your cat's eaten everything and all that's left is a single bagel."

"How is Boxy?" asked her Aunt Sue.

"His mass has begun to affect the tides," answered her father flatly.

"Don't be so mean, Cy," scolded his sister to which both the girls and Josh giggled.

The conversation died down as the various dishes made their way around the table and the eating began in earnest. As Alexandra buttered a second muffin, she watched her dad drain his cup of coffee and the restlessness emerge.

"Alright, Sis, can I help clean up?"

"Oh, Lord, he's got the willies! No, you get on the road, I've got this ragamuffin you're leaving behind to do the dishes."

Alexandra squealed her displeasure and moved toward her dad with her arms outstretched.

"Sorry, ragamuffin, you're on your own," teased her father skipping toward the living room.

Alexandra caught up to him on the front porch, and following several hugs, the predictable last words about best behavior and following directions, and the promise to return in two weeks with Audrey, Alexandra's dad stepped toward their car. Then he paused, and as soon as she saw him swing one arm up slowly, she knew what was to follow.

"Dad," she warned but to no avail.

"So long, farewell, auf Wiedersehen, goodbye,
I must return… to a cat…
That's very, very fat."

"Dad!"

"Good… bye," he sang as he sank into their car and pulled away. She watched the car follow the bend of the drive, disappear, then reappear smaller as it drifted along the main road.

"Ragamuffin niece!" cried her Aunt Sue from somewhere inside the house.

Whatever lingering concerns Alexandra had about her second-sight faded in the face of the Dwyer day. There was laundry to be gathered, schedules to coordinate, Mr. Dwyer got a call about a possible plumbing job, Josh had a soccer game, the dogs needed feeding, and on and on. Alexandra was happy to be in the middle of the bustle. She sometimes tired of being an only child and loved the feel of chipping in with the chores, hearing the thanks from her aunt or uncle, anticipating a squabble between Becca and Josh, listening to why she should take one or the other's side, watching it work out and being privy to the peace – simply being in the mix. Early on after her parents split up, the summer visits here kept her wishing for more family. When her mom remarried, she thought maybe there would be a sister or brother, but that hadn't happened, and her dad just never seemed much concerned about finding anyone else, so over time Alexandra resigned herself to being an only. She grew more competent with the role she played in each house, and let these dreams of a larger family fade. In fact, for these last few summers, she found herself glad to return to the quiet of her other homes, but not always at first. At first it was too much like having left behind your new best friends from a favorite summer camp.

The day wound down to another home cooked meal with Alexandra helping chop vegetables and set the table. Before dessert and the dishes, there was a pick-up game of ultimate

Frisbee, adults against children, with Muffin as designated monkey-in-the-middle, and Gruff as audience until another snooze seemed more promising. They played until Becca's dad complained that he was having trouble seeing the Frisbee. They all headed in for a late dessert. Then by the time the dishes were done, Mrs. Dwyer announced bedtime, and the girls followed Josh upstairs.

Already Becca's room was taking on the look of a dorm with a second mattress along one wall, a dresser drawer half pushed in draped with a discarded first and second choice shirts, magazines open, and a small stack of books by the head of each bed.

"I like our little nest," proclaimed Alexandra.

"Me too!" Becca quickly agreed then just as quickly added, "Which means we have to keep Mom out of here and the Josh from ratting us out."

"No Aunt Sue, no Josh," confirmed Alexandra with a salute. "What about Uncle Bob?"

"The Dad dares not enter where women rule," added Becca dramatically as she flopped down on her bed to watch her cousin root through a drawer of colored t-shirts. She still stewed over Alexandra's height, so she played back in her mind the times during the game of ultimate where she had bested the younger girl.

"You gonna wear this one tomorrow?" asked Alexandra holding up a light blue shirt.

"Maybe. Is there another one you could choose?" answered Becca knowing that she had no intention of wearing that particular shirt.

Alexandra shrugged and refolded the top. "I have one or two I brought," she added quietly.

"We better get the light off before Mom comes up."

Alexandra nodded and busied herself getting ready for bed. Once her eyes adjusted to the dark, she studied the dim shapes in the room, the geometry of the posters and pictures, the odd forms of draped and discarded clothes. She found Becca sprawled on her back on top of her sheets, her elbows splayed as she rested her head in her hands.

32

"Will you know a bunch of people at the lake tomorrow?" Alexandra asked, a little worried that she would find herself on her own, abandoned by her cousin in favor of her school year friends.

"Don't know… but don't worry," she added, feeling a little guilty for denying her cousin her choice of shirt, "I'll hang with you no matter what."

"Thanks, cuz."

"Solid," snapped back Becca.

Both girls burst into giggles then tried to outdo the other in shushing themselves. Alexandra fell asleep thinking of how things might have played out differently that first day if Muffin hadn't caught up with her in the woods.

Usually Alexandra was a sound sleeper, but an unfamiliar bed in an unfamiliar house kept her mind more alert, so when Becca stirred and opened the door to the hallway, Alexandra rolled over to see what was afoot. A band of weak light from the hall sliced through the room. Becca heard her roommate shift and turned to see if she had been seen.

"Gotta pee," was all that Becca's silhouetted figure said as it disappeared into the soft light of the hallway.

Alexandra rolled back over, and as her eyes quickly sought to recover from the shock of even that little bit of light, the after image of Becca's figure began to fade. Settling back into the rhythm of own breathing, Alexandra drifted in that moment before sleep where sense and nonsense commingle, where randomness rules, and disconnect seldom disturbs. *Carrying shoes*, thought Alexandra as her cousin's silhouette pulsed one last time. *Carry shoes to the bathroom*, followed the next thought but without the question mark it might have carried. *At campgrounds carry shoes to bathrooms*, came the answer though no question had really been asked, and that was when Alexandra decided not to fall back to sleep so quickly. *We're not camping*, she thought with more consciousness and her breathing changed. Her body pulled in a deep breath, the rush of that oxygen denying sleep any further hold. *Who takes shoes to their own bathroom?* And with this question mark, Alexandra sat up and listened, for two minutes, for five, for nearly ten. No water ran, no floor board popped, no door opened, either down the hall or to their room.

Before she thought to ask herself if she should follow, Alexandra dressed and collected her own shoes in hand. She paused at the door as her thoughts caught up with her, and she became fully aware that she was getting ready to stick her nose in where it didn't belong, nevertheless her hand still reached for the door. She passed the dark bathroom with its door ajar, then scanned the living room for Becca's shape, but the couch and chairs were empty. She surprised herself how quietly she made it to the kitchen where Gruff and Muffin waited with tails wagging as if a quick sneak was a nightly event. She petted them both then tested the back door. It was already unlocked which she immediately reminded herself was unremarkable out in the country with dogs in the house. She held the screen door as the air escaped from that contraption to keep the door from slamming and let its clasp click quietly into place. At the base of the back steps the dark expanse of the fields and mountains loomed and the potential guilt of her actions knotted her stomach. She wondered what she might catch Becca doing. *Well, what do you think you'll be doing in three years?* she asked herself then immediately wondered what she was supposed to do if she did catch Becca, and then what Becca would think of her if she found out she'd been caught. *And she will find out*, Alexandra had the courage to admit that much to herself, *People always find out.*

Yet before she could gather her conscience to contribute to the decision, it happened.

It came this time with her eyes open, no little drama of crouching to summon it, and the compression-expansion happened quickly like a pulse or a quake or a thud her body felt but did not hear. She watched the fields and mountain shift to their other light. They loomed less and welcomed her more. She could see no threat, blackness became gray, the once continuous mass of darkness shifted toward individual shapes, bushes, trees, rocks – just as in daylight. Though not as boldly lit or colorful, everything was distinct. As she acclimated to her replenished sight and her eyes fell on the yard, the questions of consequence for what she was about to do faded then disappeared altogether.

A clear set of footprints led away from the house, their dullness growing less distinct as the time passed but as yet still clear to Alexandra. Unlike that first day in chasing Becca into the woods, this time Alexandra felt no rush, no worry, no fear of a false trail. As she stepped off the steps into the yard, she knew with certainty that she could find Becca, that if she wanted, she could creep up on her, tap her on her shoulder, and whisper *boo*.

What Alexandra did not see, what no one saw as Alexandra's vision changed, as that tiny quake shook her in a way she assumed was specifically internal, felt by her but invisible to others, was how both dogs in the Dwyer's kitchen snapped their heads up. Muffin pranced to the back door and crouched down on her front paws, rear end sticking up, tail wagging, eager for the game to begin. Gruff too sat up and beat the floor with a happy tail but soon felt the spark move away, intent on some other task. Looking at her daughter, crouched and eager, she dropped back to the floor and blew a short muffled bark as if to say, *Don't you wake this house.* Muffin dropped her hind quarters but remained intent on the door. Even when she let herself drift toward sleep, the younger dog's body sensed that something marvelous was afoot. Her ears proved the most reluctant to let that something go, refusing to relax, staying pricked for any sound. And though sleep won out, Muffin's dreams were filled with marvelous chasings.

The dream for the thing in the pressured cold of a lake bottom were not so fanciful. All cultures give name to that which lives by malice, that which intentionally harbors and nurtures evil. The thing stirring in the ice cold silt of this lake was such a thing. In this region, before other names for it were imported, this spirit was called *Matchi Manitou*, by some of the tribes of the Northeast. Sometimes a twin, sometimes a lesser brother to the great creator spirit, the great gentle spirit known as Gitche Manitou, Orenda, Ha-wa-ne-u, and Earth Holder. One account tells of how the Great Mother who gave birth to all forfeited her life in bringing these two forces in to the world. The great gentle Manitou was to be born first, but the jealous darker brother could not bear this and tore out of his mother's belly to try and claim the larger influence in the world. And because Matchi Manitou first touched so many places, he doomed his better brother to the fate of forever trying to reclaim a greater influence.

The thing at the bottom of the lake was not the full manifestation of pure evil but more like a small tentacle of this Manitou's layered reality. In fact, this particular tendril of Matchi Manitou barely stirred, thinking to itself how the pulse was, after all, still slight, and having focused on in it dream-time, its receptacle smacked of a two-legger, probably a mistake, a convergence of unlikely impulses and equally unlikely capacities. The Manitou thought that if the human persists in its willingness to let this gift-sight take root, then perhaps this age of sleep must be disturbed, if only to scratch this little itch away.

ॐ 6 ॐ

Joy Discovered

The night world lay before Alexandra in all its muted richness. With only a thumbnail moon, she relied on her eyes to discern subtle details, and they did. The mountain read like a roaming buckle of velvet, individual trees now and again catching what little breeze there was to sway and shimmer in paler shades of gray. The tall grasses and wildflowers through which she waded mirrored the night stars in how she saw their tufts and petals glimmering. It was as if she were walking through the Milky Way, and for an instant, when she looked up to see the real thing, she felt a slight wave of vertigo as if suddenly hung upside down, as if she were standing in the night sky looking from above at a field glittering with the flowering stars of her own vision. She laughed and then half-sobbed and then laughed again. She watched insects flitter and glow, all were now as fireflies to her eyes. Wiping a large tear from off each cheek, she allowed the joy to seep deep within her, at the same time as she acknowledged that none of it was really her doing. She let the question come, *What is happening?* and she let it remain without forcing an answer. She looked around her and took in a landscape charged with light, lit by the shimmer of a million tiny movements.

As she brushed her hand along the bearded tops of the tall grass, the quality of light left by her touch enchanted Alexandra. Though the effects of her touch, the dulling of an otherwise sustained glow, did not linger long as she toyed with the grass, she marveled in the fact that she mattered at all, that with her new eyes she could see that when she walked through this world she left a kind of wake. She studied the effects of her hand. The lighter the contact the shorter the span of dullness. She started making patterns with her hand, circles and swirls, then watched the various grays rebound to their original shades. She reached out, gathered a clump of fern, gently squeezed it, and set it loose. The aftermath of her touch lasted much longer, and she was still studying the pace of all this dulling and re-illumination when she noticed the tracks she had left, how much more clear they were than anything she had caused with the touch of her fingers. She bent and placed her hands on the ground, kicked her feet up into a quick handstand, then sprung back to see the result. Clearly two handprints dulled the grass more persistently than any brush or grip she had applied to the grasses and plants, but they still read differently than her footprints, yet not because of shape. As with her earlier impression, she felt it had more to do with the nature or quality of the thing making contact rather than weight. She remembered the birds' touch on the branches, the pressure from the branch she had pressed into the ground, and her footsteps. She wondered over the difference. She looked down again at her own path, a meandering line where the shimmer had been stolen and now was being replenished. Before she could chase this new thought, she suddenly realized where she was and remembered what she was supposed to be doing. She came out to follow Becca.

She took in her location and discovered that she had wandered into the field on no particular bearing. She had drifted to the South and East rather than in the Northerly direction Becca's tracks first led. For a moment her heart sank with the thought that Becca's trail had most likely gone cold, but with and odd determination, almost of as if her legs were making the decision rather than her head, Alexandra fixed on a point that she felt would intersect Becca's trail and started walking. She still walked with her hands brushing the top of the field grasses gathering some kind of energy from that contact, all the while her eyes scanning the ground in front of her in order to pick up on any hint of Becca's path. She decided that if she didn't find any indication of where her friend had passed, she would circle once back toward the house. But this strategy proved unnecessary. Almost as soon as she finished making the backup plan, Alexandra stumbled across a pair subtle imprints evenly spaced. She turned to her left and saw a few more clearly leading in a straight line away from the now distant Dwyer farmhouse. She had found Becca's trail.

Alexandra wasn't sure how much time she had spent simply relishing her heightened vision before she turned her attention back to finding her friend, and now she wasn't sure how long she had been following Becca's trail. The Dwyer's house was nowhere to be seen. It now lay hidden behind the slow bend of the hill leading up into the trees and the mountain. Becca's path kept to a fairly consistent line about thirty or so feet from the forest's edge which relieved Alexandra because even with her improved vision she didn't relish the idea of wandering into the woods by herself at night. However long it had been, the tracking got considerably easier as the evidence of Becca's footsteps became more and more obvious. With the ease that came with simply following an obvious path also came the chance for Alexandra to think more carefully about just what she was doing. She realized this was no midnight stroll for either of them. Becca was clearly going somewhere. Her footprints were evenly spaced and did not seem to wander much which suggested she both knew where she was going and was walking a familiar course. This idea prompted Alexandra to question her motives in continuing to follow Becca. At first it had been merely a matter of curiosity, then wonder at the shift in sight, then simply the challenge of being able to find Becca's trail, but now she had to admit to herself that she was sticking her nose into someone else's business. And Alexandra knew that such a course didn't always work out well, but here she was, and the trail was as clear as a bell, and perhaps most importantly Becca would be doing the same if the situation was reversed. All these excuses, however, failed to fully convince Alexandra that what she was doing was really alright.

She slowed her pace, came to a stop, and let the freshness of her sight become the focus of her mind again. She was now far from familiar sights. She could see the lights of a few houses across the valley lining the bend in the river and the river itself. At this distance, too far from it to see it with any detail, she saw how it had a shimmer to it completely different than any of the land life. For an instant the pull of the river became all she felt.

To see it more closely, to see its grays, to see the light carried in its current was all she suddenly wanted, but her feet refused to move. Alexandra looked down as if to ask them what the problem was, and when her eyes left the distant sliver of water, the hold it had on her dissipated. Alexandra felt both a sadness and a relief, the intensity of which made no sense. She closed her eyes and fought back a sob and let the confusion in, *What is going on?... Why am I crying?*

Then aloud with eyes shut, hands cupping her cheeks and eyes, "Get a grip, girl. Middle of nowhere... Not ready for water. Look at the field again. The mountain.... Land."

Immediately, her breathing slowed and her body relaxed. She dropped her hands, reopened her eyes, and stood amazed, as if she were seeing with her new eyes for the first time all over again. Everything was hers to see, steely grays glowing and details down to the antennae on a beetle just before it took flight. Looking down for some new tiny aspect of the world to examine, she saw how much more distinct Becca's trail pulsed, as if suddenly fresh again. Alexandra was just beginning to rethink what she had said before reopening her eyes – the water, the land – to try and figure out what could have contributed to this renewed vision when she heard the voices. Most likely it was a shift in the wind, but with the way her senses and emotions where jumping all over the place, she couldn't be sure. She stilled and looked again at Becca's trail and realized that for the last ten or so yards the distance between imprints increased and continued to increase as they moved off in the direction of the talking. Becca had begun to run. What Alexandra couldn't know was if her cousin sensed her coming and started to run to escape or had she been running toward something all along. A short sweet laugh broke out from the direction of where Becca's trail led. Alexandra moved along that trail trying for as much stealth as she could muster. When she crested the next slight rise, she could hear bits and pieces of conversation much more clearly, even to the point of catching a few distinct words... *don't you dare... did to... never mind then...* and the laugh again, Becca's laugh.

Alexandra crouched and put her eyes at the level of the field grasses to try and see any bodies or head that broke that imaginary plane. Nothing. Then another giggle and a short deeper laugh that was definitely not Becca's, and Alexandra saw them. They sat on the rounded top of a boulder of eight or ten feet high, and they faced away from where Alexandra crouched. She recognized Becca from her silhouette, and the boy she was with looked about her size, so Alexandra assumed he was around Becca's age. Alexandra smiled to herself to think of her friend sneaking out to rendezvous with a boy in the middle of the night. None of the boys Alexandra knew were yet worth losing any sleep over. The two figures leaned into each other then pushed playfully away, and as if she had been pushed as well, Alexandra suddenly became acutely aware of the intimacy she was watching, of the fact that she was no longer tracking but spying, of how invasive her eyes were in a moment designed to be private. Almost before she could finish this thought, the boy turned and looked in her direction. She couldn't make out his face but could tell by how his position changed that he looked, if not directly at her, then within only a few feet either side of where she crouched. Now Becca's figure turned as well. Alexandra was sure she was caught, when slowly the boy leaned in and appeared to kiss Becca's exposed cheek. This impression was confirmed instantly when Becca nearly pushed him off the rock. She ended up having to grab his flailing arm to keep him from a fall. Their laughter rang out as they settled with both their backs once again toward Alexandra.

The younger girl took this opportunity to retreat, admitting that she had no business here. Whatever the original reason for following, the gut curiosity of it, then the wonder at how she could see, and then the thrill of the tracking, it had never been about Becca's safety. Alexandra hadn't come out here to rescue anyone. Maybe she should have never followed the trail to its end, and now she knew something that Becca hadn't willingly told her. *Easy enough to sit on that juicy little tidbit*, she was telling herself when she heard the voices once again behind her but this time too clearly. *He's walking her home!* Alexandra panicked. She was still protected by the slight rise in the field. Neither of them were visible to the other for another few moments. Two options seemed available – she could head into the woods and wait for them to pass or she could try and out run them. She looked toward the woods. Even in the shimmering grays of Alexandra's sight, they loomed a little too darkly. *Forget that*, she told herself. Decision made, Alexandra broke into a sprint.

If they see me, they see me, she thought to herself as she gained speed. She was running with some confidence when she nearly tripped. As she regained her balance and stride and she also changed the style of her running to a kind of sporadic, loping gate. It wasn't that she said to herself *start loping*. It was more like she told herself to *run right*, and for her in this moment in the night fleeing from being discovered that meant a loping gate where her feet no longer dragged through the tall grass but landed and pushed off quickly, where any tangles that might trip were avoided, where she could change course suddenly by simply pivoting off one or the other foot. Without thinking it, without realizing it or trying to manufacture it, she found herself dashing deer-like through the fields and with greater speed than she had known. Had she thought about it more carefully, she would have been surprised with how quickly the Dwyer house reappeared, but her sense of her speed was easily hidden behind the fact that she had walked when going out and run when coming back. So of course the house would come into view sooner on the return trip.

When she reached the short grass of the yard, she stopped to catch her breath and to try and get a sense of how close behind Becca and her friend were. They were nowhere in sight or in hearing. Alexandra crossed to the back door pausing again to try and calm her breathing. She turned the handle as quietly as she could and stepped back into the still warmth of the house. Gruff looked up from her sleep, slapped her tail once on the linoleum floor and dropped her head back down. Muffin, who had not moved from her watch on the door, needed to rise to avoid being bumped as it opened and so was up and anxious to be acknowledged for her sleepy diligence. Alexandra gave her a loving rub around the ears. Removing her shoes, she made her way back up the stairs, hoping no boards creaked too loudly, hoping no one was crossing through the hall to or from the bathroom. Only when safely behind the mostly closed door of their bedroom did Alexandra start to feel as if she had pulled off a successful adventure. She quickly got out of her clothes and into her bed to wait for Becca's reappearance. She turned away from the door so it would be easier to pretend to sleep, but real sleep came before she could ward it off. She never heard her cousin return. Instead Alexandra dreamed rich dreams in which she was two footed but moved with the balance and speed of a four footed creature, in which she could see for miles and miles with great detail, in which she ran and ran and ran until she came upon an impassible river that appeared to both flow and not to move. In her dream, she stood and stared at the water puzzled by how at times its surface seemed to skirt past with great speed while its depths remained still, and at other times, its deeper waters tore through its channel while its surface remained both pliant and immobile. As with many dreams, while dreaming it, at some level, Alexandra knew she was in it and of it. As with many dreams, she would have no recollection of the experience when she woke.

❧ 7 ❧

Truth Will Out

The next day looked like it would play out as if nothing odd had happened the previous night, as if Becca had never snuck out, Alexandra had never followed, as if neither knew about the other. The sounds of the rest of the family and the smell of pancakes and sausage roused the girls awake. As they moved sleepily into their robes, Alexandra kept waiting for Becca to let something slip about being tired after not getting much sleep, but the only comments they exchanged were about each other's bed-hair. Breakfast came and went, and Becca's family seemed none the wiser. Alexandra detected no side glances between the adults, and Josh offered no blackmail proposals based on having heard them sneaking out or back in. By the time the girls went up to get ready for their trip to the lake, Alexandra began to contemplate the hope that she had gotten away with it all, but her conscience nagged at her to be certain. As they changed into bathing suits and decided on the clothes they would wear over them, Alexandra tested the waters.

"I had the weirdest dream last night about wandering around outside but can't remember any of the specifics."

"Me too, except all I remember is that my dream was about having this really weird girl come visit for a month... Oh no, wait, that's not a dream, that's actually happening."

Alexandra held her side as if sore from laughing while Becca giggled to herself.

"Are you wearing a two piece or one piece?"

"One piece," answered Becca with a good amount of emphasis. "Too many boys, too many eyes, and there are too many older girls prancing around in their bikinis already."

"Me too. It's all Dad would let me bring."

"Yeah, well, there's that too."

After they helped carry the cooler, towels, and other day-at-the-lake supplies, but before they were allowed into the car, they were required to slather on the sun screen under the watchful eye of Becca's mom and the hyper commentary of Becca's dad.

"Sun block and vater. Sun block and vater. Hit zee tops of your earz, girlz, and behind zee kneez, lotz on the snozzles and the tender skinz around the pitz of zee armz."

"And your bald spot if you have them," added Mrs. Dwyer much to the amusement of all the kids.

"It is not a bald spot. It's where my tremendous brain activity has burned off my hair," replied Becca's dad in a mock sob and abandoning his accent.

It was during the last scramble for the almost forgotten – water for the dogs, books to read in case of boredom, Josh's goggles – that Becca's dad stuck his head out the back door and asked about the garbage.

"Leave it for now. We'll add the day's trash to it. One of the girls can run it out later." called back Becca's mom, then while it was still just the three women around the car, added, "And if you forget, one of you could always snag it on your next midnight excursion."

Alexandra and Becca stared at each other. Alexandra felt the color drain from her face, in no small part for being discovered by her aunt, but in much greater part for what the comment might reveal to Becca. But before anything else could be said, Josh leapt from the house, goggles in hand, doors were locked and all were ushered into the car.

It was a short trip to the lake which wrapped around the base of a mountain and had a small man-made beach at one of its narrow ends. Even though it was still before lunch, the parking lot was already half full. Clumps of families and friends dotted the shore, the few predictable couples off to themselves, grandparents with zinc oxide noses and large sun hats, toddlers in their swimmies, and every age in between. The multicolored and multi-patterned umbrellas, chairs, beach towels and swimwear made it all look as if some large piñata had exploded around this end of the lake. The Dwyers staked out their plot of sand between two other families. They unpacked and settled in for a day in the sun. As they helped unpack and arrange their day camp, the girls continued to catch the other's eye and then to avoid it so as not to seem to be staring. It was some time before they found themselves able to escape Josh's company and swim out to the floating dock.

There were other older kids there as well, but Alexandra and Becca found a corner and turned their backs to the others, to the beach, and settled into an awkward silence.

Becca spoke first.

"Mom doesn't miss much."

"I can see that now."

Some part of Alexandra wanted to apologize immediately, but another part of her held that impulse in check, so she let the silence play out again waiting to see just how much Becca either knew or suspected. She found Becca was pretty good at waiting as well.

After a time which was probably shorter than it seemed to either girl, Becca offered a further observation.

"You couldn't have been right behind me."

"I wasn't... I... It took me a little while to figure out that you wouldn't be taking your shoes with you to your own bathroom."

"You saw that."

"Yep."

Becca pondered a number of responses then offered, "Well, I don't know... Josh's aim isn't always the best."

"You know, I really don't need to hear any more details on that," Alexandra blurted out as both began to laugh, but as soon as they started to calm back down, Becca was ready with the next question.

"Did you follow me?"

Sensing a keenness to Becca's curiosity, Alexandra's mind raced to settle on the right response and offered back a vague explanation.

"I wandered mostly."

"Did you try to follow me?" Becca snapped back not wanting to let the point go.

"Yeah,… eventually, but it took me a while to figure out the whole shoe carrying thing and then to get dressed and then to really decide to sneak out, so by the time I got out back, it'd been at least fifteen or twenty minutes. You were nowhere in sight."

"But you found us… me… you found me."

"Eventually."

Becca let Alexandra's explanation sit for only a moment or two before launching back into her inquest.

"You tracked me at night with almost no moonlight?"

Alexandra let the question hang while she desperately tried to see her way clear around letting on just yet about her shifting vision.

"Did you find one of our flashlights?"

Shaking her head, Alexandra admitted that she didn't have a flashlight, but before Becca could draw a more complete picture of how Alexandra had followed her or fire off another question, the dock rocked noticeably as several boys clambered onto its surface like a group of seals.

They gathered in a small circle jostling each other and smiling at themselves in recognition for having apparently caught most of the others on the dock by surprise. Alexandra noticed that Becca didn't turn back right away and then with a quick shoulder bump whispered that she'd be right back. She got up and crossed to an empty portion along the edge of the dock and dropped her legs back into the water to dangle. Almost instantly one of the boys broke off from the pack and settled in next to her. There were a few hoots from the group, but a quick glance back by the boy sitting by Becca cut short any further teasing.

Alexandra turned herself slightly so she could watch from the corner of eye. She focused her gaze on a middle distance out on the lake so that she could concentrate on the forms in her periphery. She noticed that they sat a little too stiffly as if not completely sure how to be together. Then he leaned in to cup a bit of water and must have splashed her legs because she snapped and waved one hand as if in warning. After that, they both relaxed, and immediately Alexandra tried to not let herself admit that she was now watching again the same couple on whom she had spied the previous night. Yet even as she kept her gaze out on the lake, she watched him lean back to face her after hearing something Becca had said, she knew the truth. This was the same couple. Alexandra looked over to satisfy her growing curiosity to see them together in the daylight only to find the boy staring at her. She met the boy's stare with her own hoping that if she appeared more confident and less guilty she would start to feel the same way. He had dark brown eyes and darker brown hair which was cow-licked from the water and wind. He was thin like a lot of boys who haven't started filling out, and with him sitting she couldn't tell how tall he might be, but it didn't seem he was much taller than Becca and therefore not much taller than her. He wore an odd expression, neither grin nor grimace, but a look that with a little more effort might have become half a smile. He mumbled something to Becca as he turned to look back out over the water, and she turned her glance toward Alexandra. With an ever so subtle roll of her eyes, she gently gave her head a little twitch, both to beckon Alexandra to join them, and from Alexandra's perspective, as if to say *Let's get this over with.* Alexandra rose and crossed the few feet to take her place by her friend.

"This is Will."

"Hey," said the boy leaning up to look at Alexandra directly again, only now with more obvious expression of amusement.

"Hi, I'm Alexandra."

"Yeah, I already told him."

Alexandra heard the comment knowing it meant her name but probably also meant that Becca had told him more as well. The three of them sat rather stiffly and in an ambiguous silence for a time.

"Must not be completely pale," said Will flatly out toward the lake.

"What does that mean?" snapped Alexandra. Even though she'd been found out and even though she was nervous as to how she might now be treated, included or not included, she wasn't going to sit quietly by and let herself be ridiculed quietly.

Perhaps sensing Alexandra stiffen even further, Becca quickly spoke up, "Will's mostly Abenake."

"Western Abenake… and Seneca"

"Alright, mostly *Western* Abenake."

"…and Oneida."

"Okay."

"… a little Huron, we think."

"Enough. He's a mix of tribes and like me… is curious how it is that you were able to find us," said Becca.

As she went on to explain that Will was learning a lot about his family's history from a certain uncle, Alexandra watched Will sit a little straighter and tilt his chin a little higher. It was a subtle shift, not like the boys who boasted with each other over some sports feat or new bike or which girl they were convinced now liked them. She was trying to chase the difference down in her thinking when two interruptions came.

First, Becca finished her comments with, "So we were both wondering how you found us that far from the house on a night with no real moonlight and how is it we didn't hear you coming?"

And second, a ball came skidding across the water in front of them and bounced off the wood of the dock. All three looked back along its path to find Josh treading water madly and smiling at what an accurate throw he had just made.

"What!" exclaimed Becca.

"Lunch!" yelled Josh right back at her before turning and swimming toward shallower water.

Becca reached out, grabbed the ball, and hurled it at her brother. It skipped off the water in front and off to the left of his path. He stopped, treaded water again, grinned and waved teasingly with just his fingertips, then continued on, changing his course to retrieve the ball. All three teens stood, and Alexandra watched as Will straightened up to his full height of at least half a head shorter than Becca. He didn't read that short, however, something in the way he looked at Alexandra made the fact that he was having to look slightly up at her irrelevant. There was a frankness to his eyes. They didn't waiver, they weren't shy or unsure or insecure, they simply watched. With eyes like that, Alexandra thought, who cares how tall you are.

"I'll find out more," Becca assured Will, and then she dove gracefully into the water.

Alexandra was about to follow as fast as she could when Will's voice stalled her.

"You know, I knew you were out there."

Alexandra looked into a pair of eyes full of frank curiosity and replied as evenly as she could, "Yeah… I saw that too." She turned and dove welcome for the water's encasing pressure and silence.

Had she lingered a moment longer, she could have watched Will's brow furrow as he puzzled over her admission. His words had been a bit of a brag aimed at throwing her off her game, though he still wasn't sure what that game was exactly, but her blunt admission that she saw him look for her confused him. He had only turned because of a gut feeling and had seen nothing. Come to find out, she was actually there, maybe only a few feet away. His face tightened a little more as he told himself, *This is not something Uncle's going to want to hear, that some Pilgrim crept up on me.*

Alexandra, however, was oblivious to the consternation she had caused as she burned off her nervousness in trying to match Becca's pace. About half way back to the shore, she pulled up to catch her breath, realized she could touch bottom, and decided to wade the rest of the way. By the time she reached the beach, Alexandra had calmed her breathing and her nerves. As she splashed her way through the last few steps, she quickly assessed what had almost happened. Josh's appearance had been a godsend really because it stalled her having to talk in any specific terms about how she had been able to track Becca. If she was going to continue to play around with her newly discovered ability, she was probably going to have to come clean about it to someone. And soon. Becca though, for all the friendship they shared, was not the person Alexandra wanted to confide in first. She really wanted to run it past Audrey, and that meant keeping Becca's curiosity at bay until this weekend when her dad and Audrey came up for their visit. Maybe if she apologized for the sneaking around, for the spying, which she knew she should do anyway, that might both satisfy Becca's bruised feelings and distract her from too much further questioning. When Alexandra reached the Dwyer's little camp site, however, Becca shot her a glance that suggested to Alexandra that any plan of stalling was not going to work. It was a glance that older girls had been shooting at younger ones since the beginning of time, full of judgment and condescension. And even though Alexandra knew this, recognized the glance in all its charm, she couldn't help but wince and worry.

As soon as Becca's mom distributed the sandwiches and the drinks, Becca sidled up to her cousin and indicated that they should find some place private to eat. But before Becca could steer Alexandra clear, her mom spoke up.

"Was that Will out on the dock?"

"Yes, Mother."

"I'm just asking. Did you introduce him to Alexandra?"

"She did," chimed in Alexandra hoping that any help she could lend Becca now would build up some good will in the more pointed conversation she knew was coming once Becca got her on her own.

"Boyfriend," sang Josh following it up with a series of exaggerated kissing sounds.

"Josh," interrupted his dad, "in about three years we'll be doing the same to you."

Josh made a face as if he had just had to swallow a mouthful of sand and fell silent.

"What did you think, Alexandra?" continued Mrs. Dwyer, intent on getting some kind of news.

"He seemed really nice," offered Alexandra, still hoping to curry favor with Becca, but her cousin appeared unswayed by these little shows of support and looped her arm into Alexandra's and led her off toward an unused picnic table further down the beach near where the sand ran out and the grass and trees began. They both looked out over the water to see the group of boys with Will still at the dock taking turns diving or cannon-balling into the water.

Between bites of sandwich and sips of juice, Alexandra fielded Becca's questions mostly by repeating her story that there was a lot of luck involved, which she thought there was. The more she heard herself explain her success as a consequence of luckiness, the more she began to believe it rang true enough. She hadn't asked for this strange talent, she still didn't know when it would manifest itself, so she continued to feel completely lucky in having it pop up and stick around long enough to work in her favor.

Alexandra heard her cousin's skepticism falter, so she spoke up hoping to take advantage, "Look, I never imagined you went out the front door, so I went out the back. Then it's either left or right. Left loops you around front. Not likely. Straight ahead puts you in the woods. Less likely. So I chose right and out through the fields along the forest's edge. Eventually anyone would have come across you two on that boulder."

Becca chewed her last bite of sandwich and waggled her head as if to concede the point. Sensing a chance to redirect the focus, Alexandra asked about Will. Becca admitted to liking him a lot, that they had several classes together, that they had started to talk even more now that school was out, and that though they had tried three other times, they had only met up once before at night because one or the other's parents had heard them or hadn't yet gone to bed. Alexandra was amazed. She didn't admit she was amazed, she tried to keep her reaction as deadpan as she could, but in her mind she worked to imagine sneaking out of either of her houses in the middle of the night to meet a boy and it didn't seem possible.

Still trying to keep the conversation focused on Becca and Will, Alexandra pushed on, "It's cool you're... you're...," she stumbled over the right word. "Are you dating?"

"We're just hanging out," Becca assured her friend.

"It's cool you're hanging out with a... a...," again the right word seemed tricky. "Do you call him Native American or what?"

Becca laughed and almost choked on her sandwich. "I call him, Will. But he calls himself an Indian. He says... or really

I think that it's his aunt and uncle who say that Native American is as much a made-up label now as Indian was back in the day."

"There's another odd term… aborigine… no, wrong continent."

Becca nearly spit juice out her nose, then came to Alexandra's aid, "You mean indigenous?"

"Yeah, that's the ticket."

"Indigenous peoples…, yeah, that's in the mix too. But not for Will or his family, they calls themselves Indians. Less bookish, I guess."

"Are they into all of that stuff… I mean their own stuff?"

"Like what?"

"I don't know, I mean, Dad and I have driven by places hosting pow-wows, drumming circles, camping out."

"How 'bout you talk to Will about what he's into. I tell you this though, he's wicked smart about the woods. His family's been in these mountains forever. He knows all about these trails and streams. He's been all over these mountains since he was a kid." She paused. "I think that's what made him so curious about what you pulled off. I think he thought only someone… from his… clubhouse could sneak around like that."

Still looking to avoid having the conversation turn back toward her, Alexandra suggested another swim out to the dock, and both girls looked out only to find it deserted except for a couple of older high school or college kids. Alexandra watched Becca scan the shore, but the boys were gone.

"They never stay long. Come down, see who's here, split," she said, the disappointment clear in her tone.

Nevertheless, now with the weight of their secrets off their chests, the girls enjoyed the next few hours swimming, playing monkey-in-the-middle with Josh and his mom, sunning and snacking. They helped pack up and headed home listening to an almost constant barrage of hilarious descriptions from Mr. Dwyer regarding how sand can find its way into the most inconvenient places on a person's body. Dinner consisted of leftovers as they all made plans for the coming weekend. Alexandra's dad and best friend, Audrey, were to roll in sometime late Friday afternoon and stay through Monday. Mr. Dwyer solicited menu choices from Alexandra, but she didn't have much to offer because, like herself, Audrey would pretty much eat anything once. Just before the girls cut out to head upstairs, they found themselves alone in the kitchen with Becca's mom.

"Listen you two," she began with the same tone kids have heard from their mothers the world over, "I'm not giving you permission to keep sneaking out, but be smart and be safe."

The girls nodded and tried to make a quick exit.

"Becca."

Both the girls froze and turned. Mrs. Dwyer let the silence linger.

"Yes, Mom."

"Meeting boys is off the choices of things to do at night," she waited only a beat, "Do you hear what I'm saying?"

"Yes, Mom."

The girls turned again.

"Oh, and Alexandra…"

Alexandra's heart was in her throat.

"… if you do go out, remember the garbage is under in the sink. Becca will show you where it goes."

"Yes, Aunt Susan."

The girls barely held off their giggles before they got out of the room. They scurried upstairs, brushed their teeth, and shut themselves in their bedroom. They recapped the day, relived the conversation they had just had with Becca's mom, talked a little more about how well Audrey would fit in with their days then fell into their own thoughts. Alexandra listened as Becca's breathing sunk into sleep. Audrey was on the way, and that meant she could get this secret out and off her conscience. It would mean coming clean all over again with Becca, but she would figure that out later.

As Alexandra's body gave in to its own fatigue, her thoughts took her back to the dock that afternoon and the boy with the clear, calm eyes. What was it he had said about her? That she wasn't completely pale. *I must remember to ask Dad something.* She called to mind how he sat right up when Becca talked about his tribes. *He kept listing all those tribes. Something about Grandma Stepp. Something about her Great Grandmother's dad.* She watched him sitting up again, tilting his head back, but not much, only slightly, yet didn't the smallness of the movement make it all the larger? *Smaller is large,* she thought. *More within than without,* she thought. *Within can be huge,* she thought and drifted away.

❧ 8 ❦

Tents and Trees

The next few days were misty and damp. The girls and Josh spent their time indoors helping clean in between watching DVDs and playing marathon sessions of various board games. After a good bit of debate and rechecking of the forecast, it was decided that Mr. Dwyer would find and drag out the larger tent and the girls would camp outside for the weekend. At first Mrs. Dwyer thought they would do better spread out around the living room, but once it looked like the skies would clear and the overnight temperatures would warm up, she gave into the repeated request that they be allowed to pitch the tent in the back yard. Once the decision was made, Alexandra saw the wheels inside Becca's head spinning. They were both calculating how much easier it would be to sneak away when you were already outside.

For a time however, the tent stayed hidden. Mrs. Dwyer had been sure she had last seen it in the barn, but Mr. Dwyer and Josh returned from their search empty handed. They proceeded down into the basement only to reappear gilded in dust and draped with cobwebs and still without a tent. With a shrug of their shoulders, the two started to try and clean themselves off.

"Josh, not inside," scolded his mom, "Both of you out. Robert!"

When Mr. Dwyer heard his full first name, he snapped to attention, lunged at his boy, picked him up like a large sack of dog food and made for the back door. Josh screeched and Muffin came prancing in to join the fun. Mrs. Dwyer crossed to open the door and looked sternly on as the two started to pass. Just before crossing the threshold, however, Mr. Dwyer paused and pretended to pick a speck of something off his son's dusty southern end and daintily dropped it on the kitchen floor. Mrs. Dwyer spun, snatched a roll of paper towels off the counter, and bonked her husband on the head. He did a perfect imitation of Josh's earlier screech and disappeared out the door. From the back yard, as they continued to dust themselves off with overly dramatic gestures and much coughing, Mr. Dwyer warned that if no tent could be found then the living room would have to be turned into a bunk house. The girls looked at Becca's mom.

"Oh, for heaven's sake. Becca, grab a flashlight," her mom directed. Then she turned and gave Alexandra a wink, "Let's show 'em how it's done. Gruff, get that mouse!" With the promise of a mouse hunt, the old dog scrambled to her feet and joined the rest of the women on their march to the barn.

"Out of the way dust boys!"

"Did you hear what Mom called you?" teased Josh.

"She was looking at you, son. I believe she was looking right at you," countered Mr. Dwyer.

The girls passed them by without so much as a glance, and Muffin, sensing a better game was now afoot, loped around the girls to see what Gruff might have to say. It seemed to Alexandra that Mrs. Dwyer had a particular nook to seek out and check because she crossed through the first part of the barn where most the miscellanea was stored, dust coated coolers, outgrown bicycles, discarded but salvageable furniture. She crossed out of the light offered by the large doors and headed toward the steps leading up to the loft. Gruff and Muffin crisscrossed the dirt floor of the barn in pursuit of scent nearly colliding with the girls more than once. As she and Alexandra moved to join her mom in the climb up to the loft, Becca switched on the flashlight she had brought. Instead of taking to the steps, however, Mrs. Dwyer skirted past the makeshift banister and motioned for her daughter to hurry with the flashlight.

"Swing it in behind the steps for me, dear."

Becca did as instructed. As the beam of light moved along a path from immediately underneath the first few stairs across the space that extended back toward one corner of the barn, Alexandra could see any number of boxes and crates draped in plastic. Gruff appeared to sniff along and between the boxes, quick and efficient, sniffing once or twice in each crevice, blowing her nose clear then moving on to the next. She outpaced the light, finished her searching, and was gone. Becca was moving the beam out from the corner toward the back wall of the barn when her mom called out.

"There it is. Keep the light right there. Alexandra, we're going to pull this plastic off. Watch for spiders."

"What!?"

"Quick now. Don't think about it."

"Yeah, don't think about," giggled Becca.

When the plastic had been pulled away, Mrs. Dwyer grabbed a loop of what looked like an oversized athletic bag and dragged it free. She had Alexandra pick up the opposite end and help her carry the tent out of the barn into the afternoon light. Ever hopeful that any discovery would involve a treat for her, Muffin pranced around the tent as if it were a large chew toy. Alexandra watched Mr. Dwyer's face change from a smug look of *I knew you wouldn't find it* to one of mirthful defeat.

Quickly pointing to his son, he said, "I told him to look there."

"Look where, Dad," spoke up Becca.

"Where ever it was you found it," he barely had time to say before being attacked by Josh.

"Set it right down here, Alexandra. Thanks," said Mrs. Dwyer and then turned back to her husband and son who were still locked in their mock battle. "Now you two. Bob leave the poor boy alone," she continued despite her husband's look of despair at the false accusation, "Since we completed the finding, you can complete the pitching."

Before Josh could muster the breath to protest, Alexandra and Becca both offered to help Becca's dad – Becca because she wanted to preempt her brother's inclination to find rocks to hide under other people's portion of the tent and Alexandra because she was genuinely curious as to how this compact bag was to be transformed into their sleeping quarters. She followed her uncle as he looked for a good spot. Becca brushed past her and gave her arm a squeeze.

"Not too close to the house, Dad. Alexandra said she wants it to feel like we're really camping."

"Maybe just a little more toward the field," Alexandra chimed in.

"But from here, girls, you'll have the back door light to keep you company."

"We'll have flashlights, Dad."

"We'll have flashlights, Dad," he sang right back at her much to Alexandra's amusement. "Fine," he conceded, "let's just pitch it out here with all the snakes and the scorpions..."

"Such a drama queen," interjected Becca.

"... and the pterodactyls..."

"The what!?" laughed Alexandra.

"No, Dad, we want to face the mountain," explained Becca pulling at the tent to turn its entrance away from the house.

"To increase the illusion of being out on our own," added Alexandra waving her hands about as if she were performing magic.

Her uncle stopped and stared at her. "What an odd niece. Could we just get this done? I hope a pterodactyl builds a nest right on top of it.

"Ooooh. Baby birds," squealed Becca.

Mr. Dwyer shot Alexandra a look which she met with a cheesy grin.

Less than an hour later, the girls were rolling up flaps on the meshed windows and securing the zipper on the entrance screen in order to air out any remnants from the Dwyer's last camping trip. They just stepped into the tent to get a feel for its space when a shadow darkened the entrance.

"Just so you know that I know, all this chatter about *creating the illusion of camping*," Mr. Dwyer began waving his arms in much the same way as his niece had done, "All I can say is you better not cross your mom by pulling some stunt." Becca started to protest but her dad cut her off with, "Save it, sister." He held her eyes for a moment, relinquished a slight grin, then disappeared letting the sunlight spill into the tent.

Becca looked at her cousin and shrugged her shoulders. They listened to his footsteps moving away through the grass. Then silence. The girls held their breath.

"Ooooh. Is that a pterodactyl?"

"Dad!" cried Becca, but the only response they heard was the sound of the back screen door swinging shut.

Both the girls enjoyed sitting in the warm musty confines of the tent. It was like an instant clubhouse, and even though they would never have called it by such a name, it held for each of them a sense of separation from the norm and also a feeling of seclusion. When the world quieted, when no sounds came from the house, doors closing, voices calling out to some other, no traffic was passing up or down the road, it was as if they were miles from anything or anyone, completely on their own. In one such moment both drifted into their own thoughts. Becca imagined what it would be like to live in a cabin out apart from the rest of the world. *Would it be this lovely? Would it be lonely? Would she be sharing it?* At the same time, Alexandra pursued her own concerns, working through various strategies of how to first tell Audrey and then Becca about her new sight. *Maybe if I can get her out here alone when they first arrive, maybe Becca will be called in to help with some chore, help get Dad's digs set up? But I don't think I can get through it quickly. I'm going to need to lay it out in pieces in order to make any sense of it.*

In the midst of these thoughts, Alexandra felt a shudder and turned to look at her friend. Rather than seeing her lit by daylight, she saw her as if in shadows. This time the pulse failed to bring her gift-vision. It felt the same but the details that should have shimmered in their heightened tones of gray darkened instead. Becca's figure no longer sat in a tent under a sunny sky but in shadows. It was as if she saw Becca in a cave, and then came a flash of déjà vu leaving Alexandra even more puzzled. Alexandra had never seen Becca in a cave. Alexandra had never even been in a cave herself. She couldn't remember having seen any movie or TV show in which a girl looking like Becca was stranded in a cave. *So why the déjà vu?* she asked herself. Still mesmerized by the oddness of the moment and perplexed by the implications of this waking vision, she did not realize that Becca had turned to face her. Then for an instant, she did, and she saw Becca gaunt and sad and fearful. Then in a flash, all of this was gone replaced by the common light of the Vermont sun and the smirking face of a healthy, bemused, and wary Becca.

"Are you there, Alexandra?"

"What? Yes. What?"

Becca laughed and rolled onto her side. "Wow, you were far, far away, my little friend," she said playfully in a scratchy witch's voice.

"Sorry, I guess I cut out there for a moment."

"Becca?" came the call from Becca's mom.

"We're coming! We're coming!" responded Becca then, turning back to Alexandra, added, "Let's go get the sleeping bags before she sends Josh out to find us... or worse... help us."

Alexandra got up to follow still haunted by her vision of Becca alone in a cave. For the first few moments after emerging from the tent into the open air, she trailed along behind her cousin as if in a trance, still trying to chase down what might have led to the sense of déjà vu. She couldn't remember any visits to any caves, and though she had read plenty of stories involving caves and seen movies with scenes set in caves, she couldn't reconcile Becca's appearance in such a setting, so thinned down and haggard. Within the few feet leading to the backdoor, however, the mundane immediacy of gathering the supplies for Audrey's visit, pushed these other odd concerns from further exploration.

After several trips between the house and their tent, the girls launched into making plans as to how best to settle in. First, they decided on the sleeping arrangements. Becca suggested that the three sleeping bags could parallel the three sides of the tent so that the entrance and the central space were left open and clear. Then they began to discuss what snacks would be necessary and whether or not a makeshift table should be introduced for eating, reading, and playing games. They were just moving onto issues of little brothers and security when what Alexandra thought sounded like a combination of a warthog suffering a severe cold and a coyote plagued with a toothache interrupted them.

"Josh!" screamed Becca, and the gargled braying stopped, replaced by a choked giggle and the sounds of a hasty retreat. "We can't discuss issues of security if we're being harassed and spied upon. Quick. With me," she whispered harshly, spinning and lunging for the tent's exit."

"Where are we going?" stage whispered Alexandra already caught up in the new game.

"To safety. Flee while you can, girl. Flee," giggled Becca. "But keep low and run."

Alexandra followed her friend in a dash up and across the field leading to the woods but not on the expected line toward any usual entrance. As they ran crouched over trying escape undetected, Alexandra realized they were simply heading into the woods at what appeared to her as a random point. In full but awkward bent-over stride, Becca turned to speak but in turning lost her footing and took a spill.

"Jeezlepete!" she screeched laughing.

Alexandra squealed in delight as she flew past her fallen friend.

"You're not supposed to leave a wounded comrade behind, you fiend," barked Becca as she regained her feet. Then in a whispered cry, "Get behind the first tree you can."

Alexandra made the fringe of the woods only a few moments before the older girl. Both bent over laughing and catching their breath. Running uphill while crouching down took a lot more effort than running downhill in full stride.

"Behind a tree, girl, behind a tree!" commanded Becca suddenly switching back into character as the escapee.

Alexandra did as she was told but still bent over and taking huge gulps of air. "Were we followed?" she whispered.

Both the girls peeked around their trees to answer the question for themselves. Josh was nowhere to be seen. The field flowed out, away, and down toward the tent and house, clear of any little brother's bobbing head. Becca motioned to Alexandra to follow her.

"It's just over here," asserted Becca as if Alexandra knew what she was talking about.

They moved in a path paralleling the fringe of the forest for only a few strides before Becca drew her friend's attention to a makeshift ladder leaning against the mottled trunk of a large sycamore tree.

"Safety," sighed Becca with dramatic relief.

The ladder was crafted from a long plank. *Something from a construction site*, Alexandra thought, *like the boards used for scaffolding. Pilfered from her father.* Other pieces of scrap wood were nailed to it at even intervals providing a series of steps. Becca took to the ladder like a girl who had climbed it a hundred times before. Near the top of the plank, which Alexandra noticed bowed under the shorter girl's weight, Becca stepped onto a fat sturdy branch of the tree. In a quick few moves, she reappeared at least ten feet higher, wedged comfortably on a branch and against the main trunk.

"Come on up. We have a perfect view should anyone decide to try and track us."

"But what if…"

"Just come on up," insisted Becca before Alexandra could complete her doubtful thinking out loud. "You'll see where to step before you even get to the top of the ladder."

And indeed, she did. Before she reached for the last nailed-on rung of the bowed and bouncing ladder, she found herself in easy stepping range to a branch wider round that she was. Free of the wobbly wood and physically aware that her weight didn't even register with the tree, she began her ascent. Without fully considering what she was doing, simply looking to appear too timid in front of the older girl, she climbed. The hand and foot holds seemed to appear as a matter of course, and the next thing she knew, she was up in the tree sitting on a branch opposite Becca.

"This is where I almost came the other day to hide from you. But I didn't think I could get to it and up in time to see whether or not you had seen me. So I decided to hoof it deeper into the woods," Becca explained, and then after only the slightest pause added, "but a lot of good that did me."

When Becca turned her head to see what reaction her last little comment might have elicited, she had her attention redirected by Alexandra's frantic gesturing toward the house. From their perch, both girls could see the full expanse of the field down to the tent, the house, and beyond, but what caught Alexandra's attention was the small figure emerging from the southern corner of the house, a little brother, unmistakable even at this distance. Both girls sat mesmerized as they watched the boy pause and move, pause and move, in what he clearly thought was a series of masterfully stealthy maneuvers until he reached a corner of the tent near the entrance. After only a few moments like a cat gathering itself to lunge, he sprang toward the screened doorway. The banshee cry he wailed in tandem with his lunge took a few moments to reach the girls in their perch, and when it did reach them, it sounded oddly frail and screechy. They burst into laughter then just as quickly silenced themselves, but what sounded loud to them died out long before it could make the return trip back across the field. Unwittingly, Josh provided the two girls with several minutes of what came off as well-mimed disappointment, confusion, and defeat. First he poked his head into the tent to confirm that it was, in fact, empty. Then still thinking the game might be afoot, he dashed back and forth around the tent, randomly switching directions, cutting back on his own circling in the hope of catching the girls at the same. Next he crouched and disappeared from sight below the line of cover created by the field grass, but the girls could follow his progress as his little head popped up again and again to scan for movement in the field. Finally, with visible disappointment, he turned and trudged back toward the kitchen door and disappeared into the house.

"Aww," giggled Becca causing a flutter of jealousy to pass through Alexandra's stomach.

She had no one to tease in either of her houses. *Well, there's Dad,* she thought, *and Mom… and my step dad tries, but they're not a kid brother or kid sister.* These were quick, familiar, and fleeting thoughts. Alexandra drowned the flutter as she often did by jumping back into the present moment. "This is a great spot. How long have you had it?" she asked as if to suggest that Becca had recently had this massive tree erected like some kind of summer cottage, but Becca answered in the same spirit.

"This is like the third year. I couldn't get up it for the longest time until I swiped a fat plank long enough and scrounged for the steps. We can go higher if you want."

"I'm good here."

"You can really see stuff from up top," added Becca but without any taunt or insistence in her voice.

"No thanks... I really like it here."

"Me too,... and look there," she said pointing to third branch a little forward and down from where Alexandra sat, "for your friend when she's with us."

Alexandra's stomach fluttered with pleasure. That comment made Audrey's imminent arrival and potential inclusion real. "You'll like Audrey."

"She sounds pretty cool..."

"And she'll love it here..."

The girls sat for a time following their own thoughts and listening and half-listening to the sounds that reached them. Depending on the presence and direction of a breeze, they could hear traffic passing or could watch it without hearing it. They could hear the forest sounds, the scatter of leaves as squirrels traced the floor, the sporadic pitched alarm of chipmunks, the crack of a branch giving way to decay, the call and response of any number of birds, the flowing whisper of the trees as a wind took to its chosen course through the mountains. Two tall fir trees framed the sycamore in which they sat. With both set back into the woods slightly, it was as if they cupped the sitting tree, and when a particularly concentrated burst of wind moved along the forest's face, these two firs caught it and spoke it to the girls surrounding them with the long crisp whisper of its word. Drawn from her musing by the intensity of the sound, like sitting in an amphitheater simultaneously shushed by all in attendance, Alexandra turned to look at Becca who she found was already looking at her and nodding her head.

"How 'bout that," she said with a clear sense of pride almost as if she could somehow take credit for the experience.

"That was awesome," agreed Alexandra.

"This is my whispering tree. I come here sometimes when I know it's going to be windy just to sit in the middle of what you just heard. It's like you're hearing the biggest secret that ever was... and even if you have no idea what it is,... you know you're hearing it."

"It's exactly like that," agreed the younger girl.

"It's a good place to let a secret go too...," began Becca before pausing.

Alexandra watched her friend staring into some middle distance. She waited.

"... with a good wind and the trees like they were just now, I've let out a few serious gems," she finished and looked back to Alexandra. "It's like the trees make it all right to speak them out loud. It's like they take them and pass them along but from then on in a language no one will understand. They take them and keep them safe out in all this open."

When she finished she held onto Alexandra's stare for a second longer than seemed needed until the younger girl turned her gaze back over the house and toward the valley. They drifted into their own worlds again. Becca recounting some of the secrets she had felt better about for letting out into the world while perched in her tree. Alexandra just beginning to consider what she might say aloud given the chance.

❧ 9 ❦

A Song, a Secret, and a Sneeze

Alexandra sat on the porch listening to snatches of traffic hum past and the lonely silences between. Up in her room sitting in front of her computer, Becca surfed for new favorite videos, Josh sat in his room with the dogs, in the living room Mrs. Dwyer was reading, and her husband was out on another emergency call, something to do with a wedding ring and a garbage disposal. Alexandra grew tired of beating herself up with scenarios of how her attempts to come clean with Audrey and Becca about her shifting sight were doomed to failure. Each imagined attempt started well enough but got derailed by visions of skepticism, disbelief, by her inability to summon this skill, self-doubt, and inevitably, ridicule. Alexandra's mood blackened with each subsequent daydream. She began to contemplate not coming clean at all to any of them when she heard a car decelerate, listened the gravel of the Dwyer's drive crackle, and noted the chuff of a familiar engine. All thoughts, black and bright, left her mind as she watched her father's car roll into sight presenting her with a view of two of the dearest people in her world. As the car rolled nearer, Alexandra began to sense the mischief. Even from the top of the porch steps, she saw conspiratorial mumblings and the looks of glee passing between her father and her friend. The car barely rolled to a stop before the two of them leapt out from opposite sides and burst into song, each taking solos and joining together as a chorus depending on the lyrics.

Alexandra, Alexandra, Alexandra,
She's not a peach or a pear or a panda!
She's my friend, she's my pal,
She's my buddy and my daughter…
And just like us, she's reconstituted water!

Alexandra, Alexandra, Alexandra
She's not a carrot or a parrot,
An onion or a shallot,
And she's years away from any official ballot.
Alexandra, Alexandra, Alexandra,
She's not too spicy, she's not too blanda!
She's her friend, she's her pal,
She's his daughter not an otter…
But even so we still gotta wonder
What's she doing reconstituting all that water?

They delivered this last line facing the mortified Alexandra, with great gusto as both performers dropped down to one knee, their arms raised and spread and hands wavering in their best attempt at a cheesy Broadway finale. Before she could grasp the oddity and horror of what she had just witnessed, Alexandra felt the comforting arm of her Aunt Sue circling her shoulder.

"I could have them arrested," said her aunt calmly.

"I think that would be best for all of us," agreed Alexandra.

Just as Audrey and Alexandra's dad were rising to their feet, Josh and Becca emerged from the house. Sensing the need for an encore performance, Mr. Stepp cried, "One more time!" but was waved down by Audrey who was no longer as keen to perform in front of the new audience, most of whom she didn't know. Hugs were delivered and introductions made. Audrey and Becca had heard a lot about the other from Alexandra. And while both were glad to finally meet, both were still a little intimidated by the other and remained a little reserved. Becca was relieved to find that she wasn't going to have to look up to Audrey as well. Yet while Audrey was the shortest of the three girls, she carried herself with confidence, and her dark brown eyes were both sharp and warm. For her part, Audrey was simply glad to be out of the car and didn't try to get too much of a read off Becca just yet. Not wanting to waste a minute now that her friend had arrived, Alexandra quickly suggested that she and Becca show Audrey their sleeping arrangements.

With sisterly cunning, Becca immediately turned to her little brother and asked, "Would you like to come too, Josh?"

Josh went a little pale, spun on his feet, and dashed back into the house.

"Run, boy, run. Save yourself!" encouraged Mr. Stepp. "But I'd love to join you," he then offered up to the girls with mock sincerity.

"Dad, make yourself useful and unpack the car," fired back Alexandra.

"Now, see, that's the loving voice I've so missed."

Alexandra's only rejoinder this time was her back and the giggles as she and her two friends rounded the house to head toward the tent. Mr. Stepp waved away the chore of unpacking until some future time and looked to his own little sister to join him on a quick stroll to work the car trip out of his legs.

Each of the girls welcomed the tour of the tent. It gave them something to focus on while they figured out how this new mix of personalities would look and feel. The girls gave Audrey first choice of sleeping bags, and while she tried to defer, slightly unsure if there was an advantage to one or other of the locations, an advantage unknown to her but already discussed by these other two. In the end, she opted for the middle one which stretched beneath the back window directly across from the entrance. Becca plopped herself down on the one to the left, Alexandra on the one to the right so that her head would be nearest Audrey's, perfect for quietly sharing their thoughts. Audrey didn't immediately take to her would-be bed but instead pirouetted.

"I can't sit down yet," she said executing another turn.

Becca was back on her feet in a heartbeat, "We could take her to the tree."

"We could," agreed Alexandra, "It's this great…,"

"Sycamore," filled in Becca.

"… up on the hill. Perfect limbs for sitting and watching," Alexandra finished thinking to herself, *and for sharing secrets.*

"Let's go," agreed Audrey.

Becca led them through the field up the hill away from the house. Instead of heading directly toward the tree as they had the day before, they headed toward the main path. They talked of videos they had seen, songs they knew. Soon they were in the woods taking the fork to the left as if to troop around on the short hike ending back at the Dwyer's drive, but about two hundred feet down this path, Becca took another sharp left.

"See this split pine?" she asked her two friends. They both nodded at her gesture toward a pair of pine trees that shared a trunk. "About ten feet in," she continued ducking under some brush, "there is another path I've cleared that'll lead us right to the ladder."

Within a few steps after mimicking Becca's bobbing and weaving through the undergrowth, they found themselves standing upright and on a narrow trail following Becca in a slow arc back downhill. Just as the forest began to thin, Becca dashed ahead and took to the ladder. Alexandra offered Audrey the chance to follow, but she indicated that she'd rather watch so see how it was done. With some familiarity but not as confidently as Becca, Alexandra climbed the ladder. When she stepped off onto that first main branch, she waited for her friend. Audrey climbed right up trying to appear more relaxed than she felt, not that she minded heights, but she felt the eyes of those above. Her dancer's coordination served her well. Her physical grace frequently offset her tendency to imagine how others judged her.

"Just step out here when you reach me. It's easy going, big limbs from here on," Alexandra assured her.

"Got it," replied her friend glad not to feel too much on her own, and when she got to where Alexandra had been, she realized with her sure footedness that the tree was infinitely more solid than the bowing and bouncing ladder. She scrambled past the other two. Her lithe body moving branch to branch as if she were being poured upward.

"Whoa!" cried Becca clearly impressed.

"Squirrel girl," cooed Alexandra, and Audrey felt a flutter of pride in her stomach.

Audrey chose a branch several feet higher than the branch originally designated as hers and found herself almost directly above Alexandra sitting on her branch as if riding it side-saddle so that she faced the same direction as the other two. All three girls sat looking out across the valley. Assuming the overly pleasant voice of a bus tour guide, Becca talked about what they could see, which direction her school lay, where the road rejoined the highway, where the river narrowed and a set of rapids began. In the spirit of the moment, the other two girls *Oooohed* and *Aaaahed* appreciatively. Becca turned their attention to landmarks nearer their location when they all three heard voices somewhere along the path below them. Instinctively, they grew silent and gleefully threw each other hand gestures to try and agree on exactly where these other people were. Suddenly one of the voices broke out in a laugh and Alexandra immediately mouthed the words *my dad* to the other two. Becca nodded vigorously and responded with a silent but overly dramatic mouthing of *and my mom* so that both Audrey and Alexandra almost burst out laughing. All three struggled to stifle their giggles as the now familiar voices passed below and behind them along the path toward where it exited out into the field above the Dwyer house.

Once the voices faded either from the distance or because of a shift in the breeze, Becca offered up a suggestion, "Let's climb down and follow them, or better we could circle round and meet them."

"Or we could let them go for a bit, and then I could track them," blurted out Alexandra.

"We could see how close we could get to them without them knowing," agreed Audrey.

Alexandra was crestfallen. She had offered up what she felt was an important secret, but in choosing this moment, it had come off as just one more suggestion for a modified game of hide and seek. Then she caught Becca's stare.

"So are we going or not?" asked Audrey.

"Hang on," said Becca.

Alexandra shifted nervously in her seat. Her secret had been heard after all. Audrey was still not in the loop, but Becca clearly latched on to the possible significance of what she heard.

"That's how you found us that night? And me, when you first showed up?"

"Yes."

"Stop talking code," Audrey said flatly just before an arm of wind moved through the two pine trees that cupped their hideout and shushed all three.

Once the calm returned, Becca retold her side of events so Audrey wouldn't be left out. She described how easily Alexandra found her on that first afternoon, though it was the dog who actually flushed from her hiding place. Even as Alexandra started to defend her success, Becca moved on to tell of how she and Will had been discovered by Alexandra on what was essentially a moonless night.

"Maybe she just heard your voices," suggested Audrey.

"No way, and it was a fifteen minute walk for me, and I knew where I was going," countered Becca.

"So she followed you."

"How, when you can't see a thing?"

"How 'bout you let me explain," said Alexandra sounding a little disgruntled at having become the odd girl out.

"Yes, young lady, please tell us exactly what it is that you've been up to," shot back Audrey in best school marm voice.

All three girls relaxed. Becca hadn't realized just how tense she had become in having to admit that maybe, just maybe, Alexandra had tracking skills beyond hers. For her part, Alexandra heard each comment looking to explain away her gift as an attack on her truthfulness. And Audrey, simply didn't want to be left out, not right away, not after a four hour car ride.

"Let's hear it then," smiled Becca.

And they did. Alexandra took her two friends through each episode of her shifting sight, from that first night in looking for Boxy to unexpectedly being able to find Becca upon her arrival to successfully tracking Becca to her rendezvous with Will. When finished with the retelling her version of events, she felt greatly relieved. Whether or not they believed her, the strain of keeping the truth hidden was over. She looked at Audrey first and found a mixture of wonder and skepticism on her face. Audrey had a hard time fully believing much of what she had just heard. If she had the time line right, the first episode was back in early spring, and her friend had said nothing for months. That

72

seemed odd to her, as did the descriptions of an internal shift in sight that cast the world into a glistening mix of muted colors. She met Alexandra's look with raised eyebrows and a shrug of her shoulders. Alexandra then looked to Becca who looked back at her with what read to Audrey as a kind of stern admiration.

"You don't really believe her, do you?" Audrey asked.

For a moment, Becca kept silent, trying to reconcile the sound of truth in what Alexandra said with the weak but persistent thought that this could be some elaborate ploy devised by these two to trick her. Finally, her gut won out. "I believe her," she said flatly. "So would Will. He knew someone was out there, and he wouldn't believe that you could just stumble onto us like that."

"Prove it," said Audrey trying not to sound bossy but wanting to push the point in order to find out exactly what was going on.

"Can you?" asked Becca.

"I could try," answered Alexandra, both glad and nervous for the chance to show them that she wasn't making any of it up.

"What if we take off and hide," started Audrey, "and you have to find us *and* tell us the path we took to the hiding place. That way it's not hide and seek but you being able to see our path the way you say you can."

"Alright," agreed Alexandra, "I can try."

All three girls picked their way down to the ladder and back onto the forest path. They agreed to let the tent be base, that it would start off like a game of hide and seek with Alexandra waiting in the tent, eyes closed, slowly counting to a hundred, and that she would have to not only find her friends but tell them the path they took in getting to their hiding place. The only condition Alexandra insisted on was that they stay together. She argued that if they split up then she'd have to find one then back track to look for the other. She made her case by repeating that a trail did not last forever, that part of what she seemed to be able to see was the energy or disturbance of a footfall slowly being reabsorbed by the ground. Once they agreed upon the rules, they made the rest of the trip back to the tent in silence.

73

When they reached the tent, Alexandra unzipped the flap and disappeared. She had a knot in her stomach like never before.

Audrey's figured appeared beyond the mesh of the screen. "If you do this, it's going to freak me out," she said quietly.

"I know," agreed Alexandra just as quietly.

"Let's go, Audrey," insisted Becca.

"Good luck," whispered Audrey.

"Thanks," said her friend with a rush of gratitude.

Alexandra turned her back on the entrance to the tent and its view of the field and began her slow count to one hundred. There was no temptation to peak or cheat. In spite of her nerves, she was beginning to believe in her ability. Even with a slow hundred count, if she could summon her sight, their trail should still be bold and bright. The question was whether or not her sight would come, and her sense was that it would if she put her mind in the right place. If she treated this like a game, she suspected that she'd come up dry, but if she put her mind to the idea of having to find these two friends in a more earnest context, as if they were genuinely lost, then she felt more confidence that her sight would shift. At the count of fifty, however, the doubts came knocking. This was a game, she admitted, and whatever it was that granted her the heightened sight would know it, would see through her ploy to prove her story to her friends, and deny her, leave her to wander around the field and woods without a clue. She wouldn't find her friends, they'd see her as a fraud, or maybe just deluded, an only child looking for one more way to get attention. Her body sank into itself in defeat. She realized that she had forgotten to continue counting. She started over at fifty and tried to fight the fear. Slowly, for first time, she found herself thinking with more care and concern of the relationship among her, this gift of sight, and whatever it was that she was tapping into to get it. She knew that it had happened, that what she had seen she had in fact seen. When granted, she knew that her eyes saw differently, maybe even more clearly. In pursuing this idea of being granted her sight, she had once again stopped counting, but before she could think of a number from which to start again, she felt it come. She felt the compression and release

74

and found that even the general uniformity of the tent's fabric now shimmered as it billowed with the breezes moving around the house and through the fields.

Forget the count, she thought. The sight had come and she wasn't about to waste it. She stepped out of the tent to find both Gruff and Muffin standing perky-eared and ready. They both approached her sniffing and prancing as if they could see the change in her as clearly as she saw the change in the light surrounding them, but Alexandra couldn't chance them coming with her and doing any of the tracking for her.

"Stay!" she commanded as firmly as she could then stepped toward the field.

Becca and Audrey's trail was faint but perfectly clear. Alexandra didn't dare turn to see if the dogs obeyed her until she was nearly halfway through the field. With a quick glance back, she saw them both still standing by the tent, alert and intent on her progress. She snapped her head back toward the forest hoping that her glance had not been read by the either dog as an invitation to now join her. From the angle of the footsteps she followed, the girls headed directly toward the main path again. Alexandra trotted along trying to decide which pair of prints belonged to which friend When she reached the point where the field gave way to forest, her heart sank. They did what she had specifically asked them not to do. The two trails of foot prints diverged. They had split up.

Into the dream of the lake cold sleep of Matchi Manitou came the curious image of a child able to summon the pulse of the great-sight, a frail wisp of a two-legger calling down this power and not being crushed by its granting. The Manitou chuckled to itself as it held up this image to its mind's eye. *What a wonderful oddity*, it thought. *What is this thing we've found, Brother?* it asked in its dream-time, the question carrying its own pulse through the deep and the dark and into the shallows and the light, addressing nothing and everything at the same time.

Audrey made her way up the path. She had not wanted them to split up. They promised Alexandra that they wouldn't, but Becca insisted and finally cajoled Audrey into a compromise by suggesting that they rejoin each other at a particular hiding place. This way, she explained, if Alexandra succeeded in tracking them, it would appear as if they had been together all the time. As she strode up the path, Audrey mulled over her decision to go along with this deception. She repeatedly pulled back out of her thoughts to look for the one sharp turn then the uphill portion and then some other split pine that signaled the location of the boulder where she was to hide and wait for Becca to join her. Becca explained that it was the same place she had hidden from Alexandra on the first day and therefore was the least likely place Alexandra would choose to look first. Audrey actually like the idea of that logic. The path took a clear sharp turn and then led Audrey up a noticeable rise. She figured she had walked for at least the fifteen minutes Becca said it would take to arrive at the pine when she saw it. She halted on the path and looked to her right. About twenty feet into the woods, she saw the massive rock. She picked her way toward it. The closer she got the larger it loomed. It was big from a distance, it was huge up close. She circled around behind it only to find no sign of Becca. *This was the place*, Audrey told herself, the turn, the climb, the pine. She settled in to wait.

Audrey quickly reacquainted herself with the elasticity of waiting time, time that takes on a different feel, time that slows down and speeds up according to the thoughts and passions of the one waiting. In her isolation, Audrey heard twigs snapping in all directions, thought she saw Becca's figure at least twice only to have it dissolve into the short waving branches of distant underbrush. For a time, she considered whether or not she had been the one duped, whether Alexandra and Becca had put her up to this as a way of sending her out to hide for no purpose, see how long she'd stay hidden, and then have a good laugh when she emerged from the forest half a day later. She should be enjoying this. She loved hide and seek. She loved being in the woods. She loved the chance to imagine herself on her own, a pioneer woman, an Indian, last of her tribe avoiding capture, a government agent on some secret rendezvous in the dark woods of Russia, but she might just be the fool on a snipe hunt. The waiting time worked its spell. Audrey's mood blackened as doubts and suspicions joined in like a chorus to the twigs that snapped for no apparent reason. She and Alexandra had been friends since forever. She should never have agreed with Becca to split. Who was this cousin compared to her best friend?

Then Becca appeared. She popped out from behind a clump of bushes slightly out of breath and grinning.

"Been waiting long?"

"No, … couple of minutes maybe," replied Audrey working to keep her voice level and not show the great relief she felt at having the last twenty dark images and doubtful thoughts dissipate like so much fog burned off by the sun.

Now the two girls shared a new kind of waiting time. Now they had time to whisper their doubts as to whether or not Alexandra would succeed, time to quietly consider whether or not she had put them both up to this and was going to let them hide indefinitely, a pair of dupes. Periodically between topics, they would try and estimate how long they had waited and how long they should give their friend before calling it a failure and tromping back down the path. Twice in these breaks to figure time, Becca waved off a mounting sneeze. Twice Audrey found the face the girl made and the frantic waving terribly funny. Finally, as they first began to consider calling off, Becca's sneeze emerged. With the hope of stifling any detectable noise, she pinched her nose.

"Bless you," whispered-giggled Audrey.

"Bless you, indeed," boomed a deep and menacing voice from the woods behind them.

☙ 10 ❧

The Gravity of Sight

The two girls spun in unison, each barely containing her scream, only to find Alexandra leaning casually against a birch tree wearing a snide grin.

"You scared the crap out of us!" yelled Becca.

"You two split up," snapped Alexandra still in good humor but not in the mood to back down from the fact they tried to cheat. To buttress her resolve, as she crept up on her two friends, she replayed in her mind her thinking when at the field's edge she found the one trail that led directly toward the path in the woods and then the other that cut off to the right skirting the fringe between the field and forest. After a few moments of consternation, she figured Becca would send Audrey along the surest route to the designated hiding place and Becca would take the trickier path. Then finally, as more of a challenge to herself, she decided to track the less certain path along the field and bushwhack through the woods.

Neither Becca nor Audrey tried to deny the accusation, partly in fact because each was trying to decipher how it was that Alexandra even knew that they hadn't stayed together.

"I'm guessing you…," Alexandra continued nodding her head at Becca, "suggested the split," silently completing the thought in her mind, *Audrey wouldn't break a promise so quickly*.

Not wanting to be put on the defensive, Becca spoke out immediately, "Yes, we split up… and it was my idea. She didn't want to. Fine… but I want to know how you know that."

"Because your trails split right before the woods."

"But how," asked Audrey.

"I told you… when my sight shifts, I see differently… completely differently."

"So you're really not talking about snapped twigs or scuffed lichens or leaves pushed back into muddy patches," offered Becca.

"Yes and no. I mean I can see those things because I see the light that each touch of your feet or hands obscures," explained Alexandra again. "I see your trails in light or where the light's been interrupted. At the entrance to the woods, almost as clearly as I can see you now, I saw your paths split. I guessed you had a hiding place in mind, explained it her and then sent her up the path and then you took some vicious windy route up the back way."

"You really can see footsteps," said Becca quietly, more to herself than to the other two girls.

"You jumped from rock to rock for a while which might have lost me if I was following scuffs and snapped twigs. But I don't," explained Alexandra and then to press her point home added, "You almost lost your balance at one spot, had to grip a small tree to keep yourself from falling off one of the rocks you had jumped onto."

Becca was staring at her friend with a mixture of disbelief and something almost like fear.

Alexandra answered the question Becca couldn't seem to articulate, "It's not just footprints, it's any touch you or anyone or anything else makes. There was a handprint on one tree," she continued making her hand mime as if she were gripping something about as round as a soup can, "four fingers and a thumb. You only hopped onto a couple of other stones before you gave that tactic up."

"How?" mumbled Becca.

"Great question," interrupted Audrey smacking the side of her neck, "but could we start moving? The mosquitoes have found me."

"Your way or the path?" asked Alexandra.

"OMG, the path. I nearly killed myself getting up here."

"OMG, the path," echoed Audrey.

"OMG, let's go," chimed in Alexandra.

"OMG, cut it out," shot back Becca.

As the girls made their way around the boulder and back onto the path, the realization of what she accomplished and revealed in accomplishing began to sink into Alexandra. Her secret was out and she had proven her ability or gift or whatever it was. She saw the shock on their faces and not only because she found them but because she found them in the way she said she did, with her sight.

As if to confirm Alexandra's thoughts, Audrey brushed up against her shoulder and whispered, "You know, you're freaking us out a bit."

But her whisper carried enough to prompt Becca to spin and add, "Serious freak out." Then continuing down the path backwards, she stared at Alexandra and added, "Are you still doing it? Is your sight thing still going on?"

"No."

"Can you see that footprint? Can you see that one?"

There was a cattiness to Becca's teasing and Alexandra felt a kernel of anger being planted in the pit of her stomach. Sensing the same, Audrey suddenly looped one of her arms through one of Alexandra's and pulled her nearer. At this show of solidarity, Becca spun back around and continued picking her way back down the path, but Alexandra wasn't ready to let the challenge go completely and addressed her comments to Becca's back.

"I don't know if I control it really. It comes and goes. It disappeared as soon as I got close enough to see you... as soon as the tracking was done."

Becca made no response.

Audrey broke in, "How does it happen exactly?"

Before Alexandra could answer, Becca turned back, paused, waited the moment it took for the other two to reach her, then looped one of her arms through Alexandra's other free one. Alexandra grinned and let that kernel of anger dissolve.

"How does it happen... exactly?" echoed Becca with a nod toward Audrey.

After a moment's pause in which the girls found a cadence to their stride which allowed them to continue on with linked arms, Alexandra tried to answer, "I think I have to want

80

to… or need to track or hunt or look for something or someone. Then I think of it… call for it… and if the time is right… or the way I ask is right…" Her words faltered as she tried to explain what couldn't be explained. "I don't know how it happens. I look for it to come and it does and I go with it."

"You can feel it?" pressed Audrey who began to try and imagine what such a change would feel like.

"At first, it's like a kind of pressure. All over but that you feel mostly in your head or in your chest. Like going up in a plane… or diving into the deep end of a pool… it's a little like that until I'm inside it or it's inside me and then I feel okay. I don't think about it when it happens. I'm too caught up in looking… too caught up in using it."

"Do your ears pop?" asked Becca in earnest.

"No, but it feels like they might."

"You could chew gum," blurted out Audrey only to have the other two girls look at her with bemused concern.

"You could wear those motion sickness bands on your wrists," offered Becca.

"Dramamine," shot back Audrey.

"Chewing gum, wrist bands, and Dramamine," summed up Becca.

"You two can shut up any time now," responded Alexandra shaking her head.

The three girls continued on their way back to the house. Where the trail narrowed, either Audrey or Becca or both would relinquish their hold on Alexandra's arms, only to reestablish it once the path widened and could accommodate all three again. Alexandra let herself be escorted. She felt as if they too were now helping carry her secret. Each time one or the other girl had to release her, she anticipated the return and welcomed the contact. As they continued, the girls separated and rejoined without conscious thought. Each was aware in her own way that something unique to them had happened and somehow this contact prolonged that moment. Each was aware without thinking it that such tight and right moments do not, by nature, last. Each felt a slight flutter in her stomach upon re-looping her arm with Alexandra's and re-completing the link among them.

Each was aware of the thrill in their unity, and each somewhat sorry to see woods give way to field, knowing that the ordinary was once again imminent.

What little of the day was left the girls spent in expected ways, chasing Josh away from their tent, helping set the dinner table then clear it, chasing Josh and the dogs away from their tent, dividing up the stages of dishwashing, drying, and setting the table for breakfast, surrounding Josh and making him promise upon the threat of a group hug that he would stay away from their tent, arguing over who would have to sit in the middle on their way to get ice cream, brushing teeth, and reassuring parents both as a group then individually that they would not wander too far from the tent or out of sight of the house no ifs, ands, or buts. In between all of this, there had been any number of glances among the girls as if to reaffirm that whatever passed between them in the woods was still potentially there. Once the evening began to die down, each of the three experienced an eagerness to leave the house and the others behind and to seek out and relish their triad.

The three of them settled quickly into their respective sleeping bags then just as quickly found their bedding too warm and constrictive and kicked themselves free to lie on top in the cooler air as they talked. In the course of the faltering drift toward sleep, each girl sought to reconnect with the rush of friendship she experienced earlier.

Becca looked to it in an almost proprietary way. Because Alexandra's skills were manifesting themselves so clearly here and now on what Becca considered her home territory, she felt oddly responsible for steering the outcome of it all. She could admit, reluctantly, that Alexandra appeared to be a more successful tracker but only as a result of a kind of cheat. *Anyone who could heighten one or more of their senses should track better*, she reassured herself. With the same hint of jealousy, Becca also wanted to know more about how, in addition to her tracking skills, Alexandra had been able to sneak up on them so easily. *I'll bet she's got a cheat there too,* Becca told herself, yet these dismissive thoughts came even as she hoped Alexandra would continue to look to her for validation of what she could do. *I'm the oldest, by two plus years*, she reminded herself, *and they should both need me when they're wandering around in my woods.* Without being able to name it as a driving motivation, Becca sensed that the closeness of the connection they had all experienced earlier in the day was the surest route to the disclosures she felt she was due.

For her part, Audrey was pleased Alexandra had waited for her arrival before revealing her secret, and as she let this pleasant realization take deeper root, she reached out and gently flicked her friend's shoulder. In response, Alexandra softly tapped a knuckle on Audrey's head. She didn't fully know what to make of Alexandra's apparent gift. She half believed it, half didn't, but more than either impulse, Audrey took it at face value and let it stand for now. Alexandra had, after all, found them via Becca's route and showed up knowing that they'd separated from the start of the forest path. Audrey had always been open to possibility. As she lay in the dark occasionally adding her two cents into the conversation about boys or music or food, she connected with her own belief that the world, that Nature with a capital N, was more alive in some people, and that some people were more responsive to being alive in it than others. She recalled a dance workshop where the woman leading it talked endlessly about recognizing gravity as a kind of second floor on which to move, that when a dancer leaves the stage in a leap or lift, they immerse themselves in gravity, that the best dancers use that constant pull as another platform for expression. Audrey remembered being irritated by the giggles she heard among some of the other students in the face of what she recognized as a useful truth. With this memory in mind, Audrey listened to her closest friend shift on her bedding. *Maybe,* she thought into the dark, *Alexandra has simply found a way of launching herself into the gravity of sight.*

As she was listening to Becca's description of one of Muffin's early escapades, Alexandra felt a little flick on her shoulder that put her stomach in a flutter. She stretched her arm out and tapped Audrey on the head. Free of her secret, Alexandra basked in the mixture of relief and fatigue that can follow true confession. What made the moment more remarkable was its normalcy. Each of these two girls had taken

Alexandra's proof of her gift in stride, and now they were back to simply hanging out in the same way as they would have been had Alexandra not had any shifting capacity for seeing. *But I have changed*, she thought to herself, and with this admission, simple as it seemed, Alexandra expanded her understanding of her gift from something that was limited to the working of her eyes to a capacity that involved her entire self. Her shoulder tingled where Audrey had tapped, and Alexandra chased her thoughts round and round. *We're all changing*, she thought, *and we know it,... bra sizes,... pimples,... old parents and boys,... and now me seeing footprints and handprints, seeing touch,... actually seeing it.* She wanted a connection to emerge that would bind all these circling thoughts into a coherent pattern, some link between her sense of change and the changes they all were in the midst of, some logic behind her sharing of that change and the apparent ease of their acceptance of her sharing it, and some coherent direction for how to use her new skill and still be just a girl with just these friends in just a tent under the stars of just another night.

But it wasn't going to be that easy.

"Alexandra!" came her name along with a chorus of giggles.

"What?"

"Where were you?" asked Becca.

"I don't know... what do you want?"

"I was asking how you managed to be so quiet."

"When?"

Another bout of giggling.

"This afternoon... when you found us," answered Audrey.

"We've been talking about it for the last five minutes," chimed in Becca.

"What happened to the story about Muffin and your mom's shoes?" asked Alexandra trying to regain a sense of the present.

"Leave my poor dog alone. We want to know how you stayed so quiet."

"I don't know," Alexandra admitted as she tried to think back to what she did when tracking Becca's path. "I think... I think…" Giggles. "It was like I could see the best places to step, Becca," she answered realizing that in fact her method of approach had clearly been tied to how she could see, that firm ground or rock pulsed differently than a dry stick or fallen leaves.

"I'm having a hard time wrapping my little mind around all this," said Becca flatly.

"But there it is," added Audrey.

"Yeah, I know," conceded Becca.

"So what happened with Muffin and your mom's shoes," blurted Alexandra.

All three girls joined in the laughter, and much to Alexandra's relief, as they wound down toward sleep, the conversation did not return to anything anyone had seen or claimed to have seen that afternoon.

As she listened to the even breathing of her tent mates, two last thoughts crossed Alexandra's mind: how she had not consciously thought of where she stepped in order to remain silent and how it must be for Becca and Audrey to be spectators rather than participants in whatever it was she was experiencing.

❧ 11 ❧

Troubling Water

All three girls dreamt of water. The next day, had any one of them mentioned her dream to either of the others, it might have initiated a conversation which in turn might have changed the course of what happened. Instead, each one of them for her own reasons decided to keep the images and the impressions of her dream to herself, and the day took its turns.

Had they spoken to each other, they might have found it odd how similar all three dreams were. All three involved the dreamer as audience watching some action or feat by one of the other girls. All three produced in the dreamer a mixture of exhilaration, bafflement, and concern. Perhaps most remarkable, all three involved water.

In her dream, Becca stood on one side of a smooth, slow flowing river watching Alexandra on the opposite shore standing calmly at the base of a mountain range. Even though Alexandra never took a step forward or backward, she seemed to Becca to be moving toward the water. For a time Becca couldn't make sense of this until she realized it was the mountains behind Alexandra moving her, either by drawing back the ground at Alexandra's feet or by rolling up incrementally. Each time that Alexandra was moved nearer the edge of the water, in empathy Becca could feel her friend's stomach tighten with concern and fear. In her dream, Becca perceived nothing unusual in such an extreme connection. With each new wave of anxiety, Becca looked to Alexandra's figure for some kind of reaction or reassurance, yet each time she looked at Alexandra's face she found only calm resignation. In spite of her concern for her friend, Becca found herself angry at what she knew was a duplicitous reaction. She knew she was feeling Alexandra's fear yet saw no evidence of it on the girl's face. The closer the mountains pushed Alexandra toward the water, the more Becca found her friend's lack of concern infuriating. Alexandra was only one more pulse or push away from being dropped into the water when Becca woke. Though she desperately tried to fall asleep and reenter her dream, it was gone. When she woke again at daybreak, she remembered no other dreams, only her frustration with Alexandra's complacency and their shared knot of fear.

Becca, in turn, was the focus of Audrey's dream. Again a river was involved, but this one was wide, rushing, and spanned by scattered boulders both large and small. In her dream, Audrey stood on the edge of a boulder overlooking the river watching Becca moving away from her as she crossed the water by jumping from rock to rock. Each time Becca launched herself into the air, Audrey felt her stomach lurch with her as if she too were jumping. More odd and wonderful was the sensation of the wind that Audrey experienced with each of Becca's jumps. With each leap, Audrey watched Becca's hair blow back with the force of her momentum. An instant later, a cool commensurate breeze pushed past Audrey and blew her hair back in the same manner. Becca was almost halfway across the river when Audrey sensed things were not well. It took her a few moments to realize that the rocks were shifting, and while Becca seemed unconcerned by this fact, Audrey feared the worst, that a boulder would shift when her friend was in mid-air and rather than finding safe landing, Becca would be plunged into the rapid water. Yet each jump was a wonder to Audrey, so in spite of her growing sense of dread, Audrey found herself willing Becca to make larger, bolder leaps so that she could feel her stomach thrill and her hair stream back. With only a few jumps left before reaching the safety of the opposite shore, Audrey watched the boulders shift faster and watched Becca's realization of the same. Becca stood poised trying to gage when and where to make her next attempt at completing her crossing. She looked back to Audrey, and Audrey heard herself say quietly, too quietly to carry across the roar of the river, "Just jump again. Jump anyway." As if she heard, Becca turned and leapt with no rock in sight for a landing. Audrey felt the thrill in her stomach and what she thought was the wind in her hair, but the wind this time was real caused by her sitting bolt upright from her dream to find herself surrounded by the darkness of the tent. She listened to the breathing of the other two girls then lay back down. For a long time, Audrey fought off sleep for fear of returning to her dream and finding Becca swept away by the river. When she woke again, it was light, no other dreams had come, and she felt spared.

As for Alexandra, she dreamt of standing by a large body of still water, its surface smooth as glass. She was waiting, but for what she did not know. Then without a sound of warning, a figure dropped from high, pierced the surface of the lake, and disappeared from sight. There was no splash. The water remained as smooth as a drum skin. Alexandra felt pressure all through her body as if it was she who was below the water. She waited until without a bubble of warning Audrey's head popped into view from beneath the water's silent, waveless expanse. As she tread water, she smiled, waved, and spoke one word in the form of a question, *Again?* Alexandra tried to answer but she failed to say anything, so Audrey nodded and swam away until she was lost from sight. Alexandra found herself once again waiting. Just as she began to squirm within her sense of time as if waiting for a dentist to be done, or for a mother to come, for a party to start, the figure of Audrey shot past and was once again swallowed by the strange water. Suddenly, with that same all-over pressure pressing every inch of her body, Alexandra found her voice and she cried out her protest to the void above the lake, but as soon as her friend's head appeared, Alexandra lost command of her voice and could only stand silent as the question was repeated. *Again?* asked the smiling Audrey before nodding and swimming away. As this pattern repeated itself, the Alexandra in the dream quickly realized that she only had a voice when Audrey was submerged. Once Audrey's head appeared, Alexandra could not command the air in her lungs to utter a sound or the muscles in her body to make any gesture. As her friend waved and swam away, Alexandra tried but could not bring herself to look up with the hope of locating where exactly Audrey perched before dropping into view. Again and again Audrey dove and emerged to ask if Alexandra wanted to see this act repeated one more time and then swam away to dive again.

Alexandra's puzzlement and frustration grew with each repeated dive as did her sense of the crushing pressure throughout her body whenever Audrey was below the water's surface. It began to occur to the Alexandra in the dream that she might find herself in this loop of action endlessly unless she did something about it. As she struggled to decide on a plan of action, Audrey dove past and disappeared below the lake's surface. Alexandra closed her eyes and willed herself to turn and move away from the shore. With this thought, the pressure throughout her body took on a burning quality. She suddenly realized that with her eyes closed, she was not breathing, that with her eyes closed, it was as if she were underwater, and the panic of drowning took hold. Suddenly she could not reopen her eyes. Her lungs were bound shut. *Shutting my eyes was the wrong move,* thought the dream girl. *I have drowned myself,* thought the dream girl. Her lungs burned. Her mind could not focus. She was drowning. Then as distant yet as clear as the scuff of a mouse in walls of a night-quiet house came her friend's voice asking, *Again?* And Alexandra was awake, sitting bolt upright in her bed with her vision-gift in full force.

She looked around the tent and found her two friends fast asleep, their bodies and particularly their heads alive with light, pulsing with a wavering light like embers. Without the filtered light of day to obscure her gift-sight, Alexandra both felt and understood that what she was looking at was a light as core as sunlight, light burning of its own accord, light for the sake of light. She watched the emanations around these two precious heads as she might the dancing light of a fire, relishing its pulse and rhythms, enchanted by the mysterious act of its burning. She lay back down hoping not to sleep for fear of re-waking in her dream, but sleep came. Thankfully, however, Alexandra's dreams for this night were done.

Thus it was at breakfast when Becca announced that she wanted to take Audrey and Alexandra up river to see a stretch of rapids, the idea appealed to each of the girls because of experiences they only half-remembered having half-had in their dream lives.

At first none of the parents were keen on the idea. Becca's dad spoke up first, "This is not a good river day. There've been rains up north, and you can't trust the currents or the levels. The crest of the river tide hasn't reached us yet."

"But the whole point of having friends stay over is to let us get out on our own. There are three of us. It's a buddy system. Mom, we can pack a lunch and make it more of a picnic," pleaded Becca.

Mrs. Dwyer shared her husband's concern and worried that the temptation to find a swimming hole would prove too much, but as she looked at the three girls, she remembered the rag tag friends she had.

As if on cue, Audrey struck just the right note, "What if we promise to steer clear of the water."

"Stay way up on the banks," chimed in Alexandra.

When Mrs. Dwyer looked at her husband and brother with a half-grin, the girls knew the battle was won.

"The emergency phone goes in the backpack and you stay on the banks. All three of you together," Mr. Dwyer insisted.

"Pinkie swear," offered Alexandra gleefully.

"Put that thing away," snapped her uncle, "I don't know where that thing's been."

The three girls and Mrs. Dwyer gasped with offense.

"Men!" said Audrey flatly.

"Don't get me started, sister," agreed Becca, sending her mom into a fit of giggling.

None of them intentionally looked to deceive, but all three were aware that even as each was promising to keep herself and the others clear of the river she was holding in her head a dream-image of one of the others very much at risk with water.

As if to escape the house before the parents could even consider changing their minds, the girls broke into a flurry of action. Becca worked with her mom to make and pack the lunches. After being sworn to not divulge the list of ingredients, Audrey helped Josh in making his secret recipe trail mix which Audrey soon realized was like most any other trail mix except for Josh's insistence on including pieces of strawberry licorice. Alexandra took on the job of arranging the backpacks which meant she needed to negotiate the input of both her and Becca's father as to the best way to distribute the contents and weight between the two packs that the three of them would share. In less than three quarters of an hour after first asking, the girls were cutting through the field on their hike to find the river. Before they could reach the woods, however, they heard shouting behind them and turned to see Josh running full tilt toward them waving what appeared to be narrow rectangle of bright white. The three girls stood mesmerized by the odd urgency of Josh's approach.

Suddenly, Audrey spoke, "I think it's toilet paper."

"It is," asserted Becca immediately, "Dad and Josh never think of it. Mom never forgets it."

Perhaps wary of what manner of reward might await his delivery of this *necessity*, as his mother called it, Josh drew up short of the girls, and before Becca could warn him not to throw it, he did. It cut a lovely arc through the air, an arc that all watching could follow because Josh released it so that it spun and unwound extending a tail to mark its path. In the distance, all three adults winced in unison like three parents watching a favorite child muffing an easy play or just missing an important score. All three girls moved as one toward the now comet-like missile hoping to cut short any further unraveling. And Josh quick to realize his error spun and started his dash back toward the house before any of the girls could think of how to mete out retribution.

"That's just great," scoffed Alexandra as Audrey laughed and Becca snatched up what was left of the main roll.

She quickly tore off the tail then divided it into three relatively equal lengths saying, "One for each of us. No, don't roll it up just yet, wave them, ladies, wave them toward our adoring fans."

The parents watched as three little streamers of white drifted back and forth then turned and floated above the heads of the hikers as they appeared to skip toward the woods.

Mr. Dwyer interrupted the bemused silence, "Heaven help anyone else out for a hike in these mountains today."

"Should we call the authorities now or wait for them to contact us?" asked Mr. Stepp.

"I think I'll have a cup of tea… and see if the local yellow pages advertise bail bondsmen," added Mrs. Dwyer as she turned to go back into the house.

The hikers made good time. They traded off the backpacks every quarter of an hour or so taking advantage of each pause to grab a snack or drink of water. Much of the travel time so far had been taken up with how Becca and Will first took notice of each other. As she recounted the series of messages passed between common friends, the lunches taken together in the safety of larger groups until trays were side by side, and the first time they arranged to meet outside of school, both Audrey and Alexandra listened intently. The two younger girls tried to imagine themselves in Becca's place and both failed to find any particular boy just yet who seemed up to the task of becoming their *Will.* For her part, Becca enjoyed her role as the more experienced among the three and felt, in spite of the challenge cast by Alexandra's odd ability, that she had reestablished her position as first among equals.

Perhaps this attitude led Becca to talk back as she did when they encountered the first group of other hikers, a family of four, a mom, dad, two girls, the oldest clearly younger than Alexandra. At first, when the two parties approached each other, the three girls stepped a little off the path to give the family easy passage, but in nodding and speaking, the father asked if he should expect to meet their parents farther down the path. For reasons even Becca could not explain, she suddenly got defensive.

"We don't need our dads to take a path through the woods."

"I think it's just that none of you seem that much older than our oldest," offered the mother in compromise.

Becca looked her in the eye and snapped, "Well, I'm fifteen and all combined, you're looking at over thirty years of experience here, lady."

Both the adults stiffened visibly. The mother turned her girls and ushered them on their way. The father caught and held Becca's gaze until beckoned by his wife. He began to say something, thought better of it, turned, and marched off to join his family. Becca stared after him for a few moments as if to drive her point home both to the man who challenged her and to the friends still watching her. Then as if to dismiss the awkwardness of the exchange, Becca mugged a bit for her two companions by widening her eyes and clenching her tongue between her teeth. Finally muttering, "Tourists."

"Jeez, Becca," said Alexandra.

"Oh, what. We're obviously way older than her kids."

Audrey and Alexandra shot glances toward the other and decided, each for her own reason, not to continue trying to figure out what just happened. The group turned back to their hike in silence, a silence that lasted for many minutes as each girl replayed the exchange and reaffirmed her right to have reacted as she did. What brought them out of their respective reflections was another party coming down the path. This one consisted of an older couple with their equally old dog. Leading in silence, Becca was the first to reach them, and she immediately knelt to welcome the dog as it lingered to pursue the scents it found of Gruff and Muffin on her socks and shorts.

"Look at your old gray face," cooed Becca then added, "He looks just like my oldest. She's gone white all around her muzzle."

"Don't we all," said the woman as she rubbed her companions back. He responded with a deep chuckle.

Audrey and Alexandra joined the group and the dog moved among all three seeking out other odors of others dogs it might know or like to meet.

"You coming or going?" asked the man.

Alexandra half expected to hear Becca tell him to mind his own business, but she was as nice as she could be.

"We packed a lunch and plan to have a picnic above the rapids," Becca answered then asked, "Did you come that way? Are we getting close?"

Audrey caught Alexandra's glance. Both girls were puzzled by the same notion, that Becca most likely knew exactly where she was, so the question had some other purpose.

"We did and you are," answered the woman adding, "and if we get quiet you can hear the river."

They all stilled and immediately could hear what sounded like a stiff breeze moving through the trees, but it was too steady, too constant of a sound for wind.

Each girl felt her pulse quicken as each watched a dream image from the night before flash across her mind. Each suddenly wanted to be done with this bit of chat and get to a point where the water could be seen.

"That's really cool," said Becca and turning to her friends added, "Come on. I'm getting hungry."

The girls wished the couple well, gave the dog a last scratch and pet, and turned their collective attention to getting on with the hike. With Becca still in the lead, they moved single file and in silence, keeping the company of their own thoughts while listening to the song of the water they had yet to see.

Becca felt vindicated and in control. She hadn't let that woman dismiss them because of their ages, and even if she had been rude, she'd made up for it with that old couple, even asking them a question that she already knew the answer to so they could feel important. Now she was leading them at her pace and with her stride through her woods toward her river, a river she fully expected to be swollen with runoff from the northern rains, unyielding and magnificent. Right behind Becca came Alexandra staring at her cousin's back listening to the persistent call of the distant water trying to figure out why her friend had gone from sassy to sweet in a matter of a few feet of path. She sensed that Becca had something to prove, but she couldn't decide what exactly that might be. Clouding her thoughts was her anticipation of seeing the river, and clouding her concern for what the river might bring was her consideration of Becca's erratic behavior. Audrey too puzzled over Becca's shift in attitude. To her that first woman's comment about their ages didn't come off as argumentative, more of an observation, even simply conversational. Then came that saccharine nonsense with the other couple and their dog. She finally decided that Becca must be working through some stuff that had nothing to do with her. Then just as she let her mind go clear, the trio crested a small knoll and the sound of the water rose. The new immediacy of the river sent Audrey back into a memory of the whitewater rafting trip she'd taken with her parents the summer before. The guide had explained to everyone in the rafting party, kids and adults, that if thrown from the raft you were to keep yourself facing down river, bring your knees up and use your feet to ward off any contact with the boulders until you got pulled back into the raft. As she had that day, she now played with the image of bouncing off the rocks as if in a dance, using the water as gravity and the rocks as her stage.

Almost in unison, the three girls caught their first glimpse of the river as the whitewater flashed like signal mirrors through the patchwork of trees. Becca turned and grinned at the other two girls.

"Come on, ladies!" she yelled happily and broke into a longer stride.

Still caught up in her daydream, Audrey pushed past Alexandra to keep up.

Alexandra moved along in their wake, hurrying now and again in order not to be completely left behind, although for her the lure of the river began to turn. As she watched her friends competing in their dash toward the water, Alexandra's misgivings deepened. The situation itself seemed to hold a double nature. Like knowing that there was light emanating beneath the light everyone else could see, she began to feel that this situation, this day, this hike, this running toward the river, was double-edged. As she watched her friends disappear around a bend in the trail, Alexandra found herself more unsettled. Suddenly as if the day itself had sent out a wail, Alexandra could not decide if what she was hearing was a baby's cry or a cat's angry warning, a weak human's need or an animal's gut response. And just as with hearing a cry in the night, Alexandra was torn between whether or not she should pursue the truth of it or block it from her mind.

Suddenly, she heard her name gleefully called in unison and she hurried down the path. When she turned the bend, a spectacular view of the river opened up. Lit boldly by the sun, the water offered a moving quilt of blues, greens, pale grays, and sharp whites. Against this wavering backdrop, she could see her friends. They turned and waved, and she waved back.

Becca had tossed her backpack at her feet and Audrey had already taken off her shoes. Alexandra couldn't believe what she saw. Audrey acted as if she was going to leap right into the river. And then she did, onto large rock, then again onto another. Becca whooped and cheered. Alexandra froze and watched with growing fear as Audrey took two more leaps farther out.

Then Alexandra felt the day showed itself for what it was. She felt the horror of it before either of her two friends would, but the knowledge came with no time to warn or call out. Instead, Alexandra watched her best friend leap, land, and then slide from view into the singing rush of the river.

❧ 12 ❧

A Slim Shard of Empty

Before Alexandra had time to think, Becca appeared in her face blocking her view of the river and the slim shard of empty where Audrey had been standing. She pulled the pack from Alexandra's back, let it drop to the ground, then grabbed her shoulders, pressing her fingers into her cousin's flesh until the focus came back into Alexandra's eyes and they locked onto Becca's.

"We move down river now. Alexandra! Now!" she yelled.

Without waiting for even the slightest nod of comprehension or consent, Becca spun and dashed off along what little shoreline the woods afforded. Alexandra looked to the river, caught a flash of color in the water, already many feet down stream and with an urgency driven by a great fear dashed to follow Becca's lead.

In the first few seconds after going into the river, Audrey nearly broke beneath the cold pressure of the water, the white noise of its roar, the bruising blows as it shoved her into and scraped her past the first few boulders, and its cuttingly quick and complete insistence that it might not forgive her slip or relinquish its control of her body. Then she was thrown back into the air and all of her focus and energy turned to keeping her eyes and nose out of this horrible rush.

At first she flailed, spun around, was pushed against and bounced of boulders of all sizes. She tried to scramble onto several of the larger boulders, but either the water simply moved her past them too quickly or she was turned wrong as they approached and couldn't reach the dryer portions where she might have found some purchase. Suddenly she was pulled back under the surface, dragged into a channel between two massive rocks, and dropped into a series of smaller rapids. She coughed and flailed again. Instinctively, as another chain of boulders loomed, she finally drew her legs up to her chest, used her arms to rotate the little human ball she had become, and angrily pushed off the rocks with her feet.

❖

On shore, the girls were finding it difficult to keep up with Audrey. No clear path cut along the river bank. Becca was still in the lead doing her best to help them pick their way quickly downstream, but often she found the most open avenues leading them sideways back into the woods or straight down to the river.

"Becca."

"Just come on. I'm doing the best I can. This way now."

"Becca!" insisted Alexandra.

"What!" snapped Becca spinning to face her cousin.

"Let me in front. Let me lead."

Becca began to protest, but Alexandra cut her off.

"I can see the tunnels we need to take."

"Tunnels?" sputtered Becca.

"I'm not seeing by daylight only," explained Alexandra pushing past the older girl and ducking and disappearing into what appeared to be thicket of brush.

"Alexandra!?... You mean your vision thing is turned on?" asked Becca as she ducked and pushed into the thicket.

Alexandra did not answer. She was already several feet distant and moving quickly. The thicket had given way to much less dense underbrush, and Becca had to struggle to keep up. There was no pause or equivocation in Alexandra's path. She made minor shifts in direction but consistently kept the river in view on her left. When her way was clear, she would take the time to locate Audrey's figure as it fled downstream. She saw that Audrey was more in control of herself, that while she was still trapped by the current, she was seemingly able to keep herself facing forward and was using her feet to brace herself against whatever obstacles the water forced her toward. She could also see that Audrey was drawing farther and farther in front of their progress on shore. If something didn't give and give soon, Audrey would out distance them.

Water circulates like the blood of the earth, pumped to the surface to nurture the land and foster the rains and then returned to the deep to be cleansed and offered up again. When Alexandra opened herself to receive her gift vision so near the river, the pulse of its coming resonated through the water, downstream and up. As with the butterfly wing beat that can eventually be felt on the other side of the world, the pulse of Alexandra's sight arriving rippled far and wide through the waters of the Northeast. Fish leapt as if it were early spring, people swimming in rivers and lakes felt a sudden urge to laugh, beavers slapped their tails and looked to take a roll and tumble as if they were all yearlings again. But deep in one lake a thing stirred without joy, troubled by the clarity in the pulse it felt. With the pulse of Alexandra's vision-gift still ringing in its ears, it decided the time had come to wake and take a look around.

Thus this finger of the great dark Manitou sent out a thought, sent it up and around the shores of the water in which it dwelt. The thought found a host, a coyote in its prime come to drink. The animal shuddered as it tried to host strong and disparate impulses. Something in the coyote wanted to bolt from the water as if the lake was one huge predator, but something else in its mind held it planted an overwhelming desire to abandon its pack and wander beyond its normal range. There was something that needed hunting, something that needed to be sniffed out and seen. Another few laps of cool water and it turned and trotted along the lake shore until the direction seemed right and it cut away into the forest.

The river was relentless. Audrey once again lost her bearings and began to lose her strength and her will to fight. Without fully understanding where her thoughts were, she began to sense how completely the current gripped her. Her breathing became shallow as she lost faith in her ability to keep her head out of the water. She gulped air every chance she could even when she might have had time to take deeper more sustaining breaths. She found it more and more difficult to keep her legs

99

drawn up and ready to fend off each subsequent impact with the rocks. She fought to keep her fear at bay, but without any sense of control she could feel the temptation to quit build within her.

A large rock loomed. Audrey tried to pull her legs up in order to fend it off but was too slow. She was going to hit and hit hard. Suddenly a plume of water rose up turned her away, spun her around, and pushed her into the clear. In the middle of her spin, Audrey found herself facing the nearer shore and saw people. They were behind her, but they were there. With her dancer's instinct she spun her head on point and confirmed that her friends were in pursuit, both of them moving along the shore.

She was not alone and the thought of giving in suddenly became ridiculous.

She paddled and swam and beat against the water as best she could. She drew her knees up and pushed off a small boulder. She worked to face forward to see what was coming and in the distance caught sight of a large flat rock. If she could maneuver herself a few feet to her right, she might be able to scramble up onto it and be rid of this river.

Even though she and Becca moved faster under her lead, Alexandra's hope that they would catch up to Audrey faded. The river's current outpaced every effort she made to close distance. Each time she glanced toward the river, Audrey's bobbing figure drew farther away. With her gift-sight revealing the path of surest progress, Alexandra broke into a staggered run. She ducked and sliced her way with greater speed. She stopped worrying about the smaller branches that whipped against her face and legs or caught and tugged at her clothes. Scratches, nicks, and bruises were nothing now. She gave her hope over to her sight. She poured her will into the path it revealed and let herself move like water through a channel.

Behind her Becca doubled her efforts to match Alexandra's pace. She tried to memorize each twist and turn she saw her friend make because the girl seemed to know just when to pivot or when to duck. In spite of her effort, nevertheless, she lost ground to her cousin and soon accumulated the scratches to prove it. She missed seeing a small hop Alexandra had made over a leaf covered root, tripped and went down, but like being tripped on the soccer field, she rolled, sprung up, and sprinted forward. Twice she had to stop herself from shouting for Alexandra to slow down, realizing both times that slowing down could likely mean losing Audrey to the river.

Then to her surprise, Becca found herself running through grass and fern. She looked to find Alexandra already at the far end of the glade about to disappear back into the woods. As if sensing Becca's presence, Alexandra stopped, spun around, pointed to the river, and frantically beckoned for Becca to hurry before she launched herself into the woods once again. At first, Becca shook her head angrily at the thought that anyone would think she needed reminding to hurry. Then she scanned the river where Alexandra had pointed, and saw nothing but white water until she saw a flash of color, and that flash of color was connected to a person, and that person was standing on a rock waving and waving.

Even though Audrey had managed to pull herself out of the river, Alexandra did not slow the pace of her pursuit until she drew even with her friend and then a little forward of her as if to make the point to herself, to Audrey, and to the river, that she had finally caught up. Becca soon emerged out of the woods to stand beside the girl who she was beginning to understand really could see in a way that defied any easy explanation. All three girls spent the next few minutes catching their collective breath.

"What now?" asked Alexandra.

"I don't know," responded Becca. Then after a moment she shouted out toward Audrey, "We go for help?!"

Audrey shook her head *no*.

"Why not!" yelled Alexandra.

Audrey again shook her head.

"I think because she did this to herself," offered Becca.

"Then how do we get her out ourselves?"

Becca wandered the shoreline. She pondered Audrey's distance from their side of the river, watched the current, then began picking up any larger sticks she could find and launched them toward the rock where Audrey stood stranded. Audrey gestured with her shoulders and arms as if to ask why Becca had decided to throw sticks at her, but Becca only waved her confusion off as she watched the progress of each stick. Soon she strode past the place where Alexandra was standing and moved further downstream. She stopped a point where a small brook fed into the river. The embankment where she stood rose about ten or so feet above the water line. She looked back toward Audrey and watched the currents. She scanned the shoreline where the two lines of water joined and noted several saplings whose roots had been eroded by the convergence of the waters. One young tree that was at least thirty feet tall was already leaning out over the river at an angle that suggested its own weight was slowing pulling its roots free of their hold. She crossed back into the forest and emerged with a large chunk from a fallen birch. It would be easy to follow the path of its white papery bark. She trotted back up to a point even with Audrey and launched the branch on a path directly toward her. Audrey flinched as it hit the water only a few feet from where she stood. All three girls watched the white bob and weave and drift. The current forced it up against a large rock and it seemed as if it might get stuck, but the pressure of the water changed and pushed it free to resume its down river course. On the bank, Becca matched its progress watching where it moved until it passed beneath the half-uprooted sapling. She stood measuring with her eye the distance between the edge of the bank and the main thin shaft of the tree. Alexandra moved up beside her.

"She's going to have to go back into the water and work her way to this side," explained Becca.

"Yeah, okay," said Alexandra with no small tone of sarcasm in her voice.

"No. That's exactly what she has to do. But not until we've pulled that tree down so that she can grab it," she explained pointing to the sapling she had been studying.

Alexandra turned to look back at her friend stranded in the rapids. Then turned to speak to Becca, only to find that she had trotted back away into the glade. Alexandra watched the older girl stop, then step back a few more feet, then pause. She started to speak, to ask how they were going to get the tree down

102

into the water and to ask what guarantee there was that Audrey could even get close enough to reach it, but she never had the chance. Becca struck the pose of a standing start like a runner in a long distance heat and at the sound a starting gun only she could hear began to sprint toward Alexandra. For the briefest moment, Alexandra actually thought this girl was going to run her down or knock her into the river, but soon realized that she was not the target but the measure. Becca was using Alexandra as the jump point, yet even as Alexandra realized this, she had no time to consider it implications or question its need. She could only watch with amazement as Becca dashed up and launched herself off their little bit of cliff and out over the water.

❧ 13 ❧

Watermarks

Becca arced through the air briefly before she began to fall. Alexandra instinctively stretched her arms out as if to pull the girl back safely onto the embankment. From her little island of rock, Audrey watched the figure of this strange, bold girl leap and plummet.

Becca gauged her jump perfectly. While she was still moving more outward than downward she reached for the thin trunk of the leaning tree. Both her arms cleared the top of it so that they guided the momentum of her body. It was a playground moment, a little girl, a chin up bar, other kids watching what she could do. Becca's body slammed into the tree. She drew her arms down to create the vice that would counter the swing of her legs. She winced at the pain of the punch her own weight produced against the wood, and she held on for the ride. The tree shuddered and bent beneath the impact. Something down low popped and the tree arced a bit further so that a few of the leaves on its topmost branches nearly brushed the water. Then it hit its point of resistance and lurched upward. Becca road the trunk like a short carnival ride almost with a sense of joy in not being thrown clear. As the tree settled with its lean toward the river considerably more noticeable, Becca let out a whoop and began to plan in her mind how she would now bring the tree the rest of the way down.

"Go tell her the plan!" yelled Becca over her shoulder as she started to bounce her weight, working against the tree's resistance, trying to break whatever hold its remaining root or roots still had to the shore.

With her heart still pounding from the shock of seeing Becca launch herself off the embankment, Alexandra turned and ran back to where she could shout out to Audrey with some chance of being heard. Audrey crouched on her rock dividing her attention between watching Becca cling to the tree and watching Alexandra's progress along the shore. With her attention so strongly focused on her two friends, what Audrey failed to realize was that the rock she sat on was slowly being swallowed up by the water. The river was still on the rise, but the changes in its depth and height, proved too subtle to mark.

Alexandra drew even with Audrey and shouted, "When the tree goes down, you need to swim this way!"

Audrey shook her head *no.*

Alexandra wasn't sure if her friend meant that she didn't hear what she had just shouted or that she didn't want to go back into the water.

"Tree goes down! You go in! Swim this way! Grab the tree!" Alexandra shouted, breaking the instructions into their most essential parts while simultaneously doing her best to mime the essence of what Audrey needed to see and do.

Audrey had heard her the first time and was going to shake her head *no* again but realized that in spite of her dread, if she was ever going to get back onto the shore, she was going to have to give herself over to the current in order to escape it. After a short moment, as she looked into her best friend's worried face, she nodded *yes* and turned back to watch for the tree to go down.

It did almost immediately, but not in the way all the parties involved understood. Becca meant to fell the tree so that it stretched out its length into the river like casting out a rope. Alexandra too thought the tree was to drop completely but more like a floating jetty that would scoop Audrey into its bay. Audrey, however, simply thought that she was to dive in with the first contact that the tree made with the water, that her friends had found a way to maybe swim out to reach her if she could just get closer to shore and that the dipping tree was the signal to put the plan into action. These misunderstandings soon became clear.

While Alexandra had been miming her version of the rescue plan to Audrey, Becca had been maneuvering her way farther out along the trunk where she thought her weight might do more to stress the tree and get it to relinquish its hold on the shore. She found a good place where she could wedge one arm around the thinning trunk and grip one of the few branches with her free hand. Although her arms were already beginning to ache with fatigue, she once again began to bounce her weight. Beneath the persistent tug of Becca's body, the tree arced more and more until at times it looked like the shaft of a fishing rod bending beneath the catch of a lifetime. Finally some of its topmost branches slapped the water's surface. Audrey took this as the signal for her to move, and without checking for any confirmation from Alexandra, she crept over to the edge of the rock, tried to visualize the course she needed to take, and slid back into the awful rush. On shore, Alexandra couldn't believe her eyes. She didn't even have time to shout. Instinctively she began to run along the shore hoping to keep pace with her friend. She looked toward Becca only to see the tree bent but not broken. Clearly, its remaining roots were holding fast.

Becca was beginning to doubt her choice of rescue plans. She was nearing exhaustion and the tree showed no sign of further weakening. When she took a moment to catch her breath and reestablish her grip, she looked to the shore and found Alexandra moving quickly toward her and staring out into the river. She followed the girl's gaze and to her horror saw that Audrey had left the rock. Her body was again caught in the current and gathering speed. Becca didn't understand what could have happened, but she knew that without the tree down, Audrey would simply shoot past the point of rescue. She also knew that this might be the only best chance to pull this girl out of the current. She knew that these were the wide picturesque rapids and that a few hundred feet farther downstream, where the river narrowed, began the real rapids. She knew no one would survive those without serious injury or worse. At a very deep and distant point in her mind, Becca began to toy with the notion of her complicity in this situation. She had been careless in bringing them here, careless in letting Audrey dance out over the water, careless in wanting to test them both against her own sense of woodcraft. These doubts and accusations flashed briefly but were overshadowed by the immediate crisis.

Alexandra watched Becca see Audrey then watched Becca look back to her with real panic in her eyes. Things were coming unglued. Alexandra suddenly felt nauseous. As she began running toward the little cliff above the river, she watched Becca swinging her legs furiously in an attempt to bring the tree down and realized that her friend had moved too far out along the tree and that the trunk was, by simply bending, absorbing most of Becca's energy. The tree wasn't going to come down without another good blow delivered to its midsection. Alexandra broke into a sprint.

In the brief time she had been allowed to rest, Audrey regained some of her strength and was doing better with controlling her body and keeping herself moving diagonally toward the bank where her friends were. For the most part, she was able to draw her legs up toward her chest and use them to pivot her body away or around the larger rocks, time and again pushing herself farther from the center of the river. This was not to say, however, that it was easy going. The current had a will of its own, and as the crest of the rain tide continued to build, the water drew new channels through and around the boulders. After being dunked briefly, Audrey reoriented herself as best she could and found herself being pushed toward a large, wide boulder. She could see that she needed to pass to its right side to avoid being driven back into the main current, but it was far from certain that she would be able to position herself far enough to the right to pull this maneuver off. Everything was happening so fast. The water drove her forward and toward the river's center. She worked against it with all her will, and when the boulder rose to meet her, her legs landed exactly where she needed them. She pushed them out, and the force of the water drove her up almost to the point of standing. Then even as her feet began to lose their grip, Audrey leaned slightly to the right, instinctively turning her body into a sail to catch the current she needed, and she pivoted toward the shore. In the frantic split second as the river came to claim her once again, she looked for her friends and saw Alexandra oddly poised in midair. Then she went under.

Becca had stopped trying to watch either of her friends. She was completely focused on bending this tree to her will, so she never saw Alexandra's running leap off the small cliff and was unprepared for the jolt sent up and through the tree when Alexandra's body made contact. All Becca felt was a strong vibration that nearly shook her free and then the weightlessness that comes in dropping. *I've pulled it down,* she thought as she and the tree crashed into the river. She was underwater then above it. The current pushed her into the trunk. She looked back toward the shore to see if the tree had snapped or fallen whole, and it was then that she saw Alexandra only a few feet away holding on to the trunk with one hand and gesturing frantically toward the river with her other. Becca snapped her head around expecting to see Audrey but saw nothing other than fast water and rocks. She looked back to Alexandra and saw the panic and disbelief in her eyes. They had lost her. Maybe the tree hadn't come down in time. Maybe she had been pulled back out toward the middle beyond its reach. Both girls held fast to the tree which had begun to swing back toward shore like a gate. A few of its roots were still anchored it to land but the current would not stand for any resistance and pushed the bulk of it out of the way. Both girls were just beginning to snap out of their stupors of disbelief, both just beginning to think of taking to shore and continuing their search at some point downstream, both just beginning to grasp the finality of what had happened, when they heard it.

Clear as a bell and near, much too near to believe, and oddly gleeful.

"Hey! Hey, you two!"

Alexandra and Becca looked up toward the top of the tree and there among the tangle of its topmost branches were Audrey's head and shoulders.

The screams of joy that followed were a mixture of disbelief, triumph, relief, and release, and for a moment their collective joyful noise bested the general roar of the rapids.

As the girls continued to celebrate their reunion the river continued to swing them closer to shore. Alexandra was the first to feel her feet hit upon river bottom, and soon she scrambled over the tree, found some purchase on the shore, and working with the water pulled her part of the trunk more toward the river bank. Becca was next and she followed suit so that two girls now pulled the top of the tree closer to shore. It took Audrey a bit longer to extricate herself from the branches. She seemed reluctant to put her head any nearer the water than she absolutely had to and so struggled to climb over each of the branches rather than take the sometimes easier route of ducking under them. Finally all three found themselves on dry land and locked in a hug full of tears and joy. Becca broke away first to let Alexandra have the chance to console Audrey on her own. She watched as the weight of what might have occurred came crashing down onto the two friends. She watched Audrey sob into Alexandra's shoulder and listened to the humming consolation as Alexandra whispered over and over again – *It's done. It's done. It's done.*

With a huge deep breath, Audrey stepped back from her friend and asked, "Can we please move a little farther away from the water?"

All three laughed and turned their attention to picking their way up the bank and back to where they could cross the stream that fed into the river. Once up on the grassy knoll, Becca stopped and removed her shirt, rang it out and spread it flat in the sun then proceeded to do the same with her shorts and ended by pulling off her shoes and wringing out her socks. The other two girls followed suit. Audrey sat and examined her arms and legs for bruises and scrapes. Alexandra looked out over the river and in spite of what she had just been through was strangely taken in by its beauty. As Becca poked at her ribs finding the tender spots from when she had first hit the tree, she watched Audrey.

"One question..." Becca started.

Both Alexandra and Audrey looked up.

"... Why did you even start jumping onto the rocks?"

Realizing the question was not directed toward her, Alexandra went back to contemplating the view.

"I don't know... I had this stupid dream about water."

Alexandra snapped her head back.

"What?" begged Audrey in response to the stares, and for the next half hour the girls took turns describing their various water dreams from the night before. While the coincidence of such kindred dreams each struck each of the girls as a little more than strange, in their fatigue and relief, none were ready to mine the odd convergence of imagery for any deeper significance. By the time they finished hearing each other out, their clothes were merely damp and their stomachs ached from hunger. They rose and dressed and turned to find their way back to their packs where the food and water waited. When they got to edge of the glade where the grass and fern gave way to the saplings and thickets of the woods, the girls paused. Audrey looked to Becca as the one to lead them through the forest, but she found Becca looking to Alexandra.

"Can you do it?" Becca asked quietly.

There was a pause in which Alexandra turned and faced the upriver woods, she had barely begun to form a desire to see a way clear when the wave of pressure ran through her and her sight doubled, the light from within augmenting the daylight. The tunnels again appeared. A way was clear.

"Come on," she said in quiet response, "We don't have to go so fast this time."

Becca grinned sheepishly and dropped in behind Alexandra as she bent and entered the thicket.

"Monkey see, monkey do, Audrey. Whatever you see her do, every duck and jump, you do the same," instructed Becca then continued, "She's the reason we didn't lose you. Cut through this mess like she was on I-91."

"You've got your second set of eyes turned on?" asked Audrey loud enough for Alexandra to hear over the rush of the river.

"Yep," came a distant matter-of-fact reply, and the girls fell silent, each returning to her own thoughts of what had and hadn't transpired over the last hour.

Soon they emerged above the bit of accessible river bank where Audrey had first danced onto the rocks. They all noticed that the water level had risen slightly. Some of the rocks on which Audrey hand first mounted offered much smaller targets now. In fact, as she looked over the available footholds, she could no longer see a way out into the river at all and marveled at her own audacity, a word she preferred over stupidity. They had shed their packs far enough back from the water's edge that neither of them had gotten anything close to wet as the river widened in its cresting.

In unspoken deference to Audrey, they did not linger near the river but ate as they returned to the path and began their hike home. Becca took one pack and handed the other to Alexandra. They each went for a bottle of water first before unwrapping their sandwiches. None of them ever tasted water so delicious or enjoyed a sandwich as much. They even fought playfully over sharing Josh's trail mix, especially the secret ingredient, the corn syrup sweetness of the licorice providing the closest thing to dessert they were going to get.

After they finished eating, they paused to divide the empty bottles and plastic bags between the packs. Audrey asked first one then the other of girls to let her take a turn carrying one of the packs. Both gently rebuffed her offer with the same unspoken understanding, that Audrey was still in need of special consideration. Even when again Audrey repeated her desire to share the lightened burden, this time about half way back, she found that neither Becca nor Alexandra were of a mind to do anything but let her continue walking unencumbered.

After lunching and except for the occasional *heads up* on a low branch or high root, there was little talk. The food and drink gave them the energy to keep moving, but their minds were still dizzy with the mixture of disbelief and relief. At different points along the path, each of the girls felt the full weight of what might have happened. Each had the notion nestle into her mind and memory that this was a day that does not get taken back or rearranged to suit one's fancy. What had happened had happened. Irrevocably. The fact that it turned out well did not lessen the gravity of the chain of events. At different points along the path, each caught herself looking at the other two and being swept away by a sense of gratitude. In one way or another, they had refused to abandon or to be abandoned. They had chosen to find the link among them stronger than the temptation to despair or to panic or to quit. At different points along the path, each felt and accepted the mark this day would leave.

They emerged from the woods onto the field above the Dwyer's house in a huddled line.

"Not a word," Becca half-asked, half-stated.

"Not a word," confirmed Alexandra.

"Just a picnic by the river," offered Audrey.

They would hold to this story for years until it became necessary to say otherwise, but for the rest of this day into a night filled with pasta and ice cream, they let Josh's afternoon of mischief and mayhem with Muffin overshadow their little hike up to the see the rapids.

When Alexandra ducked into the tent for the night, she found Audrey had rearranged her sleeping bag so that it was in the middle paralleling the other two, all three heads at the back, all three feet pointing toward the door. None of the girls commented on it. It seemed a perfectly sensible change. They settled in and let the exhaustion of the day come. After about a quarter of an hour of tense silence, Alexandra spoke.

"I swear to God, Becca, when you jumped off that cliff, I nearly peed myself."

All three parents as well as Josh, Gruff, and Muffin heard the great peal of laughter burst from the backyard. Up in their bedroom, Mr. Dwyer rolled over and looked to his wife.

"We don't even want to know," she said dryly.

❧ 14 ❦

White Lies and Bandages

The next morning started off much the same as the night before had ended – with a fit of giggles as each of the girls discovered for herself just how sore she was from the previous day's bumps and knocks. Becca woke first, but when she tried to sit up a bolt of pain raked along her left side from hip to shoulder. She dropped back down onto her sleeping bag only to have this maneuver fire off another bolt of pain. She inhaled slowly and found she could only manage about half a deep breath before her chest tightened with the discomfort. Imagining herself lying in this spot for rest of the day, she got giggling and then crying out as each little convulsion and the following intake of air made her feel as if Josh was rabbit punching her up and down the length of her torso. Thus it was that Alexandra was pulled from her sleep by an odd series of yelps which only increased when she tried to sit up and immediately dropped back down because of the painful stiffness in her back, stomach, and arms.

"You can't move either," laughed Becca only to cry out again.

"I can't and don't make me laugh… it hurts," answered Alexandra.

This response intensified Becca's giggles and the volume of her cries. So it was that Audrey woke up to the sounds of her two friends caught in the throes of what seemed to be a painful inside joke. Yet when she tried to roll over on her side to question Alexandra, she winced and lay back down.

"Her too!" squealed Alexandra sending Becca into another wracking bout of giggles and cries.

Audrey joined in the laughter at first, but as she stretched her arms and pushed herself back into a sitting position, she discovered that she had seriously bruised the area behind her right shoulder. She tried but failed to recall the specific impact that might have caused it. While in the river, there had been so many bangs and scrapes that it was impossible to isolate any one particularly bad blow. Yet it was Becca's growing discomfort that cut their giggling short. Her cries turned to whimpers and she found catching her breath after each bout of laughter more and more difficult. Audrey first recognized the change in Becca's tone and gestured to Alexandra.

"It really hurts, and I can't get a good breath," said Becca shakily.

"Don't try to breathe deeply, try and breathe slower," offered Audrey as she caught Becca's eye and worked to help by demonstrating what she meant.

Under Audrey's guidance, soon the two girls were breathing in sync and Becca was feeling less severe pain with each intake, but she still could not manage more than these slow shallow breaths.

As Becca continued to calm herself and minimize her movements, the other two girls took more careful stock of their own injuries. Audrey found small bruises and scrapes on both knees and along both arms. She had a particularly nasty bruise on one shin, but it was the area on her back that troubled her most. She had Alexandra check for any outward sign of injury. Though none could be seen and while she could raise her right arm all the way up, it was a slow and painful process. She silently chastised herself for the day before but was reluctant and even careful not to let the full weight of what might have happened come crashing back into her mind. It was ample punishment that her injuries could not be easily explained away to her parents and that they felt severe enough to last for weeks and get in the way of her ballet camp. As Alexandra helped her pull her shirt back down, Audrey looked over at her new friend. Clearly Becca's injury was the more serious and this too helped keep Audrey from dwelling on her own pending troubles.

Alexandra had fared the best which only made sense since she had spent the least time in either the tree or the water. She too had bruised her chest and ribs but not anything close to the degree that Becca had. As she watched her friend trying to find a more comfortable way to lie still, Alexandra imagined that even if the impact of Becca's first jump hadn't been enough to do this much damage all the subsequent grinding she did as she swung her legs would have added to it, and then there was the fall when the tree came down. *Maybe she had gotten crushed briefly between the water and the trunk,* she thought. In any event, Becca was not doing well.

"I think," Becca said trying not to let her emotions spill out and in crying cause her pain, "we need to tell Mom and Dad. I don't feel right."

Alexandra was up and almost out of the tent before Becca could manage her next breath and thought.

"Wait," she whispered as loudly as she could. "Just wait. We need a story. Need to stick to it. Need to believe it. And need them to believe it."

After a quick frantically whispered debate, they settled on the explanation that during the return trip there was a good bit of horseplay, pushing and shoving and racing to be in the lead, and that in the middle of all this, in addition to some other scrapes and knocks suffered by all three girls, Becca had both been nudged and had lost her footing and fell sharply onto a larger rock. She had hit it the act of getting her arms up to stop herself, and although it had hurt like the devil when it first happened, it wasn't until this morning that the injury showed itself to be as bad as it was. If pressed, she was going to argue that maybe she had slept on it in such a way as to make it worse. They rehearsed the details a few times in case any of them got cornered into telling the story outside the presence of the others. It was clear that Becca was the most comfortable in proceeding, maybe because she was in the most pain and wanted to get it all over with, or maybe because she that in sneaking out to meet up with Will, she had become more confident in her ability to deceive in little ways. Audrey and Alexandra, on the other hand, seemed only half-heartedly convinced this ploy would prove successful, and Alexandra looked a little green as she went to find one or both of Becca's parents. Left to their own thoughts, each of them started to sense that this initial little concoction of a story could well prove to be the first of many complications to follow from their trip to the rapids.

As should have been expected, everyone came running. The Dwyer's took their daughter to the nearest emergency room. The three remaining kids and Mr. Stepp stayed near the phone and played cards to pass the time. Alexandra could see that Audrey favored her right side, keeping her right arm resting in her lap and reaching with her left hand only. When Audrey would catch her friend's worried stare, she would dismiss the concern with a half-smile and little shrug as if to say *It's nothing really*. Neither Mr. Stepp nor Josh seemed to notice anything in terms of Audrey's stiffness or Alexandra's concern.

The mothering instinct of Gruff, however, proved keener, and she easily maneuvered her way through the forest of legs until she pressed up against Audrey. The girl stroked the dog's neck and matched her stare of concern. She leaned in gingerly, trying not to let her discomfort show. "I know you know, momma dog, but we're keeping it a secret for now," she whispered. Gruff responded with a chuff that sounded to Audrey a lot like a scolding. The girl sought out Gruff's eyes again, met them, and was rewarded with a swift full lick along her cheek. "Saucy girl," she squealed happily.

After a few more hands, Mr. Stepp decided to call Audrey's parents to let them know about Becca's situation and to let them know that if one or other of Josh's parents didn't return soon their return trip might be delayed. Almost as soon as he hung the phone up, however, a car came rolling up the driveway. Dogs and all rushed to the front porch, Audrey moving a bit more gingerly than the rest. Becca's mom looked tired but relieved as she helped her daughter out of the car.

"A pair of cracked ribs," she announced as she continued to steady her daughter. Becca's dad seemed his usual self and asked right away if he had missed any work calls. As Becca emerged slowly and stiffly from the back seat, Audrey and Alexandra looked to each other for reassurance that their story survived not only a doctor's examination which most likely even included x-rays but worse, her parents' questioning, yet all the reassurance they needed soon came from Becca herself. As the

116

two girls looked back to the car, they caught the older girl's expression. With eyes twinkling, Becca wore a wolfish grin complete with the tip of her tongue peeking out from one corner of her mouth.

As soon as the injured girl settled on the couch, Mr. Stepp made another call to Audrey's parents to let them know everything was back on schedule, and this set off a small flurry of activity as bags were packed and offers made to linger and break down the tent. Mrs. Dwyer insisted on making snacks for the road. The girls kept trying to find a moment to put their heads together but were continually interrupted by one demand or another. Audrey was called to double check that she had collected all her things. Aunt Sue needed Alexandra's help in the kitchen. In the little time the three girls managed alone, they found that Audrey's injury now loomed larger. She was clearly in a great deal of discomfort, but they decided that if she could just make it back for the drive, she could tell her parents that she too had fallen and get the injury addressed on that end, maybe just maybe, without alerting Becca's parents on this end. As they climbed the porch steps to get the last few bags and take them out to the car, Alexandra's dad pulled her aside and let her know that he felt he needed to make the offer that she come home with him now in order to let Becca fully rest and recover. Before she had time to react, they entered the living room and the words were out of his mouth.

Even as Becca's parents looked to each other in consideration of this offer, Becca spoke up, almost too quickly, almost as if she anticipated such a possibility.

"She's not going anywhere. She was the one chasing me when I fell, so she's got to stay here and keep me entertained," she commanded adding, "Maybe even until I'm *fully* recovered."

Getting the nod from Becca's mom, Alexandra's dad retreated, "Okay, okay. It was just an idea. She stays. Do your penance, girl. Keep this patient entertained."

All exchanged goodbyes and promises of return trips. The adults confirmed plans for Alexandra's departure in a little over a week. Reminders about good behavior and expectations of helpfulness were delivered. As her dad and uncle stood by the closed trunk talking about whatever dads and uncles always find it necessary to talk about before one or the other drives away, Alexandra lingered by Audrey's window.

"You look terrible," said Alexandra quietly.

"I'll be okay. I think sitting down is what I need to do. It'll be smooth sailing once we're on the highway"

"What are you going to tell your mom and dad?"

"Same story... that in running around the woods, I took a spill. I think for this... I'll need to have fallen... maybe out of tree."

"Out of a tree?"

"Tell Becca, so we're all on the same page. Maybe I ran ahead to hide, climbed a tree, and in trying to keep out of sight, lost my footing and came down hard on my back... How's that sound?" asked Audrey looking a little pleased to be joining in with a white lie of her own.

"You've got that story down pretty well."

"I'll need to."

"It should work. I'll let Becca know the details," grinned Alexandra as her dad opened the driver's side door.

With waves and a series of honks, Alexandra watched her friend and father disappear down the driveway. She stood for a moment before going back into the house with more than an inkling of regret for not returning with Audrey to see that she too was going to be alright. A gleefully weak cry from the house, however, soon pulled her back into the moment.

"Lemonade! I need lemonade! Where's my nurse?!"

Before the novelty of it dissipated, Becca milked her invalid status as much as she could that first afternoon. Upon returning from estimating a job, her dad brought her a handful of teen magazines and a six-pack of her favorite root beer. Her mom disappeared into the kitchen and soon the smell of baking filled the house. Less than an hour later a plate full of warm chocolate chip cookies appeared on the coffee table within Becca's easy reach. Even Josh offered the care he thought most essential by bringing down his favorite stuffed animal to keep his sister company.

Eventually, each time they had a moment alone, Alexandra would get Becca giggling by chastising her for taking too much advantage of the situation. And each time her giggling reached the point of causing her pain, Alexandra would feel terrible and fall over herself to apologize which as often as not put Becca into further fits of giggling as she watched her friend fall into the same trap that her family had in placing her at the current center of the world.

This dynamic changed, however, with a phone call. Becca's dad answered it, stayed on the line for a time listening, then called Alexandra over to speak with her dad. Becca watched her friend's back, heard the concern in her voice, and then saw it in her face when she glanced back to where Becca sat reclining on the sofa. As soon as he had handed off the phone, Mr. Dwyer had sought out his wife, so when Alexandra quietly replaced the receiver and turned to face the room, she found that Becca had been joined by her parents on the sofa. Mrs. Dwyer's face was drawn and stern.

"You tell Becca what you've heard, and then I have some questions for the both of you," she said almost sadly.

Becca and Alexandra both immediately picked up on the tone. It was a mother's disappointed voice – her *I'm not angry, I'm just saddened that it's come to this* voice. Worried that Alexandra might not be able to hold to their story, Becca only half-heard what had happened to Audrey, that she had been taken in for x-rays as well, that while there was no apparent evidence of any break or fracture, there was clearly deep bone bruising on her right shoulder blade, that it would be weeks if not months before she fully recovered, and that she would miss her ballet camp and maybe even the start of her dance classes in the fall.

"But she's going to be alright?" asked Becca.

"Yes," said her dad very quickly, "Cy said that they expect her to be fine and to be back dancing before you know it."

"She never keeps her feet still anyway. She'll make her fall classes. I know she will," insisted Alexandra hopefully.

"How did it happen?" Mrs. Dwyer asked before the conversation could move too far away from the accident itself.

Becca started to answer, but her mother cut her off with a glance and looked to Alexandra. Alexandra repeated the story she and Audrey had concocted: that Audrey ran ahead to hide, climbed a tree, lost her footing, and fell onto her back. Becca nodded her head in agreement with each detail.

"And why did no one mention this earlier?" asked Mrs. Dwyer.

Again Becca started to offer a response, but again Mrs. Dwyer made it clear she wanted to hear it from Alexandra. Smooth as silk, the other girl explained that since Becca's injury seemed the more severe, it became the focus, that they had all been stiff from running around so much and that Audrey hadn't complained that much to either of them.

Another phone call interrupted Mrs. Dwyer's pursuit of a truth she could accept. This time it was Alexandra's mother and step-father. The Dwyer's sat as Alexandra repeated abbreviated accounts of what had happened to both of her friends and reassured all listening that she was fine and that with Becca laid up they wouldn't be doing anything like it again. Finally, Mrs. Dwyer rose and stood beside Alexandra motioning to the girl that she wanted to speak to her mom before she said good-bye. Alexandra was relieved to pass the receiver off to her Aunt Sue. She and the others listened to Mrs. Dwyer's apologies and reassurances that everyone was fine and in safe keeping.

After years of shuttling between homes, Alexandra learned to play down the scale of any drama that happened in one house when talking to the other. Her parents were cordial with each other, but it was clear to her that they were no longer friends. She found it mostly an issue of tone. What they said of each other was generally supportive, but it was done either in such a overtly polite way or with such a monotone that the words carried little conviction. At first, when she was younger and they had just broken the marriage off, Alexandra toyed with the power of seeing one or the other parent react to news of some carelessness or oversight in the other house, but in the last couple of years, she discovered how that game left her feeling isolated, in a kind of limbo between allegiances and with homes that felt more and more like temporary houses. The alternative, however,

120

had its drawbacks as well. When she decided to keep to the middle, play things down, not look to stir the pot excessively, she was left with more to carry on her own shoulders, bits of the fuller truth that maybe should have been shared but that seemed to her too potentially volatile or upsetting for one or the other parent to hear. And now came this situation where she keeping another kind of truth from all parties. *Maybe it'll be easier than the usual little lies*, she thought to herself as she watched her aunt hang up the phone.

That interruption put an end to Mrs. Dwyer's inquiry. Whatever she felt she needed to say to Alexandra's mom and step-father exhausted her desire to hear any more about any of it. After a little bit of discussion, she and Mr. Dwyer agreed that the girls would camp out in the living room right where they were since the couch and pillows offered Becca the most comfort and support for her injury. It wasn't until Becca's parents were out of the room that either girl felt as if she could finally breathe again.

"She'll be fine," Becca said quietly after a long pause.

"I know," agreed Alexandra, "I'm just trying to figure out whether it would have been just as well to come clean from the start."

The girls sat in silence for a time.

"Maybe. But I don't really think so," Becca said finally, "If we'd told them the truth we'd be in such trouble and it wouldn't have made our getting banged up any less. I'm laid up. Audrey's laid up. You're all battered and stiff. It's enough we're dealing with that."

They decided to put a movie on, but neither of them really watched it. Mr. Dwyer came in to help get an air mattress situated for Alexandra. He sat on the couch for a while gently stroking one of Becca's shins. Mrs. Dwyer crossed through the room, said a quiet good night, and headed up the stairs to her bedroom. Soon after, Mr. Dwyer gave each girl a quick kiss on the top of their heads. At the base of stairs, he paused and turned.

"No handstands or back flips tonight, okay?"

Both girls looked at him and smiled weakly.

"Glad we understand each other," he said.

At some point, well before it was over, they decided to turn off the movie. Each of the girls took a long time settling in, and each fell asleep waiting to hear the other drift off first.

❧ 15 ❧

The Dark Shawl

The next few days passed without incident. The girls spent most of their time in the living room watching videos, playing board games, or reading. Becca's ribs began to mend. She was capable of a good deal more movement and complained almost constantly of the itching she felt just below her skin. There had been numerous calls back and forth between Alexandra and her parents, Aunt Sue and Mr. Stepp, and Alexandra and Audrey. Becca was relieved to hear that Audrey was recovering nicely as well. Already she could move her arm much more freely and even snuck in a few pirouettes when her parents had been out of the house.

The most unexpected event came with Will's appearance at the front door toward the end of the third day of Becca's convalescence. Josh was the first to hear the bike tires on the driveway and assumed it was one of his friends stopping by with either an invitation to dinner or to ice cream afterwards, so he rushed to the door only to announce that it was Becca's friend Will. He was welcomed by Mr. Dwyer, offered something to drink by Mrs. Dwyer, complimented on his bike by Josh, sniffed by both the dogs, and finally allowed to sit in the arm chair nearest where Becca lounged. He didn't stay long that first visit, leaving soon after he passed along the best wishes of his aunt and uncle with whom he now lived, but he did offer to come back and Becca made it clear that would be a welcome addition to her daily routine.

Nevertheless, while much of the house seemed to resume its normal, pre-rapids trip routine, the girls still sensed that Becca's mom continued to have her doubts about what exactly had happened. Once the first batch had all been eaten, she baked no more cookies, and when she joined them to watch part of a movie, play a game or two, or read, the girls agreed she was less talkative than during the earlier days of Alexandra's visit. Every chance she got, Becca reassured Alexandra that everything was going to be fine, that her mom would come around eventually, and that sticking to the story and letting time pass was the best strategy.

To escape from the boredom of routine and her sense of the tension between Becca and her mother, Alexandra began looking more and more to find time to be on her own. She found that for an hour or so each evening after helping clear the dinner table and dry the dishes that she could step outside without being missed and watch the forest as the sun set. Becca and her dad got into the habit of sitting down to an after dinner game or games of chess or backgammon. Josh chose a video, and Becca's mom worked on her computer at the kitchen table.

With only a few more nights before she was to return home and wanting to make the most of each evening, Alexandra would drag one of the lawn chairs out into the center of the backyard, face it toward the mountain, and sit and watch and think. It was as if she was trying to memorize the shape of the field and the line of the trees. Here her gift-sight had come on full force and opened up the world to her. She wanted to take these shapes with her when she left. She wanted to have them at the ready to recall what it was like when she first moved within her heightened vision with complete confidence. She wanted to be able to tap into that confidence and to remind herself that hers was an ability beyond Becca's woodcraft. She didn't need to know these woods like the back of her hand. She simply needed to know how to ask them to reveal their pathways and passages.

On this night, she was glad to find that there was a breeze to keep the mosquitoes at bay. In fact, cool gusting winds moved in front of a long line of storm clouds. She watched the storm approach, watched the few early stars being blotted out by the front, when the mountain range was suddenly back lit by distant lightning, lightning so far away that no thunder followed. Behind her the back door opened and she turned to see Mrs. Dwyer framed by the light of the kitchen.

"Just don't get hit by lightning," she said firmly, "I don't want to make that call to your folks."

Gruff scooted past her and trotted out to join Alexandra.
"I won't be out much longer. It's still really far away."
"If it starts to rain, please come in."
"I will, Aunt Sue."

Gruff sat by Alexandra's chair sniffing the air. Alexandra wondered what curious scents the wind carried from up the range and out of the woods. She gently stroked the soft hair on top of Gruff's head as another course of lightning silhouetted the mountains.

As her eyes readjusted from the distant flash, she returned to the matter of memorizing this stretch of land. Like an artist returning to a favorite subject, Alexandra found herself moving beyond contour and shape and letting the play of colors and textures settle into her mind. Perhaps it was the odd mix of lights, the lingering daylight competing with the creeping shadow of the storm, the sudden backlighting provided by the distant storm, but the landscape seemed to flatten. Instead of seeing the field as if it receded back to meet the woods, she saw the woods as if they had been pushed forward bringing the back edge of the field with it. She found herself staring at the scene like a canvas, the world in two dimensions, the muted colors held up for closer inspection. It was not like a photograph, however, the world had not stilled, the wind continued to bend the tops of the trees as if they were tall grass, the storm front pushed its shadow farther over the range, but it seemed as if the world had tilted itself in order to present Alexandra with the details she needed to cement a more complete image of this place in her memory. Even in the growing dimness the many greens shone through as did the all the different pale yellows of the field. She seemed at times to see both an entire tree and its individual leaves, an entire section of grasses and its individual tufts and flowers. Still stroking Gruff's downy head, she let these images and their impressions drift into her mind's eye. Another flash of distant lightning and the world wavered. The mountains receded and the field lay back onto its sloping run toward the woods. Then suddenly, unsummoned, the crush came, Alexandra's gift-sight swept into her eyes, and she found herself looking at the landscape before her relit by the quiet light within.

Gruff stiffened and wagged her tail furiously as she sniffed and licked Alexandra's hand. Whether or not the dog experienced any change in its sight, Alexandra was uncertain, but clearly Gruff sensed its emergence within the girl. Why her sight had descended, how it was the dog sensed it, what was it she was to seek in this moment, all of these questions rose in her mind and were just a quickly forgotten because in the next moment the dark behind the mountain forest flashed, and it nearly took Alexandra's breath away.

In addition to the usual brilliant flare, Alexandra saw the sky and the bottoms of the clouds lit by soft tendrils of pale lavender and a faint, creamy green. She watched the web of these colors dance and recede northward following the charge shooting up from the earth as it move along the storm front. Again the mountain rose and the field tilted and Alexandra watched the pulse of the wind worked its way southward, the flutter of individual leaves as they resisted and released the push. Soon the entire forest billowed as the mass of air cut its channels through the trees. Then something of the light that had lingered after the lightning gathered and took form at the point where the path emptied from the woods into the grasses. The girl stood up from her chair and turned all of her attention toward that bundle of light. Without a doubt, she could see the shapes of people, five or six of them, but nothing solid, only their shapes outlined by pulses of pale lavender and faint green. Gruff suddenly crouched down and pushed up her hind quarters. Her tail cut a swath of joy as if she were a puppy ready for a game of tag.

Two valleys over the rains had already come and falling water played against the leaves and by rivulet or drop by drop the forest sang its song. Drenched but undeterred a coyote trotted along it way. A few moments earlier, it paused in its stupor of purpose, held still a moment as if robbed of all will to move, think, feel. The dark Manitou whose wish possessed it paused to take account of the pulse sent out by the onset of Alexandra's gift-sight. Deep in the lake, Matchi Manitou itched to know the source of this pinprick. It released the coyote to continue on its quest, filling it with new thoughts as to how to find paths across rivers, how to coerce brothers in order to muster a pack when needed, what to look for in its victims, what to smell, what to taste. The coyote struggled to manage the jumble of such knowledge. It trotted along glad to be moving even as it tried and failed to turn its new mind to wishing itself back by that lake again.

The storm moved in. With the next flash, the first distinct bolt of lightning cut the sky behind the mountain. When its brilliance retreated, Alexandra found herself face to face with the form of an old woman wrapped in a shawl. Only a few feet separated them. It was an odd moment completely void of normal response. Alexandra was surprised but not startled by this vision. Even as she began to take in what she was seeing, she also became aware that she felt no fear. The woman's features came and went with the pulsing of the lights that defined her. Her faint hair fell across the front of her shoulders in two long braids. Her faint face was weathered and warm. When it could be seen clearly, she wore an expression of curiosity and at the same time something like recognition, or perhaps the expectation or desire to be recognized. Alexandra responded to that desire and felt within herself a commensurate need to know this face. She felt as if she should remember it but could not.

The storm moved in. The old woman's countenance faded and returned, her body faded and returned, and suddenly, in all the ambiguity of this fluttering, Alexandra noticed that the shawl she wore held firm in its appearance. It held its form as if it were the only real thing left in the world. She could see the detail of its rough weave and the dark red and black of its simple striped pattern.

In the next moment several things happened.

The storm arrived. Several streaks of lightning broke only a few miles away. The spectral face of the old woman seemed to draw matter from the charged air and came into stronger focus. Alexandra saw the hint of smile and felt as if she was being told *yes*… but *yes* to what was uncertain.

Alexandra heard the back door swing open and the stern voice of her Aunt Sue, "Girl, get-in-this-house!"

The old woman and the other forms at the wood's entrance vanished, the mountain and field tipped back into their rightful positions, and Alexandra's vision-gift began to falter, but not until she looked down to find Gruff happily sniffing at a set of footprints in the grass a few feet away from where Alexandra still stood, clear as any imprints made by one of her friends but in complete isolation, no suggestion of any tracks leading up to the point where they lingered as their dullness was slowly fading into the faltering luminescence of the surrounding grass. It was as if the person who had made them had simply dropped from the sky.

Like a rough whisper, Alexandra could hear the rain beginning to blanket the forest, and she and Gruff spun and dashed gleefully toward the light of the house.

❧ 16 ❧

Questions and Plans

When Alexandra first entered the house, she immediately joined in with the flurry of closing windows before the blowing rain wetted their sills and then helped in retrieving and positioning fans to insure everyone would sleep comfortably. It wasn't until the Dwyer's retreated to their bedrooms and she and Becca turned off their light that Alexandra had any chance to reflect on what happened and what she saw in the moments before the storm's arrival.

Her thoughts, however, were muddled as she tried to understand how it was her gift-sight had descended without her having summoned it and to understand the significance of what she witnessed. Even in the dark and with the rain's soft patter, her restlessness filled the room. *Had I been seeking something?*, she asked herself. *Why was the shawl not ghostly as well? No, I was memorizing the tree lines. Did they come with the lighting? In it? Because of it? A blanket's not a living thing. Can stuff carry the light I see?* And on and on it went as if her mind seemed intent on undercutting its own logic.

"What's the deal, girl. I can hear you thinking all the way over here," broke Becca's voice into the strained half-silence.

Alexandra poured out her story, trying to tell it in such a way that it would make better sense to her, but rather than offer any answers, its retelling merely served to underscore the questions of who the woman was and why she had appeared and what was it that prompted Alexandra's heightened sight to descend in the first place. As if on cue, as she reached the end of her tale where she was describing how Gruff's sniffing had directed her gaze to the footprint evidence, the old dog emerged from the kitchen and sauntered over to rest her head on the couch near Becca's head.

"Did you see the old woman too?" Becca asked the dog and in answer heard Gruff's tail beat against the floor. "And she didn't bark at all?" asked Becca into the dark.

"No. It's like she got all happy when it started... like she could sense the change in me when my vision-thing kicked in... And when that woman showed up, she got all skippy-jumpy like this was going to be the best game ever." Gruff's tail beat a faster rhythm on the floor, and Alexandra couldn't tell if it was in response to the tone of what she said or if Becca had at that moment decided to treat her to a scratch in one of her many favorite places.

"So did she look just old old, or was she scary old?"

"I don't know... It's hard to say... It was getting dark and she was pretty faint. I know she was old and she had braids... but it was her wrap, the blanket or the shawl or the whatever... that was the most solid thing about her."

"That just seems weird to me."

"I know." agreed Alexandra.

"So who do you think she was?" asked Becca then waited as patiently as she could listening to Alexandra's silence. "I know you don't know, but what if you had to guess. What does your gut say?"

"She was an Indian."

"Yeah, I was thinking that too."

"What's going on with me?" asked Alexandra, but before Becca could answer, both girls heard a door upstairs open and then Mrs. Dwyer's voice, quiet yet firm.

"Girls, it's late."

"Okay, Mom," responded Becca quickly.

"Thank you," she said as she turned to go back to her bedroom. Gruff pulled herself away from Becca's touch and trotted up the stairs as if she too had been told to settle down and find her place. The girls listened to the door close and whispered their *good nights* before turning inward to their own thoughts.

Becca tested her ribs and found that it was only when she pushed really hard that she could feel a dull ache. She imagined that she was well enough to take a walk with Will if he were to show up again. To set the stage for that eventuality, she decided to help with breakfast and the laundry. If she could help with the chores, surely she could take a short walk around the fields.

For her part, Alexandra was still holding to Becca's suggestion that she trust her gut, and her gut told her that the old woman had been a Native American, that she was not malicious, that the shawl was somehow significant, and that there was some connection to be found among the woman, the shawl, the storm, and Alexandra's gift-sight. In fact, as she poured back over how she felt and what had happened as the storm approached, she was gut-led to realize that whatever it was that was the source of her gift-sight had dropped it on her in order for her to believe what she was about to see, that if there had not been footprints visible to her on the ground, she might have been able to dismiss the vision, even with Gruff's happy sniffing insistence that something had indeed been standing in front of her. Again came the odd notion her heightened sight was both within and without her, that while she could summon it, it could also summon her. This was a large admission.

She fell into a fitful sleep wanting answers to questions she had yet to fully form, wanting to know what exactly it was that was both open to hear her call when seeking and willful enough to demand that she seek the hint of an old woman and the shawl she wore.

The next morning, Alexandra woke thinking Audrey was still in the house and anticipated the relief of telling her about her vision from the night before and to getting some help deciding what it all might mean. For Alexandra, Audrey was already the friend that Becca was yet to become. Becca would always be the cousin she saw once or twice a year and would always be those few years older. Alexandra had grown up with Audrey. She had been the one constant in an otherwise divided life as Alexandra moved between her two houses, her two sets of rules, her two sets of expectations. It's not that Alexandra didn't talk to the adults in her life. She told her parents about school and the petty gripes with friends, this new interest or that new dislike. She talked with her mom about the girl stuff and with her dad about most everything else, but she talked with Audrey about things in a way that went beyond reporting. She talked about how she felt in the face of those petty gripes, the pending girl stuff, characters in books and movies, and a horizon populated with boys. Most of all, when she was with Audrey, she didn't have to try and be what was expected, she could simply be.

As she ventured further into the waking world, however, she realized that any discussion with Audrey would have to wait a few days until she traveled back home. A knot of disappointment gripped her stomach. She took a deep breath working to remind herself that a few days wasn't forever.

She rolled over and found Becca watching her.

"Yo, Chickee," blurted out Becca with no hint of a whisper.

Alexandra laughed out loud, "You are so weird."

"I feel great," said the older girl sitting up and stretching both arms out and up showing no sign of any lingering stiffness in her ribs until she started to reverse her movements, and then there was a noticeable hitch and pause in her movements suggesting that from a certain angle all was not a hundred percent.

Nevertheless, Becca was determined not to spend another day lounging around on the couch. She insisted that they get up and explore what if any damage the storm had done before the rest of the house woke up. Quickly and quietly they dressed and exited through the front door. Almost in unison, they both shuddered from the cool air scrubbed and chilled by the rain. Alexandra took a deep breath and the crisp air spilled into her lungs like cold water on her face, and she felt that however awake she had been before, she was infinitely more awake now. She looked around at a sky already evenly lit by the coming sun and was surprised by the distance and detail she was able to see. Halfway down the driveway, she watched a cluster of chickadees chasing insects and chatting as they scurried from tree to tree or hopped from branch to branch. Even at this distance, she could see both the flashing white of their tiny breasts and the sharp black caps of their little heads.

As she followed Becca's lead and tip-toed down the front steps, Alexandra found she suddenly wanted to look again at the ground where she saw the whisper of the old woman the previous night. Maybe in this clean light some proof of her presence would yet be evident. Then just as suddenly came an urge to obscure that evidence, and with this urge Alexandra found herself again wishing for Audrey's presence, for the friend she could trust absolutely with this new twist of events. As she crossed from the gravel and scruff of the driveway into the cool dampness of the grass, Becca's actions pulled Alexandra back from her own thoughts. Her cousin Becca seemed equally intent on circling the house toward where Alexandra had been sitting before the storm came, and the desire to avoid any further exploration or discussion of the old woman and her shawl surged through Alexandra's mind. She picked up her pace to try and come even with Becca as they rounded the house.

"Slow down," she whispered harshly.

Becca spun and shushed her, pointing to the second story and her parents' bedroom window that she instinctively knew would have been pushed back open by one or the other of her parents once the storm has passed. Indeed when Alexandra followed Becca's gesture, she saw a window pushed up and the dark square cut by the screen.

Becca stepped back and whispered, "I want to check out the tent. See if it's still dry."

"Why?"

At first Becca did not answer, then she leaned in closer and spoke even more quietly, "I want to meet Will again tonight. I'm feeling fine. I'm going to chip in around the house all day, sneak a quick call to Will, then we're going to get permission to sleep out here one last time because it'll be a lot easier to cut out from back here than to worry about squeaking doors and dogs."

Before Alexandra could respond with concern or questions, Becca turned and strode toward the tent. Alexandra followed but with her own mission now, to move the chair she that she used the night before away from where it sat, to move it back into the circle of other chairs so that maybe the topic of what she saw would get forgotten in the shuffle of other people's plans. As soon as Becca unzipped the tent's main flap and leaned in to see what she could see, Alexandra half-walked half-ran over to the folding chair, snatched it up and half-walked half-skipped over to where a few other lawn chairs sat, and added it to their rather haphazard semi-circle. In turning to check on where Becca's attention was, Alexandra again found herself mesmerized by the clarity of the early daylight. Forgetting about the older girl altogether, she sat down in the chair she had just replaced and began again to memorize the landscape. She focused on the where the field gave way to the forest path. She noted how it was framed by birch trees, a pair of two larger ones on the left and a cluster of smaller ones on the right, their bright slashes of white seeming to float free of both the forest and the ground.

"Jeez, my feet are frozen," came Becca's whisper, sudden and near, "I forget how cold the ground gets in the morning."

Like being pulled from a deep sleep, for a moment Alexandra was confused as to where she was and what she had just heard. She turned to find Becca sitting beside her in one of the other chairs vigorously rubbing her wet feet. With the next breath Alexandra was fully back in the present.

"How did the tent look?" she asked as quickly as she could, afraid that Becca might want to know what it was that had her so distracted.

But Becca was fully focused on her own dreams.

"Dry as a bone,… so we just need to convince my folks that we want at least one more night sleeping out in the tent before you head home, and if they start to waffle because of my busted rib, then you've got to take up the slack and sell it to them," Becca whispered then added in as loud a voice as she dare, "Don't leave us hanging."

"I don't think it'll be that big of a deal," stated Alexandra after a short pause, trying to sound more sure of herself than she felt.

At that moment they heard the back door open and turned to see Becca's mom step out carrying a tray of mugs each trailing a line of steam in the cool morning air. Becca turned back and gave her friend a wink. Alexandra just shook her head.

❧ 17 ❧

The Lake

Alexandra sat back sipping her hot chocolate and watched Becca work her magic.

"How 'bout I do the breakfast dishes?" Becca sang after a first sip.

"You're feeling that much better then?" asked her mom.

"Absolutely!"

The girls' were too busy giving each other the eye to see the gleam of amusement in Mrs. Dwyer's own eyes. She had come down to find the living room empty and so had moved to the kitchen to start the coffee and heat the water for the hot chocolate. From the windows over the sink, she had watched Becca make a bee-line for the tent and also her niece quickly and rather strangely dash to move a folding chair back among the others.

"She stretched her arms over her head without flinching," added Alexandra.

"Wow, that much better," Mrs. Dwyer cooed, "Then maybe I'll let you do those dishes."

Becca gave her cousin a wink. "And, Mom, I was thinking... seeing that Alexandra goes home soon..."

"You'd like another night in the tent," said Becca's mom as she stared out toward the woods. She relished the silence her remark caused. "You know I can see the back yard from the kitchen."

"You saw us?" asked Becca.

"Yeah, but only from the great big windows... in the kitchen."

"The ones that overlook the back yard," offered Alexandra.

"Oh, you know of them, do you?" quipped her aunt.

"Rumors mostly," teased Alexandra. Alexandra didn't know what had changed or why, yet she was glad to have the old Aunt Sue back. And in spite of her coy glances and winks, Becca seemed relieved as well.

"I really don't see how you'll be comfortable," Mrs. Dwyer continued.

"I will with a bunch of pillows."

"We can recreate the cushions just like on the couch," insisted Alexandra.

"We'll see," said her aunt into the steam rising off her coffee.

With one last shared glance, both girls clearly took encouragement in the fact that her first response had not been a flat "no."

The back door shut and Josh and the two dogs made their loping appearances. Gruff pranced over to where the figure of the woman in the shawl had left her footprints the night before, and Alexandra held her breath thinking that Becca would see this and be reminded of events. Becca, however, was too busy fending off Muffin's repeated nuzzlings to take any notice of what Gruff was up to. Josh sprawled one leg across the arm of his chair sipping his own mug of hot chocolate.

"Make that yourself?" asked his mom.

"Dad's up too. He boiled the water..." he stated then added before she could ask, "And we turned the burner off."

"Always turn the burners off..." came Mr. Dwyer's voice from behind the screen door of the kitchen, and then as he emerged to join the group, he added, "Any man who can't remember to turn the burners off shouldn't be allowed to own a house."

"He ruined two of Mom's pans," explained Becca.

"Doom and despair!" shot back Becca's dad with great drama. "I think we should see the up side... Your mother had the chance to replace *two* used pans with *brand new* ones of the make and size she most desired."

Alexandra looked over to see her Aunt Sue's eyes roll skyward.

"Right, Dad," concurred Becca flatly.

"Thank you for your support… though I question its sincerity," continued Mr. Dwyer cocking one eyebrow as he shot his daughter a villainous glance. "Just as today when I found out that the sink fixtures the Colson's ordered haven't come in, I could see it as lost work or a chance to take my loving and adoring family to the lake."

A shudder of excitement rippled through all three kids. Mrs. Dwyer mumbled something into her mug of coffee that sounded to Alexandra a lot like *Drama queen.* Becca must have heard the same because she scolded her mother immediately.

"Don't you make him mad. I'm on your side, Dad. Those were lovely new pots and the lake sounds wonderful."

"Thank you favorite daughter."

"Only daughter," added Josh.

"Careful, boy, I could replace you with a bit of copper tubing and some elbow joints," shot back his father.

"You always say that," came Josh's defiant response.

Ignoring his son's recalcitrance, Mr. Dwyer turned his attention to Alexandra, "And you, girl who has been sleeping here for weeks, what do you say?"

"Oh, yes, Uncle, a trip to the lake sounds wonder…" but the rest of the word was replaced by a scream as the now unobserved Gruff had sidled up and decided at that very moment to lick the water off Alexandra's feet.

Mr. Dwyer gave a mock scream to match Alexandra's sending kids and even his wife into a fits of giggles.

For Alexandra the rest of the morning took on a strange feeling of prolonged déjà vu as the lunch supplies and drinks were packed, bathing suits were put on, the cooler, towels and other day-at-the-lake supplies were carried to the car, and especially when Mr. Dwyer once again repeated his performance as his wife, the Czar of Sun Screen.

"Sun block and vater. Sun block and vater. Behind zee kneez and lotz on zee snozzles."

"What about zee spotz that be baldee?" broke in Alexandra much to the amazement of Becca and her mom.

"Ach! Zee leetle girl'z wordz go bitee bitee," screeched her Uncle Bob.

Mrs. Dwyer checked and double-checked the collection of picnic and beach supplies, and soon the Mr. Dwyer was pretending to race the car toward the lake. Alexandra felt a different and welcome dynamic in the car. Whatever tension there had been between Mrs. Dwyer and her daughter had clearly been acting like a damper on how comfortable the others were when interacting with each other, but now with the spark back in her voice and the sparkle back in her eyes, the reserve that Mr. Dwyer and even Josh had imposed on themselves for the last couple of days disappeared. Laughter and release filled the car. Soon they pulled into an almost vacant parking area. They had their pick of spots along the small arc of the beach, and Mrs. Dwyer suggested a location that would stay sunlit but that also sat near to a small clump of shade trees where she could send whomever she felt needed a break from the pending heat.

All was well until Alexandra turned to look at the lake. In spite of its beauty beneath a crisp blue sky and the sounds of play and laughter, the sight of the water stretching toward its other shore tied a knot in Alexandra's stomach. If she had been able to speak of this tightness in the core of her, she might have described it as a mixture of dread and pull. Without a thought as to why, she waded out until she stood waste deep, her mind filling with images, old and new. First, it was as if the slight pressure on the lower half of her body pulled her back into her water dream where she had watched Audrey diving again and again into a splashless skin of water. The press of the water on her thighs soon led her to feel again as if she were entirely immersed. Then suddenly she was, but now the water raged and pulled her along in a current she couldn't fight. Even as she struggled to escape this water, to right herself, orient herself to its surface, Alexandra tried to tell herself that this was Audrey's experience, that she should be watching from above, from the helpless and horrible safety of the shore. Then suddenly she was above the water or at least the top half of her was, but before any sense of relief could take hold she looked down. She was not back in the lake, she was still caught in the whirlwind of imagery, but worse than this realization was what she saw happening to the part of her immersed in the current. It was as if she was

138

losing her solidity to the way of water. She felt it in her legs, that they had become sieve like, porous, semi-solid. She tried to tell herself that what she saw was a trick of her eye, that what she saw was simply legs magnified and warped by the water. Yet she knew otherwise. She could feel her feet against the small stones of the riverbed and was aware of her body above the water line, but there was at best only a wavering sense of everything in between. She was filled with horror and wonder as she tried to disbelieve what she knew was true. Then it occurred to her that what she should do is dip a hand into the current and see what change came to her fingers. She watched as she moved one hand delicately above the water's surface half-expecting her finger tips to simply wash away. She watched her hand lower to within an inch above the silken current when she was lightly but firmly tapped on the head.

She found herself back waist deep in lake water watching the beach ball that had bounced off her head land and bob a few feet from her. She turned to see Josh grinning and behind him Mr. Dwyer and Becca. Becca shook her head and pointing to her face as if to be sure that Alexandra didn't miss the puzzled expression.

"I've been yelling at you for the last five minutes," called Becca.

"We'd thought you'd turned to stone," gasped Josh as he splashed passed her to retrieve the ball.

"The opposite actually," responded Alexandra, but the boy didn't hear as he dove into the water. She turned back toward Becca and her dad saying, "Daydreaming, I guess."

"Ya think," shot back Becca.

Alexandra was debating whether or not she should try and offer up some other response, when she sensed the silence behind her, or maybe she picked up on the glance that Mr. Dwyer shot past her shoulder, but whatever it was, Alexandra smelled mischief. She spun back toward the silence that was Josh right at the moment he hurled the ball at her for a second time. Had she turned a moment later, it would have already been in the air, but turning when she did Josh couldn't stop his throw and she had plenty of time to react. She caught the ball easily and in one fluid motion spun and sent it speeding toward Mr. Dwyer. Caught completely off guard, Mr. Dwyer could only turn to the side and let the ball bounce off his shoulder.

"This is a sad, sad day," lamented her uncle, and with a gleam in his eye, he turned and lunged to retrieve the ball.

Before Becca could start to join in the chase, her mother called from shore and warned her off any rough play. Becca started to protest but didn't want to ruin the mood, especially since she had already managed to get permission for what she understood as another night in the tent. Instead she waded back toward shore to find one of the magazines she had brought along. As she sat flipping through its pages, she replayed in her mind her plans on how to arrange for another late night rendezvous with Will.

For the next half hour or so, Alexandra was in heaven. As they splashed and pushed and pelted each other with the ball, Alexandra gave herself over to the fantasy that she was the big sister and that this was her family, her dad blowing bubbles as he emerges from the water like a wanna-be sea monster, her little brother squealing in fear under her attack, and her mom under the umbrella talking with her friend who was here for the summer. Although she loved her parents and although she and her dad had spent plenty of afternoons in horseplay of one kind or another, this felt different. This felt like family in a way Alexandra had only ever known in spurts and starts. Even though her mom had remarried soon after the divorce, her step dad didn't look at her or engage her or seem to know her like her own father, and the play in that house seemed like playing at play. Since her dad apparently never planned to remarry, it was always only him, and if he was in one of his moods from a hard day in the classroom or a disappointing day in his workshop or studio, then Alexandra had to tiptoe around that situation with no one else to turn to. As she dove and dodged, these were not her conscious thoughts, rather these were the conditions of her thinking that allowed her to relish so completely this brief experience of what she imagined it could have been and should have been like had her folks been able to manage keeping the family they once had together.

140

Becca's dad gave out first. He simply couldn't keep up with the two youngsters. Left on her own to battle Josh, Alexandra soon got bored and excused herself to go and check on how Becca was faring. Josh claimed himself the victor and spent the next half hour trying to balance himself on the ball without rolling off into a dunking.

As she sat down next to her cousin, Alexandra found herself a little saddened by the failure of her fantasy to hold. She, in fact, was the visiting friend. Her Uncle Bob was not her dad nor Aunt Sue her mom. Becca was the big sister, and Alexandra was the kid on vacation playing at family. Whatever pool of self-pity Alexandra planned to dive into, however, never got the chance to fill.

"Look at the dock," whispered Becca as she handed Alexandra a sandwich from the cooler.

Alexandra looked out over the water, saw the cluster of figures on the floating dock, and tried to recognize one or all. Then she caught Will's profile as he emerged from the water and stood in line for another turn on the diving board.

"You need to swim out there," whispered Becca as she pretended to drink from her cup.

"Why?"

"To tell him ten thirty."

"Ten thirty?"

Becca did not respond beyond giving Alexandra a look that all younger girls dreaded getting from an older girl. A look that carried the complaint that *If I have to spell it out for you then you're really not going to get it anyway.*

"Tell him ten thirty," confirmed Alexandra hoping that her quick acquiescence would counter her initial mistake.

"He'll know what it means," whispered Becca into her cup.

"Now?" asked the younger girl.

"Eat your sandwich first..." shot back Becca, "... but make it quick."

Alexandra chewed on her ham and cheese and watched the line of boys take their turn diving into the lake. She tried to imagine who she might arrange a rendezvous with, but it was never any boy she really knew. It was always some lead singer in a band she'd listened to or seen on You Tube, or some long dead movie star from the black and white films she'd watched with one or the other parent. Will's profile became more distinct as she watched. He wasn't as tall as some and tended to hang off to the side even as he kept his position in the line. He wasn't alone. He was part of a group. Probably the same group of boys he'd been with the other day Alexandra thought as she finished her last bite, but he didn't join in their jostling and pushing. He remained outside of it. She tried to picture herself just swimming up and having him crouch down to hear her whisper *ten thirty*, but at the same time, she doubted it would be quite so easy or direct. She turned to find Becca staring at her.

"What?" asked Alexandra.

"You're done, right?"

"Can I swallow?"

"I don't know. Can you?"

"Jeez!" shot back Alexandra quietly. "You know they've invented this thing called a phone."

"Are you going to do it or not?"

Alexandra didn't respond to Becca's accusatory plea. Instead she stood and turned to Josh, "I'm going to swim out to the dock and back. Do you want to come?"

Josh shook his head *no*, and Alexandra turned to Becca to find that she had cocked one eyebrow as if to say, *well played*.

"Don't cramp up," reminded her Aunt Sue.

"I'm fine. I just want to keep moving," explained Alexandra hoping she hadn't appeared too eager, but Becca's parents went back to their lunches as if it made no difference. Without any further silent communication with Becca, Alexandra turned and waded into the water.

At first Alexandra was mostly nervous simply because she was expected to swim up to a dock full of people that she didn't know and pick out the one she had met and deliver an ambiguous message. Yet as she moved from wading to striding to actually swimming, she began to have flashbacks to her earlier daydreams, and she began to worry about crossing water that was over her head. What if what she had imagined actually happened and that without being able to be in contact with the lake bed her body did, in fact, melt away, first her legs, then her torso and arms, and then her head would simply drop beneath the water's surface, and never to be seen again. She pulled up and let her feet drop to the bottom of lake. She found that she could still stand with her head above water. She turned and looked back to shore. Becca was watching her progress. *This is ridiculous*, she thought to herself, but still she turned and looked to the dock hoping that maybe Will had seen her and that he had dived in to meet her half way. No such luck. For a moment, she equivocated. She weighed the need of Becca to use her as messenger with her own paranoia about dissolving. Irrational as the one option seemed in the face of the other, she had seen it and felt the odd horror of it, in her mind's eye, and it had been real. She held her position. With her toes touching the silty lake bed, she considered turning back and was almost ready to give in to this desire when she saw Will watching her as well. He had stepped out of the line and had sat down letting his legs dangle in the water. She felt his eyes on her and Becca's eyes on her back and figured she'd no real choice now but to press on. *At least between the two of them, one of them should see me disappear if I melt away.* Yet as with many situations, Alexandra found the worrying worse than the doing, and once she started swimming, it was her fears not her legs that melted away.

She swam up alongside the dock and grabbing hold of the wood with one hand continued to tread water with her legs as if she still didn't fully trust their permanence.

"How is she," Will asked with genuine concern.

"She's fine. She's just afraid of overdoing it by accident and ending up back on the couch."

"Should I call her?"

"She sent me out to tell you 10:30."

Will kept his eyes locked onto Alexandra's as he took in the meaning of the message and the fact that she had been trusted with it.

"You two camping out?"

"Yeah."

"Tell her I'll see her at 10:30 then," he said and before Alexandra could turn away added, "but just her, right?"

Alexandra grinned, shrugged her shoulders, and pushed off the dock to start her swim back to shore. The return trip seemed to take no time at all, and soon she was wading toward then crossing onto the stretch of beach where the family sat still finishing their lunches. Before Becca could pull Alexandra down to discuss what had been communicated, Mrs. Dwyer spoke up.

"Was that Will out on the dock?"

"It was."

"I thought I recognized him. How is he?"

"He's fine. He asked after you, of course," teased Alexandra nodding to Becca.

"Yeah, thanks for that," she shot back.

"How sweet," chimed her mom.

"You two are a real hoot," said Becca trying to sound both stern and bored.

Something the mixture of her word choice and tone tickled her mother who tried to stifle a laugh but ended up snorting instead which sent Alexandra and Becca into a fit of giggles.

Soon after speaking with Alexandra, Will and his friends swam back to shore and left, and the rest of the afternoon passed as days at the beach will with cycles of getting wet and drying off, grabbing a snack, putting on more sunscreen, and getting wet again. Becca made Alexandra repeat the entire conversation that she had with Will at least twice. When she asked for a third time to hear again how he had first wanted to know if she was doing well, Alexandra waved her hands in surrender and suggested that she wait until she saw him that night and have him repeat it.

As the day wound down a touch of melancholy crept into Alexandra's mood. She started to sense that this part of her summer was coming to an end. She only had a couple of days left and didn't think they'd be back to the lake with her. When she thought of them coming back without her, her stomach dropped and the earlier fantasy of being a permanent part of this family disappeared completely. After the expected jostling and jockeying for position for the ride home, Alexandra found herself milking this feeling of pending isolation and was on the brink of throwing herself a nice little pity party when the oldies station that her Uncle Bob had tuned into began playing "The Lion Sleeps Tonight," and in spite of knowing little more than chorus, he began to sing along at the top of his lungs. Soon everyone in the car was swaying and singing, and Alexandra found herself happily back in the fold.

⮔ 18 ⮕

Notes and a Disappearance

Back at the house amid showers and rinsed suits hung outside to dry in the lengthening shadows of late afternoon, the sense of ending crept back into Alexandra's heart. This time, however, it was compounded by a sense of homesickness which she had not felt for most of her time in the Dwyer's home. As she dressed and puttered about Becca's room gathering some of her things to put aside for the packing that would soon take place, she found herself desperately wanting to hear her father's voice singing her one of his ridiculous songs and her mother and step dad's voices above the clatter of pans and drawers as they talked about their days at the college while making dinner. Her sense of being a guest in someone else's house, even if it was a house as dear as this one, suddenly seemed overwhelming. From downstairs, she listened to her Uncle Bob and Josh getting scolded by her Aunt Sue for some mischief, but instead of wanting to fantasize that she was part of it as she had at the lake, she perceived them as the surrogate family they were. She wanted to bump up against her real parents again. This was not her room, not either one of her two rooms, she corrected herself, and that was a telling correction – that having two distinct rooms in two different houses was now the norm for her, that the idea of just one room in a single house was now, by definition, an oddity.

In moving a pile of folded clean clothes away from her growing pile of dirty laundry, Alexandra uncovered a small spiral bound notebook that she packed intending to keep a diary or jot down song lyrics or poems. On impulse she sat down and started writing. She didn't hear when Becca came in to gather a few more things for their night in the tent and didn't hear her when she left the room. The task of cataloging the events that had taken place since her arrival completely absorbed her.

Perhaps this impulse grew out of her sense that time in this place was short and growing shorter. Whatever it was that had released the muse, she was fully in control and Alexandra's hand moved across the page without hesitation. At the same time, however, she showed caution in what she wrote. For instance, she never spoke of her heightened sight but simply referred to the time when she *tracked successfully*. She did describe the three dreams in as much detail as she could remember, thinking that since they were dreams, their significance would remain qualified by the lack of description about the river adventure. In fact, she referred to the river adventure in exactly those terms, *the river adventure*, rather than Audrey's near death experience. Even as she coded that day's event with innocuous terms remembering all the what ifs that could have led to disaster tied her stomach in knots. She found she skipped lines and left space on certain pages, such as the page with the dreams, sensing that she would want to come back later and fill in other thoughts or link other events to prior experiences. She was just starting to jot down a description of the evening that brought the storm and her vision of the old woman with the shawl when Becca poked her head back in the room and demanded that she come down and help with the dishes.

After the dinner dishes were done, Alexandra helped Becca gather extra pillows from the couch to use in the tent to help prop her up in whatever position provided the most comfort for her mending ribs, briskly said their *good nights*, and were nearly out the door when Becca's mother quietly but firmly called her daughter aside. Alexandra stepped up to take the pillows from Becca and headed out the back door glad to avoid witnessing whatever conversation was to follow. She made herself busy in the tent arranging their beds and checking the flashlights and the little halogen reading lamps to make sure their batteries still produced a strong enough beam by which to read or write. Then she waited.

Finally Alexandra heard the back door open and the swish of feet approaching the tent and then saw Becca's figure as it appeared beyond the scrim of the tent's doorway.

"Don't even ask," was all she said to Alexandra as she entered the tent carrying two plastic bottles of water. Then, of course, she proceeded to tell her everything that she and her mom had gone over. The main theme that Becca swore was repeated at least half a hundred times was not to sneak off and meet up with Will. How her mother knew, Becca had no clear idea beyond the fact that her mother always seemed to know what she and Josh were about to do or wanted to do or were even just starting to think about doing.

"Does your mom or dad know that kind of stuff?" she asked. Then before Alexandra could begin to answer, she launched back into what else had been said about *age appropriate* behavior and *levels of trust* and how *privilege carries responsibility*. "I swear to God, I thought she was going to pull out the *Where Babies Come From* book," and at this Alexandra found that she couldn't hold her mirth in any longer.

She reached over and took one of the bottles out of Becca's hand and offered it back to her, "Here, have some water."

Becca looked at it, took it, looked at the other bottle in her other hand, looked at Alexandra, and handed that one to her, "Thank you, and here's some for you."

Both girls drank several small sips to let the tension and amusement die down. Then Alexandra looked at the older girl and half-asked half-stated, "But you're still going out."

Becca responded with one of those looks as if to say *Don't be so stupid.* Immediately Becca could sense that this gesture stung the girl.

"I'm sorry. It's just that she was really in my face. What I told her was that I wouldn't do anything stupid. And I'm not… but I am going to meet him because I don't see that as stupid or anyone's business but my own."

Alexandra appreciated the apology and let it and everything else that had been said settle for a moment before speaking just as plainly back to Becca.

"What if after you leave, she sticks her head in the tent?"

"Then I'm busted," said Becca with as much casual bravado as she could muster. "I'm not asking you to cover for me. To be honest, I'm really tired and still pretty sore, but I'm not in the mood to back out or back down. My guess is we'll meet up, say *Hey*, then he'll walk me back to the top of the field, and that'll be that. I doubt I'll be out of the tent more than half an hour, forty-five minutes maybe."

The girls sipped more of their water as each took in the significance of this clear decision to defy her mother's wishes. Even though she appeared calm and comfortable in her defiance, Becca hoped the water would dispel the growing lump in her stomach. Alexandra was less able to disguise her concern with Becca's decision. When she wasn't sipping, she was twisting the cap on as tightly as she could then fighting with it in order to take another sip. She wanted to find some argument that would allow Becca to consider the possibility of missing her meeting with Will, but she knew that it would be pointless to try and talk her out of it. More to the point, Alexandra was just as busy convincing herself that it really wasn't her place to try and change her cousin's mind any more than it would be Becca's place to try and reverse her thinking about a decision that she'd already made, a decision about which she might feel just as strongly.

"I'm going to read a while. Then I think we should kill the lights to convince Mom that we've gone to sleep," said Becca relieved that her younger friend hadn't found it in herself to offer any advice against going out.

"Sounds like a plan," agreed Alexandra and pulled out her notebook. She reread what she had written so far then picked up her description from the previous night, the storm, the figures at the wood's edge, and the woman with the shawl. In order to continue to protect herself, she wrote this section as if it had been a daydream. She described how *As the storm approached, I* imagined *a group of people appearing at the point where the path into the woods began and then* imagined *the friendly face of an old woman appearing within just a few feet of where I sat.* She knew that these visions were more than figments of her imagination, but she wanted to give no hint of this to the outside world. Not just yet. She still needed to decide what exactly she saw and, more importantly, why.

Caught up in her own thoughts, Alexandra was oblivious to Becca's fidgeting. The older girl was having difficulty concentrating on the book she had brought out to read. She continually checked the time on her cell phone and looked over toward her cousin wondering what in the world she could be writing that was so fascinating, but before she could think of a remark to interrupt her, Becca wondered how much time had passed and checked her cell phone.

Alexandra finished her notes up to the point where her Aunt Sue had called her in and she had *imagined* turning to see Gruff sniffing at where the woman had been standing. She flipped back to the start of her notes and tried to come up with what the next step would look like, how she might proceed in going back and filling in her thoughts on what had been happening to her. She wanted to write her reactions out plainly but still sensed that some coding was needed, that she couldn't come right out and admit to anything. She had never kept a diary of any kind, in part, because she felt that a secret written out was a secret exposed. She would much rather keep her initial thoughts private until she's had the chance to bounce them off Audrey and maybe even her dad, though what that conversation might look like, she still could not picture.

Suddenly Becca slammed her book shut and announced, "Lights out!"

Alexandra offered no resistance. She knew Becca was already wound tightly and her notes could wait. The darkness might even offer her the chance to think about these most private thoughts without the added exposure of being watched. As Becca tossed and turned and rechecked the time, the little glow of her cell phone reappearing every few seconds like a large lazy firefly hovering over Becca's bed, Alexandra began to compare each of the different times that her gift-sight descended. Thinking back she could see a steady increase in her ability to accept and manage it. As Becca once again checked the time, the glow of her phone burning brighter in the darkness and illuminating the interior of the tent almost as if in a pale homage to Alexandra's thoughts, the younger girl smiled to herself in admission that she was acclimating to the power of her new sight faster each time it came. She realized that with each new onset of heightened sight the novelty of its initial sensations wore off and she used its power more freely, like learning to swim where once the initial fear of taking in water or disappearing beneath it was overcome. The buoyancy and freedom of the experience opened to all kinds of exploration.

Suddenly Becca was sitting up and feeling around for her shoes.

"What's up?" asked Alexandra.

"I'm heading out."

"Is it time?"

"It will be soon, and I want to get out of here before something happens that prevents that."

"Like?"

"I don't know. I just want to move. Anyway, he's always there before I am, waiting for me. If I leave now then maybe I'll beat him to the spot. If not, then we'll have just that much more time on our own before I turn around and come back here."

"Don't forget a flashlight."

"Don't need one. I could find that rock with my eyes closed in a snowstorm," Becca said as she finished tying up her other shoe.

Before Alexandra could say anything else, Becca unzipped the tent's flap and disappeared into the night. Alexandra crawled over and ran the zipper back down to keep the bugs out then crawled back beneath her bedding. Her heart raced in empathy with what her cousin must be feeling. She listened but could not hear Becca's progress away from the tent, so she listened for the back door to open and the stern voice of her Aunt Sue, but that did not come either. As the silence lengthened, Alexandra's heart beat slowed and her thoughts turned back to her own situation.

Once again she let her mind drift back to that first time when she had gone out to retrieve Boxy and her vision changed. She remembered how the cat seemed to sense the change, how it seemed to even be able to see the change. She remembered how the cat looked at her and how its nuzzling attention carried a certain intensity for hours afterward. She realized the dogs too sensed the change in her. She remembered how gleefully they came sniffing at her on that first day just as she was about to reveal Becca's hiding spot and again when she snuck back in after tracking Becca's first late-night rendezvous with Will and again each time after that. She chased the idea that the onset of her gift-sight was not limited to her eyes, that whatever shift it brought resonated throughout her which was why she so clearly felt the pulse of it as it descended. The animals' behavior suggested that as well. As Alexandra reached the conclusion that Boxy and the dogs weren't simply responding to the fact that she could see differently but to a more complete change within her, she also began to tackle the notion that her shift in sight was perhaps only the first or most obvious manifestation of other changes within her, that perhaps when she was in the midst of seeing the world's inner light there were other skills present within her that she had yet to discover. She thought to herself that maybe it was an all-over change within her that the animals sensed.

Even as Alexandra began to toy with the prospect of other skills and abilities she could possess, she drifted toward sleep. She forced herself to remember the next item in her notes. She thought it was the odd coincidence of the water dreams, and even as she thought of it, she rejected the notion of coincidence. Instead she substituted the notion of connection and was on the verge of a new conclusion when she drifted momentarily into sleep. She woke a moment or an hour later and, thinking of the old woman with the shawl, told herself to remember that she wanted to ask the other girls if they'd had any waking dreams, and if they had, what they had seen. Sleep came again. Alexandra dozed off with a slight smile on her face remembering how excited Gruff had been sniffing at the footprints left by that apparition and how gratified she was to have another creature confirm her experience.

When she woke again, she woke from a sleep before dreams and clear of the mixture of the half-thoughts to which she had fallen asleep, and she woke sensing that the tent was still empty of Becca but that someone or something was present just beyond the canvas walls of the tent. She held herself still and listened intently. She heard nothing but couldn't shake the feeling that something had been moving in such a way to wake her. In the lengthening silence, sleep came knocking once again.

"Becca."

Alexandra was awake again, certain she had heard her cousin's name quietly spoken out loud. She listened to the deep silence and started to wonder if she herself had spoken it out of her sleep addled mind.

"Becca."

This time propped up on her elbows, wide awake, she knew it hadn't come from her.

"Will?" she said into the darkness.

"Yeah," came the quiet and confused response.

"Where's Becca?" asked Alexandra almost too loudly as she scrambled free of her blankets and began to pull on a pair of pants.

"She's not here?" came the weak reply.

"What time is it?" asked the girl as she pulled on her shoes.

"A little after eleven."

"What!?" shot back Alexandra now fumbling to find her jacket and the flashlight.

"She's not with you?" whispered Will with more than a note of growing concern in his voice.

"She's been gone for an hour or more," said Alexandra sternly as she found the hard plastic handle of the flashlight and now searched for the zipper to the tent's main flap.

Will joined her efforts from the outside, and soon she emerged into the cool dampness of the night air. She could see Will's silhouette against the night sky.

"What do we do?" she asked.

"She left to come and see me?"

"Yes, Will, she left early because she was anxious. Her mom got on her about not sneaking out, so she was all knotted up about that, and then she just wanted to get on with it and decided to leave early and beat you to the spot."

"I got there early too," he said, his concern bringing an unintended sharpness to his voice, "She never showed."

The two stood for a time letting the fact that Becca had actually gone missing sink in.

"You don't think she's just inside making us sweat?" he asked with half-hearted hope.

They both turned to look at the house. It was perfectly still, no curtains pulled aside with Becca's pale face grinning as she watched her prank unfold.

"I listened to her leave. She didn't cut back toward the house. She might have circled back, but, Will, I don't think so."

"Which way did you hear her go?"

Alexandra paused before she answered, "I didn't hear her at all actually." For some reason this brought a small chuckle from Will. "What?" asked Alexandra with more than a little annoyance in her voice.

"Nothing," he said then decided in the face of Alexandra's stony silence that more explanation was needed, "It's just that we've been working together on… on… moving around without being… detected."

They stood in silence again, each with their thoughts. Suddenly Alexandra realized that the trail was growing cold and with this realization and the need behind it came the pulse and shudder of her gift-sight descending. She looked over at Will and found him staring at her. He glowed faintly reminding her of the how the old woman looked the night before as the storm came, but his light from within was more consistent and even, more solid. Then she remembered waking on the night of the convergent dreams and being charmed by the light surrounding the sleeping heads of her cousin and her best friend. The light surrounding Will's head was both similar and different. It didn't seem as intense but was just as remarkable. She pulled herself back from these considerations to scan the ground around them for any hint of Becca's trail. She saw a clean set of prints circling the tent.

"Why did you go all the way around the tent?" she asked Will flatly.

"I was lissss…" he broke off his answer mid-word as he realized the full implication of her question. He stared hard at her and then looked to the ground around the tent where he could see nothing in this darkness even with his night eyes fully adjusted to what little light there was from the night sky. He looked back to Alexandra and spoke, "You're doing your thing aren't you?"

Alexandra looked around the ground at their feet, saw where Will had come down through the field, circled the tent, and then crouched to help her free the zipper and exit. She noted her footprints as well but could see no sign of a third set and therefore no sign of Becca. She sensed Will's frustration with her silence and admitted to herself that she now paused less for the sake of confirming Becca's cold trail and more for the dramatic effect.

"Yeah, I'm doing my thing," she finally said a little snidely, "and you haven't explained why you circled the tent."

"I was listening for how many people breathing I could hear."

"And?"

"Just one," he admitted then added quietly, "snoring ever so lightly."

"Jerk," she whispered through a grin then set herself to the task of finding some clue as to where Becca had gone and thus to finding out where she might be now.

She began zigzagging back and forth in a arc behind the tent. Several times she caught some dark shape that resembled a footprint only to find it was a combination of wishful thinking and uneven ground. Sensing that Alexandra was concentrating and knowing a bit about tracking himself, though never in darkness like this, Will hung back and let her have as much room as she needed to start the search.

In the silence, Will turned to punishing himself for having waited so long before coming to investigate Becca's no show. He admitted that if he had not given her the extra fifteen minutes, then Alexandra might have already found the trace of her path. Thinking back, he told himself that he should have known something was wrong after five minutes of waiting. Becca was never late. In fact, they both tended to get to their meeting places early and try to surprise the other, but they were both so stealthy at coming and so good at hiding that one or the other would have to swallow their pride and call an *All free* just to see if indeed they were both on site already, and usually they were.

When he finally crept out from behind the boulder and gave his all clear whistle, she did not respond and did not appear. He kicked himself now for not simply starting out toward her home then. Watching her cousin crouching low and increasing the swath of her arcs as she moved into the taller grasses of the field, his stomach began to tighten. It was not like Becca to pull a joke for this long and certainly not like her to let him wander down this close to her house in the middle of the night risking discovery by her family, especially given the fact that she wasn't even supposed to venture out to meet him at all. He tried not to let his mind wander through all the things that could go wrong in the woods at night. Suddenly she froze, bent far down toward the ground near her feet, straightened up and beckoned for him to join her.

"This is her," she whispered firmly and with relief pointing to what looked to her to be a clear heel print, its small dark curve nearly faded back into the wavering grays of the surrounding grasses.

"I don't see a thing," he remarked without thinking as he stared at the unremarkable patch of grass where she was pointing, and as soon as he heard himself say it with that hint of disbelief, he knew he'd made another mistake.

She turned to him and resisted saying any number of the things that immediately leapt to mind. Instead she said only, "Try and keep up," before breaking into a confident run that took an arcing path through the tall dark grass of the field toward the darker pitch of the tree line.

❧ 19 ❧

Becca's Nightmare

Glad to be on the move, Becca's stomach began to relax as soon as she found herself cutting an arch through the field toward the tree line. When she reached a point about half way between the mown grass of her yard and the woods, she paused and looked back toward her house. There was no movement. No light had gone on in her parents' room or anywhere else in the house and the tent remained dark. Thankfully, Alexandra had not decided to go back to taking notes or composing a diary or whatever it was she was doing. Stopping, however, only allowed the doubts surrounding this excursion to reemerge and reintroduce a twinge of tightness in Becca's stomach, but before her conscience could begin in earnest to kick around the pros and cons of going against her mother's direct wishes, she turned and resumed walking.

She wanted to see Will, and it wasn't wicked or wrong, they barely even held hands. She just liked talking to him, being with him, and if her mom couldn't understand that, well, too bad. Such were Becca's thoughts as she crested the first rise in the fields and left her house to the night.

While the moon was on the wane, it provided enough of a dim glow to light Becca's way, casting slight but distinct shadows where there were rocks or dips along her path. In contrast, the stars were out in force and the air was cool and crisp. As she marveled at the expanse of the night sky and took refreshment from the night air, she was lured toward the promise within the combination of her solitude and such clarity. Becca sensed the end of summer, sensed that the freedom offered by these nights were soon to give over to the routine of school and soccer practice, homework to encroach on her nights and chores to fill the weekends. All the more reason, she told herself, to take advantage of a night like this. She looked again toward the stars trying not to let the realization that she was still justifying this trek to the part of her that knew it was a mistake ruin her anticipation of seeing and spending time with Will. Nevertheless, even this inkling of cause and effect, of risk and responsibility, exposed the expansive promise of the night for the likely fantasy it was. And she was forced to admit to herself, even as she held to her course, that she was, at some level, wrong in continuing to take this action. Yet she also felt that she was in part right and entitled to wander the night if she wanted to. She took a deep breath and laughed softly to herself.

"Yeah, you're real pretty," she said to the night and its stars, "but not much good in helping me make up my mind."

In the odd silence that followed the sound of her own voice came an unexpected rustle and snap from within the woods. Becca stopped in her tracks and listened. There was a whole list of forest sounds that she might have heard without concern such as the whine of large limbs or trunks of trees that had grown together and that sang when they rubbed, the thump of rotted wood hitting the forest floor after finally gaining release, the scatter of leaves of a foraging animal, or the receding crash of a deer as it bounded away. This sound, however, did not appear on Becca's mental list of what could simply be ignored. She held her pause, and rather than look into the dark of the trees, she kept her head facing forward so that her ear was turned and tuned to any further movement hidden in that darkness. There was none. She quickly calculated how close she was to the boulder where she expected to meet Will and figured she was a little over half way, just far enough where he might have snuck down in order to let her pass then creep back up on her as she tried to hide from him. A grin crossed her face and she broke into a dash, full speed, along her original path toward the meeting place for twenty or so yards then spun on a dime and rushed toward the dark of the trees disappearing into the black of their shadows.

She crossed about ten or so feet into the woods and pressed up against a large tree. Her injured ribs pinched at her for running, but she ignored the minor discomfort and turned her attention to listening for any sound that would expose Will as he

158

looked to double back on her. She was soon rewarded when she heard the slight pad of a foot fall back in the direction where she had first heard him give himself away. Another grin broke over her face as she imagined letting him pass by her and turning the tables on the would-be woodsman.

Her grin disappeared immediately, however, when she heard a second foot fall from within the woods from up the hill where she had yet to pass. She looked back toward the field, thinking that being in the open would be much better than having to negotiate through these trees, but to her dismay she glimpsed the silhouette of a loping figure pass along the border of the tree line. *Coyotes*, she thought to herself and immediately wished that she had brought a flashlight. She knelt down and felt around the dark forest floor for anything she might use as a weapon, a rock or larger stick or branch. Her hand found a stone which she passed to herself and continued feeling until she pulled a smaller branch free of the leaves. It was less than she hoped for but better than she had a moment ago, even a small branch could potentially be used as a kind of whip to discourage the initial interest any bolder members of the pack might display. If she could get back out of the woods, she could make a dash for the boulder and either find Will waiting or scale it and wait for his arrival. With one hand holding a plum-sized stone and the other a slender branch, she turned to scurry free of the woods and regain the open visibility of the field but found her way blocked by two small dog-like forms. As if having read her mind, they stood at the woods edge clearly blocking any easy retreat toward the fields.

Becca felt the hair on her neck go rigid. Her whole body tingled as fear took root, but before she could succumb to the emotions of the threat she sensed, she was shocked into action. From behind her she heard the rustle of leaves and in one fluid motion she spun and whipped the branch across the darkness. She didn't make contact but clearly heard the retreat of whatever it was that had dared to approach her. She quickly looked back toward the tree line and watched with a growing sense of panic as one of the coyotes skulked into the woods toward her while the other remained to block her escape. *Up*, she thought, *I need to get off the ground,* and she frantically searched the shadows and their trunks for a tree that had branches low enough to offer her some purchase to higher ground. She heard another rustle and this time saw the shape of an animal lunging toward her. She whipped the branch and it disappeared into the shadows. Quickly she switched the rock to her throwing hand realizing that she could swing the branch with either arm but needed to have the rock in her right hand if it was to serve its purpose. Again she searched for a tree that she could climb. Again came the rustle of leaves this time from two directions, but nothing materialized from either. She looked to find the one still standing watch at the field's edge. She could find to hint of the other. As she scanned the woods, her mind was racing to guess how many of them there were. She imagined that she could account for at least four, *not a large number,* she reassured herself even as she heard more rustling off to one side. On instinct she spun and launched the rock hard and low in the direction of the sound and again heard a clear retreat. Now she had only the stick. She knelt and again felt for another stone and that was when she saw what she thought was pine tree about ten or so feet further into the woods. She couldn't be certain, but she if she was right in having seen some low branches tufted with needles then that could prove to be her sanctuary.

She found two more small stones, slid one in her pocket, and took a good throwing grip on the other. Suddenly the woods surrounding her came alive with the sounds of gathering, footfalls, rustling, odd whining from all quarters. She heard a particularly distinct scuffing of leaves nearby and off to her right. Instinctively she whipped her arm and release the stone low to the ground, and without listening for its effect, launch herself toward what she hoped was escape.

Behind her the coyotes collected themselves. First they had flinched from the angry object that had shot toward their leader and then from the unexpected movement by the thing they were driven to hunt. With stifled growls they fell into pursuit looking for a chance to nip and trip and then smother with their cunning.

In running Becca dropped the whipping branch to free both her arms for balance and to ward off the underbrush that now seemed to be whipping at her. She heard the small feet and the muffled grumbling of the pack. She heard parts of them overtake her on either side looking to cut her off, but she wasn't looking to out run them indefinitely, just long enough to escape them, and as she felt a first probing snap at her heels, she reached what the pine tree. She kicked back at whatever was behind her, missing it but buying her enough time to duck into the darkness beneath the tree and scramble up against the rough bark trunk and frantically seek out that first low branch.

Some of the pack overshot the mark in their pursuit. They expected their quarry to lose itself in its panic and begin to turn and attempt to cut back, but this thing only ran a short while before taking to a tree. Those who themselves had to turn and cut back found that this was not like the larger four footed things. This thing climbed like their smaller prey, and it was trying to leave the ground when their leader struck.

Becca found a branch and grabbing at it with both hands desperately pulled herself off the ground. As she swung and pushed her feet against the trunk in an attempt to further propel herself up and away from the coyotes, she felt a twinge in her ribs where she had been healing. Then just as she managed to hoist herself up to the point where her upper body weight could provide a pivot and allow her to swing her hips and legs clear, one of the coyotes launched itself into the air looking to sink its teeth into the back of an ankle. Instead it clamped down on the empty denim of her jeans, but it held on hoping to let its weight dislodge her. It nearly did. The unexpected added weight almost pulled Becca back down, but she let her body fall against the branch and wrapped her arms around it. The coyote would not let go of her leg, and as she kicked and tried to swing it loose, she felt something inside her give and a pain like she had never felt before tore through her insides. When she tried to let out a scream, she produced only a whimper as if she had no air left in her lungs. The coyote's teeth cut and tore clear through the fabric of her jeans, dropping the animal unceremoniously to the ground. With tears running freely down her face, Becca gingerly gathered her feet up and managed to sit herself on the next branch above and then with great effort to another branch above that where yet another branch provided a kind of arm rest over which she could drape an arm. But she could not get comfortable. She was badly hurt. The pain came in great pulses, and she could only manage short shallow breaths. Only intermittently aware of a commotion below her, she fought off the need to faint, panting like the pack of dogs that pursued her.

Preoccupied with not losing her balance while she suffered through each following wave of pain from her new injury, Becca failed to notice how strangely the lead coyote reacted to her escape. At first it simply paced and pawed the ground. Then it suddenly launched itself into a kind of dancing rage, at times balancing on two legs while twisting its head and snapping its teeth, at times leaping furiously into the air so that it slammed onto the ground on its side or back, at one point even attacking the trunk of the tree, tearing at it with its small fangs and scarring it with its claws, and except for a few quick guttural whines, all this was done without bark or yelp. The other coyotes flinched and paced with nervous fascination as their leader burned through its frustration. Finally the anger seemed to break. The lead coyote stilled and stood panting and switching its tail as if in rhythm to a tune only it could hear. One of the members of the surrounding pack crept toward its leader like a fawning supplicant toward its king only to be rewarded with a lightning attack of jaws to throat. One small baleful yelp escaped before the leader's jaws clamped down across the windpipe and then snapped the smaller animal's neck. There was a brief collective whine from the rest of the pack. Several of them made as if to bolt away only to turn and rejoin the rest in their nervous circle of fear. The lead coyote dropped the now dead brother at its feet and with a quick warning glance challenged any other to approach. None did. Then with a quick half-bark the pack was dismissed, and as if released from a dream, a shudder passed through them and like a startled flock they turned and disappeared into the shadows of the night woods.

Left alone, the lead coyote dragged the broken body of its random victim away from the base of the tree where Becca still

162

sat fidgeting in fear and trying to catch her breath enough to call out for help. It dropped the body some distance away, returned, paced back and forth for a time then began to trot in a small circle around the base of the tree.

This is not this two-legger I want, thought Matchi Manitou. *This is not the itch-maker but maybe it knows something. It doesn't smell strong enough. It doesn't smell like it had any remarkable powers at all. But these woods are alive with the old essence.*

At first where its paws padded against the needle covered ground there had been the slightest whisper and snap of twig and leaf, but soon an absolute silence fell. Up in the tree, Becca sensed the muffling. Slowly the night sounds of the forest faded as if she were burying her head under a pillow. The sounds of the wind faded. The clack of leaf and slow thrumming of branches as they rubbed one another faded. Soon she found herself in a column of silence where even the raspy whisper of her short gasping breaths seemed to die before they escaped her lips.

After a time, the dark mind of Matchi Manitou sensed something passing along the border of the woods, moving back along the way this two-legger had come. Without breaking its stride, it sniffed the air and again sensed no powers at play, but this thing moved quietly for a two-legger. The powerful Manitou made the coyote sniff again. *A first-people*, it thought as it continued to cut its circle around the tree's base, puzzling out a thousand possibilities, happy to wait for the next hint of a clue.

Such a hint was not long in coming. The pulse in response to Alexandra's call for her gift-sight sent a shudder through the animal and into the waiting awareness of Matchi Manitou. As if in response to the challenge, the coyote gave in to its instincts and paused to mark the circle with its scent. *Let's just see what this little would-be can do*, thought the darkness within the animal. *We'll keep the two-legger in the tree silent and see if they can find us anyway.*

❧ 20 ❦

Treed

Will was impressed, and as he followed in Alexandra's wake, his head filled with questions that he knew should wait but that couldn't.

"How long have you been able to do this?" he asked, sounding a bit demanding and gruff, his voice jarred by his need to jog along.

"What?" she shot back.

"How long? This tracking stuff?"

"Since this winter," she offered after a pause.

"How old are you again?"

Alexandra pulled up from her searching. She turned abruptly to face the boy.

"I'll be thirteen in September," she answered then added curtly, "Is there anything that you absolutely have to know or can we get back to finding Becca?"

Will winced a little as if slapped and Alexandra felt badly for her tone. They stood facing each other for a moment.

"It's just really weird… to me… watching you," Will offered.

After a short pause, Alexandra admitted, "Yeah, it's weird. But it's here. It's in me. And I keep finding ways it's needed."

"You should meet my aunt," said Will as if this statement carried its own authority.

Not certain what to make of it, Alexandra said nothing.

"She's going to want to meet you," he said in an off-handed way, as if such a meeting was out of their hands and inevitable.

"Come on," said Alexandra flatly as she turned back to the task of tracking her cousin. She listened to Will fall into stride a few paces back, her mind now divided between seeking footprints and wondering what in the world Will's aunt had to do with anything.

They were well away from the house and Becca's prints were clear but also in the process of fading when Alexandra found another set of prints fall in behind Becca's.

"Hold up," she said as she came across a second and third set of animal prints emerging from the woods and trailing along the same path that Becca had taken.

Will stopped and stayed silent as he watched Alexandra wander around the area, clearly bothered by something she saw.

"What kind of animals run around here at night?" she asked in a hoarse whisper.

"How big are the prints?"

She made a gesture with her hands that she quickly realized he couldn't see, "Size of a plum maybe."

"How far apart?"

"I don't know," she said then stepped up to him taking his arm and measuring out a length from the tips of his fingers to a point a little beyond his elbow.

"Just one set?"

"Three."

"Coyote," he said without hesitation and quickly added, "Are they behind her or is she behind them?"

Alexandra thought about the question for a moment. She bent and looked carefully at the prints trying to tell which set seemed fresher. Their scale muddled an easy conclusion, not knowing how to tell if Becca's greater weight made any difference in how long her prints lasted compared to the weight of the much smaller coyotes. When she admitted to Will that she couldn't be sure, he heard the frustration in her voice.

"Don't worry about it, but we need to find her," he said then quickly added, "Just track her prints and tell me if you see the coyote prints do anything but follow hers."

After just a few feet further along Becca's trail, Alexandra spoke up, "One of the coyotes just turned back toward the woods."

"Keep going."

After about another minute of tracking, Alexandra paused and announced, "She stopped here. Two prints side by side. Here's a small one and another. She's moving again. They're getting farther apart."

"She's running," said Will flatly, but the coolness in his voice disturbed Alexandra.

She and Will now lengthened their stride to match Becca's prints. Then without warning Alexandra moved over into a stretch of grass where there was no sign of Becca at all.

"Wait, wait, wait… She didn't come this far." Alexandra began to walk a large in the grass. "She turned toward the woods. She ran into the woods."

"Go… go," Will whispered harshly.

At the woods edge, Alexandra paused, gestured into the darkness, and announced, "Coyote tracks back and forth all along here."

The two trackers entered the mixed shadows among the trees. For Will it was like entering a cave. For Alexandra it was walking through a strange and luminous stage set. There was a stillness that felt like an empty building. Both she and Will felt the oddness but did not remark on it to the other. Alexandra's thumb played over the switch of the flashlight she'd brought, but she didn't know how its light might affect her ability to see Becca's foot prints. She found the tree where Becca had crouched and was dismayed.

"She stopped here. There are coyote prints everywhere. I can't tell how many there were now," she said. Her voice sounded odd to her ears.

Will turned unsure if he had heard Alexandra speak. "What," he said hearing the volume of his voice fall short.

Alexandra caught a hint of motion farther into the woods and without thinking switched on her flashlight and directed it beam toward that point. The light startled Will and he instinctively followed its circle of light as Alexandra swept it back and forth. It crossed over something in motion. Both of them saw it, and before Will could direct her to return the beam to what he'd thought he'd seen, she did it herself. A large coyote stopped in its tracks. Its eyes reflected the harsh light and glinted like mirrors. It turned its body toward them.

The coyote watched the sharp light hold on its face. It sniffed the air to try and determine how many of the creatures had tracked it. It gave a few low barks to call the others before the mind within it remembered having killed the one. The others were gone, retreated back to their hiding or hunting. They would not come now. The Manitou realized that it would have to work to rally them again. Their dog minds would not easily follow one that would also kill them. The light held steady and the great Manitou grew irritated.

Alexandra held the flashlight's beam steadily on the coyote. It remained frozen for a time as if thinking what to do next. Will had said nothing but slowly moved his hand toward a back pocket. A subtle wave of tension swept over the animal. Alexandra watched its head drop slightly and its fur bristle. Will slowly pulled a knife handle from behind him bringing it around in front of his waist to meet his other hand. With one thumb he pushed against the blade release as the other found the pull notch along the blade's back. As the coyote continued to bob it head ever so slightly trying to gauge the number and position of things beyond the flashlight's glare, Will slowly pulled the knife open. It clicked into place, and with that click the coyote seemed to relax. Its fur went smooth again and its head came up. For a moment its tongue lolled out one side of its grinning mouth and it took on the look of an innocent dog. Then it was gone. Alexandra looked at Will and saw the confusion on his face. They neither one saw it turn or run. One moment it had been there, in the next it wasn't. With the animal's disappearance, the air felt open again.

"Becca!" Will called out, his voice ringing clear and loud.

Up in the tree, Becca had closed her eyes to better focus on keeping her breathing and her fear under control. She could sense that the thing that had treed her still circled the trunk below and the odd silence that rose around her continued to press in against her ears. She squeezed her eyes shut, letting this tiny gesture suffice for the rage she could not fully expel without causing a fresh wave of pain to sear through her chest. Tears streaked down her cheeks and fell onto her shirt. How long she sat perched this way, she had no idea. Then without any warning the sound of the night forest descended. She heard a breeze cutting through the tree tops, the small clatter of dry leaves and branches, the swell of a greater wind as it pushed through the full body of the forest, and then like an unexpected kiss, her name in Will's voice. From her perch, Becca looked down to see a shaft of light sweeping the forest floor, drew in as much air as she could against the pain, and called out.

Both Will and Alexandra heard what sounded like a whimper and moved toward the base of the tree where they had first seen the coyote.

"Take it," said Alexandra pushing the flashlight into Will's hand, "I don't need it. It didn't change anything for me.... Will, this is strange...," she began, but was interrupted by the frail call of her cousin's voice from what sounded like just above their heads.

Will directed the beam of the flashlight up along the trunk of the tree until it lit up a pair of shoes, a set of legs, and finally the pale and frightened face of a girl. His heart nearly leapt out of his chest.

"Becca, it's me and Alexandra. You're okay. Are you okay?"

Even as he spoke he moved. He shoved the flashlight back toward Alexandra and scrambled up the tree like a squirrel. Before Becca had time to fully realize that her ordeal was over, Will appeared beside her. He tried to hug her but her cry made him pull up short. She leaned her head against his and he felt tears fall onto his arms.

As Will comforted Becca as best he could, Alexandra tried to make sense of what she saw. She wanted to turn the flashlight off completely but realized that the other two might still want to see its beam, so she let it shine out behind her back and turned to examine the ground around the tree. The path where the coyote had been trotting was pitch black, not like anything she had seen before. Usually a footprint, even a fresh one, emanated some light where the pattern of the stuff compressed

168

underneath it shown through, the weave of grasses or the mosaic of twigs and leaves, but where this animal had circled no light remained. Part of Alexandra's mind wanted to explain it away. She had only ever seen single footprints not a path or track traveled repeatedly and maybe this was what that would look like. Yet another part of her mind knew that this strip of darkness was not in any way normal, was not caused by any coyote no matter how many times it retraced its own path. When she stepped back and looked at the shape cut by this narrow line, her chest tightened. Whatever it was that trod here had scribed what looked like a perfect circle with the trunk of the pine tree as its center. Alexandra knew no animal could do such a thing. It was not an oval, or nearly a circle, or a wavering shape that suggested a circle. This line cut a clean and regular arc. Alexandra knelt and touched the darkness and found her fingers coated with a fine dust. She dug her fingers into the ground to the inside of the dark line and found that the soil she pulled up still produced the hint of a glow. The ground where that animal trod was dead.

Will's call for the beam from the flashlight pulled Alexandra away from any further consideration of this strangeness. She stepped back a little from the tree and turned the beam of her light so that it lit the branches below where Will and Becca sat. Gingerly the two of them picked their way toward the ground, Will going first to provide both encouragement and an extra hand to steady Becca's descent. Though she tried not to show how much she was hurt, by the time she had both feet on the ground her breathing was ragged and it was all she could do not to break down and let herself cry.

"She's having real trouble breathing," explained Will knowing that he was stating the obvious but wanting to say something. "Let's get clear of the woods and see how she does."

As the three of them retraced their steps, Alexandra let Will take the lead in supporting Becca while she shined the flashlight in front of their path hoping to insure that they could avoid any false step. Becca's breathing was a little less labored but still sounded as if she were terribly congested. In the darkness, neither of her friends could see how pale she was. Alexandra wanted to talk about the circle scribed around the tree, but knew that any discussion of that revelation needed to wait. Every few feet, she turned and, with her gift-sight still present, scanned the woods behind them for any sign of movement. She found none. Soon they emerged from the forest and paused to let Becca rest and to figure out how best to proceed.

"We need to mark this spot," said Alexandra as she looked back along the path of their fresh footprints only to find the lingering crisscrossing pattern left by the coyotes, fading but clear enough to send a chill of empathy for Becca down her spine.

Without asking why, Will strode back toward the woods. He chose a good sized oak, reached into his back pocket, pulled out his knife, snapped it open, and quickly cut a horizontal notch even with his eye-line. He turned and jogged back to Becca's side. He looked to Alexandra and asked, "What did you see back there?"

"It can wait," she said hoping Will would hear in her voice her sense of its importance, that he would know to ask about it again soon because that circle of dead soil was not to be dismissed, forgotten, or lost. For the moment, however, she knew they should look to Becca, and so she turned to her cousin.

"Are you okay to walk?"

"Think so," Becca whispered then after a short breath added, "It's bad."

"Well, let's get you home and go from there," said Will stepping over to take her arm.

"Careful," she whispered.

The progress back to the Dwyer house was slow but steady. Alexandra found herself itching to describe what she had seen back in the woods but didn't want to drag Becca back through her ordeal. It was clear that she had been chased by coyotes and had escaped up the tree, but the mystery of how and why the circle had been made troubled her. Will wanted to have Becca reassure him that she was alright, but he didn't want to ask for fear of hearing otherwise. Her hand in his had gone clammy and her grip was weak and sporadic. He held onto her more than she to him. Up in the tree, Becca thought only of escape. Now on the ground, she wanted only to see her way clear of having to admit to her mother that she knowingly broken her word and broken their trust. In between the lightning bolts of pain that flashed up from her stomach to her shoulder and her attempts in the aftermath to regulate her breathing, she tried to concoct a believable excuse that would placate the questions she knew she would have to answer.

"Simple is best," she wheezed.

Uncertain of what had been said, Alexandra and Will looked first at Becca and then to each other, their faces faint in the ambient glow from the flashlight Alexandra pointed toward the ground in front of Becca's path. They waited for Becca to say more but she didn't. Alexandra could see the deepening concern written across the boy's face and thought to distract him.

"Will?" she whispered but got no response. "Will?" she repeated softly.

"What?"

"Who's your aunt?"

"What?!" he snapped.

"Who's the aunt you said I should meet?"

Again no response came and Alexandra decided not to try and force Will out of his worry, but Will was simply trying to reshuffle his thoughts enough to figure out just what in the world the girl was talking about.

"Scary one," wheezed Becca.

Then Will understood and remembered.

"She's no more scary than your mom," he said, "And how do you know who we were talking about?"

Another knife of pain sliced up Becca's side. She gripped Will's hand and said no more. Will squeezed her back, looked over to catch Alexandra's eye, and shook his head back and forth. Alexandra wasn't sure if he meant that Becca wasn't doing well or if he meant that she should stop talking about his aunt. She started to repeat her question to him then she caught herself. She realized that she was about to dismiss Will's concern for Becca in order to chase down what was foremost in her mind. That Becca's condition wasn't foremost in her mind shamed her, and by way of recompense, she reached out and placed a hand gently against the small of her friend's back.

After a few more minutes of steady progress, they crested the gentle slope that lead down through the field to the Dwyer's house and they paused. A wave of relief swept through all three of them. It was done, the girls were home. Yet with the next breath, a wave of anxiety surged back through all three. It was done, the girls would need to wake the parents. Becca made the first move to continue and Will and her cousin followed. When they got within ten feet of the back door Becca spoke.

"Listen, Will, you go," she whispered. When he did not budge, she continued weakly taking short breaths between each broken statement, "Alexandra, rough housing... You landed on me... Did this." Alexandra started to protest, thought back to when she had been thinking only of herself, saw this a way to make further amends, and kept her mouth shut. "Shoes, socks, pants off," Becca continued.

"Why?" Alexandra immediately asked.

"In bed already," Becca wheezed.

Alexandra looked over at Will and said flatly, "There's no way that's happening while he's here."

Will's hands shot up as if in surrender and he turned to leave.

"Will," began Becca then once the boy had stopped and turned added, "thanks."

"Thank her and those eyes of hers... and that's what my aunt will want to talk about with you, whenever you meet her. Those eyes and how come you have them and not one of us." He turned and jogged away toward the woods and soon was lost in the darkness.

Watching Will disappear, Alexandra realized that her vision had returned to its normal limits. When the shift away from her tracking sight had happened, she wasn't sure. The last tracks she remembered seeing were back at the point where they first emerged from the trees, but she was certain it lasted beyond that time as she kept checking to see if anything was following them.

"Shoes," came Becca's slight voice.

Alexandra turned to her cousin.

"Hurry," came the quiet plea.

⮞ 21 ⮜

Spotted Elk

Will watched from the crest of the hill behind the Dwyer place. In the darkness, he would not have been able to tell which girl was which except for the fact that one moved freely while the other shuffled along, bent and nearly broken. Then their thin pair of silhouettes cut in front of the back door obscuring the dim glow cast by some little light left on in the kitchen. The door opened, they were inside, and other lights were turned on. Then a light upstairs appeared. It was done.

As much as he wanted to return to Becca's side, to help her face her parents, go with her to the hospital, that was impossible. He turned and started home, his mind filled with snippets of what had happened and what he had seen and heard and what he was and wasn't going to tell his uncle about how this girl could track at night and then about how he'd mentioned his aunt. Then it occurred to him that maybe he'd need to keep this night's events to himself as well, but his aunt would know. She always knew these kinds of things. She was the wisest person he knew.

When Will was six, his aunt became a constant presence in their house, helping to keep it clean, cooking many of the meals, making sure he got off to school on time with a decent lunch. His father needed to travel to find steady work, and his mother didn't handle being alone well. When his dad would appear after months away, they'd have a few hours, sometime even a few days, of loud happy reunion, but it would soon slide into the dark tension of anticipation of his next departure and her spiral back toward depression. By the time he was eight, he slept over at his aunt and uncle's home during the weeks and with his mom on the weekends. In the last few years, as his mother became more and more dependent on various medications to get her up and through her days and his father's jobs kept him away from the house for longer and longer periods of time, Will found himself living full time with his aunt and uncle.

They were both older than his folks and, in comparison, very Indian. She participated in the regional tribal council, was forever writing letters to this or that Representative or this or that Senator, and attended pow-wows to keep others informed on what requests had been forwarded and what responses had come or failed to come. In contrast, his uncle believed there was no going backward or forward to better days. To his uncle's mind the only way to balance the scales against having been swept aside by the European's was to live with the old stories and practice the old skills. In the house, Will's aunt filled his head with lore and politics, and in the woods his uncle showed him the value of that lore and thus how fanciful politics could be. On the few occasions that his aunt came into the woods with them, Will grew to realize what a rich compliment they were to each other and that their differences merely clarified the goal of teaching him about the mountains and the woods, the stories of his people and the stories others carried, and how he should try to walk through the world.

While none of this was in his mind yet, all of it was in his heart as he retraced his steps away from the Dwyer place for the second time that night. As the chill of the deep morning took hold, he fretted the fact that he had passed by Becca's desperate hiding place without sensing a thing. He questioned whether he had even been looking for any sign of her at that point, decided that he hadn't then proceeded to beat himself up for not having done so. Then there was Alexandra, the Pilgrim-girl, the vacationer, who seemed to be able to summon the sight of night hunters. Will's anger at his own inabilities tested the waters of jealousy. As he neared the place where Becca had been forced to hide that night, he indulged this jealousy and vented his anger by belittling the girl who had bested him. As his stride increased under the energy of his resentment, he worked to reduce Alexandra's ability from a gift to an aberration, from a glimmer of a greater light to the brief flash of a magic trick. He broke into a loping run, his mind darkening with simple distinctions, unaware of how the woods took note.

The darkness within the coyote retreated from the metallic click that the boy produced, remembering well the craft of the two-leggers to make little toys of surprising destruction. From deeper in the woods, hidden from the piercing light of the strange stick the girl carried, the coyote sat and let the thing watch the rescue play out. *The little she's power is a bauble*, it thought. *It comes and goes. She's a remnant, she's a ripple, a little wave lapping on a great shore.* Matchi Manitou let the coyote rest as it debated whether or not it was worth the effort to toy with these children any further. It watched them wander away into the fields. The coyote trotted back to the tree where the girl had been captive and sniffed at the circle scribed in dead earth. The long lost pleasure of casting a charm tickled the Manitou. It made the coyote sniff the circle again. What was left of the coyote's true self feared the circled, hated the need to sniff at it. Sensing poison and death, the coyote wanted to run, but the thing that controlled it bent its will and it sat beside the circle, wearing a strange grin on its face and panic in its eyes.

Matchi Manitou prepared to relinquish its coyote shell and return to the deep cold of its sleep when the boy returned. He moved without his earlier stealth and he brought with him an essence the Manitou had not tasted since long before drifting to sleep. The boy brought a whiff of human jealousy. Deep in its lake, the tendril of the great Manitou rolled itself back toward waking. It danced the coyote to the wood's edge to watch and wonder at the small figure of the boy as he jogged into the darkness. *The two-leggers and their thinking-needs*, the Manitou thought to itself remembering the differences in the creatures of this world, *driven so much more beyond the need to eat. What a game I had arranging these thinking-needs.*

The lake rolled its deep waters, the fish within it gathered in frantic schools, the frogs and turtles moved toward its shores, any animal near its edges that could fly or flee did so until a stillness spread in a neat ring around the dark water.

Will's jog soon turned into a true run and his running shook his mind free of its pettiness. He ran beneath many stars he could name because of his uncle and through a night-world rich with spirits and guidance claimed by his aunt. He worked to quell his jealousy. If he felt that Alexandra's talent at tracking was to his shame, he knew his aunt's response. *If a man bends to pick up a stone who should he blame when he gets tired of carrying it?* She was full of these kinds of sayings. She offered them as needed without judgment, usually as she passed through a room, going to get another cup of coffee or fold laundry or make a phone call organizing another letter-writing campaign, and she never took the time to explain any of them, to make sure he understood why that particular bit of wisdom was being offered at that particular time. Yet her insistence and belief that he would get the meaning he needed, in a roundabout way, gave him the confidence to figure it out for himself.

He breathed the chilly night air deeply. Having passed the boulder Becca and he used as their meeting place, Will would soon came up on the path he needed to take to cut through the forest to the fields leading to his aunt and uncle's house. His stride did not lessen when he took to the deeper shadows of the woods. His eyes were strong, and since he had started seeing Becca, he had learned every raised root and little dip this path held. Yet he began to feel fear creep into his gut, and though he had no idea why, he had learned from his uncle during their wandering lessons that an animal who doesn't listen to its gut *either starves or gets eaten.* Will knew that what he felt was no hunger pang and quickened his pace.

A few hundred feet before he would emerge back into the open, his inkling of fear swelled toward panic and he began to run in earnest. Something was in back of him, and for the first time in his life, Will felt the fear of being eaten.

The thing within the coyote let the boy pass then trailed along behind him reacquainting itself with how the two-leggers could be twisted around with their thinking-needs. At the bottom of the lake it chuckled as it remembered how it had orchestrated this or that rift between individuals or whole herds

176

of the two-leggers. On command, coyote picked up its pursuit and in response the boy began to run in earnest. Unexpectedly, the boy seemed to sense its presence and the amused malice of its memories and his run became a sprint. From deep within the lake the thing spurred on its host coyote to test the boy's strength of will and to further taste the spice of his fear.

Will ran for his life. Panic began to take root and he felt his breathing change. His chest tightened and his legs tired. Then he heard a new name whispered in his ear, *Spotted Elk*, a tribal name but one not yet given. His chest relaxed a little and his stride lengthened again. He sensed the path sloping downhill toward the fields near his home. *Spotted Elk*, came his name as if spoken by some other who ran beside him, and Will felt urged to sprint. The boy emerged from the shadow of the woods into the lesser darkness of the night sky running full tilt, both afraid and strong, both away from whatever it was behind him and toward the safety of his family.

Matchi Manitou sensed something was helping the boy escape. It could sense his fear but also an emerging resilience. Again, it spurred the animal on to close the gap between them. Another shudder pulsed through deep waters but other than the captive fish nothing was left lakeside to suffer its wake and to flee. Still mostly asleep, still mostly dormant, the thing that lay at the bottom of the lake searched further the folds of its mind for a memory that smelled and felt like this night, like this boy running filled both with fear and defiance. Half-asleep the search proved bothersome, so it decided instead to fog the boy's thinking and explore the source of whatever it was coming to his aid.

Will crested the rise behind his aunt and uncle's house, and for a moment could see his home, the back stoop's light burning brightly. Behind him he felt the pressure of threat and everything grew dim. Even as he ran toward what he knew was there, it was as if the house receded before him.

Suddenly spoken words pierced the air. The image of the house emerged again, the back porch light like a fallen star and in its frail glow a figure, arms raised in supplication. There were words in the air, but Will's sight darkened again. He felt as if he were running through thigh deep water. He heard bubbling laughter. The house burst through, vivid and close. The figure was a woman. She wore a dark shawl. She beat a small drum. Its leather skin droned. Its rawhide strings thrummed. She chanted their tongue, and the boy ran toward its sound. He felt the pressure from behind coming to overtake him again, but his view of the house held, his legs remained unburdened. He sprinted past the woman, catching words as he stumbled toward the back steps, words that broke over his mind like clear water filled with light, *Gitche Manitou*. Behind him, the woman's voice continued to chant deep and strong until whatever it was that pursued the boy stalled and then retreated back into the night.

Will stood in the kitchen gasping for breath. A man appeared in the doorway, turned on the light, and though his eyes were puffy with sleep and his hair mussed like a battered hayfield, his face was stern, his body tense.

"I am Spotted Elk," gasped the boy staring at his uncle without recognition.

The back door swung open and a woman stepped into the room, a worn and battered shawl draped around her shoulders. The man's face fell then immediately grew firm again.

"I am Spotted Elk," repeated the boy, this time to the woman.

"You should have woken me," the man said with a mixture of anger and urgency.

"There wasn't time. I woke in it. Called for help."

"It came?"

"It did," she said turning to face the boy.

"I am Spotted Elk," repeated the boy.

"Yes," the two adults said in near perfect unison.

"I am Spotted Elk," pleaded the boy.

"Yes," they responded as one and then watched recognition return to their nephew's eyes. He rushed into his aunt's arms and as she held him he felt the strong hand of his uncle grasp the back of his neck.

"I am Spotted Elk."

"That is your name," said his aunt.

Will pressed his face into the texture of the shawl. It pricked his cheeks and smelled faintly of smoke and the must of long storage.

"Through the Great Spirit, I was to give you that name," she whispered quietly into the boy's ear. "Now you need to tell us how it is you have come to know it."

❧ 22 ❧

Gray Lies and Hospitals

Becca's mom was completely unprepared to find her girl looking as she did. The moment she entered the kitchen, her initial irritation at being woken up broke beneath her concern in seeing her daughter doubled over and wheezing.

"Bob!" she called out and immediately the girls heard his feet on the floor above them.

"Mom," came Becca's weak plea.

"We were rough housing."

"What the hell happened?"

"Can't breathe."

"It was an accident."

"Mom."

"Alright, alright, no one says anything else," demanded Mrs. Dwyer as her husband appeared in the kitchen doorway. "We need to take her to Hilltown." Becca's dad moved to the phone. "Alexandra, in the dryer are our beach towels, get one for each of you. Becca, it's okay, honey."

Alexandra pulled two towels free from the jumble of colors in the dryer, glad to be out of the kitchen. She'd done it, she'd taken the blame, like ripping a band aid off, it was done now. She returned to the kitchen to find that both dogs had appeared and were sniffing nervously at Becca's legs. Mr. Dwyer had gone upstairs to dress and get his car keys.

"Cold nose, cold nose," wheezed Becca to each pup in turn.

As she helped secure one towel around her daughter's waist, Becca's mother spoke to Alexandra sternly, "We're going to the hospital. You're to stay here with Josh. You'll be fine. Either we'll be back by breakfast or I'll send one of the McReedy's over. He's Josh's soccer coach and she's a teacher's aide at his school, so Josh knows them."

Mr. Dwyer reappeared and stood by Becca whose breathing though calmer remained raspy and shallow.

"I'll be right back down," said his wife, "See if you can find out what happened."

"Sue, let me get her to the car. I told the ambulance we'd be on Route 100. We can't leave the kids here alone. Wake Josh and bring him if you want."

"I'm okay, Mom," whispered Becca.

"I'll start the car and then come back in and get you. Maybe lay you down in the back," said Becca's dad as he disappeared through the living room.

Alexandra watched her Aunt Sue cross over to her daughter and push a few stray strands of hair back over an ear. In her nervousness, Alexandra repeated a slightly more elaborate version of what she already said, that they had been at each other with pillows and that had turned into something more physical until she had landed wrong with an elbow or a knee and Becca had gotten hurt. Her aunt seemed only to half-listen as she tended to her daughter, and Alexandra found herself repeating over and over again that it had been an accident and that she was sorry. The dogs moved anxiously between Alexandra and her aunt as if they too were trying to carry the message of explanation and apology. When her uncle reappeared to usher Becca to the car, her aunt crossed over to Alexandra and gave her a quick kiss and a hug. The dogs nuzzled the pair happily.

"It's okay. It's not your fault. It was an accident. If Josh wakes up, we'll tell him what happened and we'll go and see how things are. Call me," she called to her husband as they all trailed through the house toward the front door.

"I will."

Alexandra paused at the top of steps leading down off the front porch and watched Becca being settled into the back of the car. Gruff licked at her hand. She and the dogs and her aunt watched the bright tail lights of the car disappear down the driveway then reappear on the highway then disappear again for good around a bend and into the night.

Mrs. Dwyer puttered around the kitchen making coffee and putting away the few things that hadn't gone into the dishwasher. Alexandra crept upstairs to retrieve a pair of pants and fresh socks then settled in on the couch. She didn't want to be in Becca's room alone. She was exhausted but didn't want to sleep, yet when the phone rang, she realized that it woke her. She sat up to find both Gruff and Muffin curled up in two other chairs. They all three listened to her aunt's voice from the kitchen. They waited together. Her aunt appeared with a mug of coffee in hand.

"Well, hello you three. That was your uncle. Becca's in the back of an ambulance and he's following it to the hospital. They think she's got punctured a lung."

Alexandra choked back a cry.

"No, no. She's going to be fine," said her aunt calmly sitting down beside Alexandra and stroking her niece's leg, "Go on back to sleep. If he calls again, I'll let you know what's what."

"I'm so sorry," Alexandra said again and met her aunt's eyes. The two looked at each other for what seemed to Alexandra to be an eternity.

"Get some sleep, all three of you," said her aunt softly crossing over to turn on a lamp before she turned the brighter overhead light off. "I'll wake you with news."

Alexandra tried to let herself relax, but sleep wouldn't come. *A punctured lung. What did that mean? How do they fix that? Can they fix it? Why did she look at me so long? Why isn't she angrier? She'll probably be angrier in the morning. I'll be in real trouble in the morning.* So the thoughts swirled, repeating themselves in various forms with various emphasis until she drifted into a fitful sleep.

The ancient Manitou walked the exhausted coyote in a circle around the house angrily. *First the two-legger she who had the gift of full sight. Then the first-people boy who ran with the legs of the deer. Now an old woman, another first-people, who spoke the ancient tongue well enough to hobble together a protective charm. I have slept too long and dreamed too little,* Matchi Manitou thought to itself as it forced the coyote to sniff the grass along the invisible edge of the charm's effectiveness. As the animal continued to patrol and test the limits and strength of the charm's barrier, the Manitou mulled over the chain of events from this night. As the coyote completed another circuit and returned to the field leading back up into the woods, the Manitou reassured itself that the words spoken by the woman were imperfect, much had been forgotten, some had been misspoken, but their effect was surprisingly strong, too strong for its coyote host to break.

In fact, the body of the coyote was spent. It had barely rested since being possessed beside the lake. Its will was broken and it longed just to be allowed to stop moving, stop having to smell this or that, stop having to hunt what it failed to catch, just to rest, to find some nook between rock and tree and rest.

The coyote let itself be led back toward the woods. The thing within it full of patient planning. *An odd mix*, it thought, *these first-people and two-legged she-girls.* It made the coyote sniff the ground until it found the boy's scent then follow that scent back through the woods to the fields that spanned the southern fold of this mountain eventually leading to the Dwyer place. By the time the broken animal neared the boulder Will and Becca used as their meeting place, it rasped for breath, its legs taking shorter and shorter steps and barely able to keep its head from dragging along the ground. The thing within it found the boy's scent strong around the rock along with that of the girl it corralled up the tree. It sensed the failing of its host and brought the animal up next to the boulder until the wasted coyote's forehead pressed against the cold hard surface of the rock. The will and awareness of the great Manitou's tendril at the bottom of the lake drew itself into the boulder releasing the coyote.

Suddenly free of any thoughts but its own simple and instinctual fears, the coyote lunged away from the rock and dashed toward the woods. It ran a crooked line along the fringe where the trees gave way to the fields, but this rush of energy granted by the freedom to flee lasted for only a few feet before falling victim to utter fatigue. The coyote collapsed. Too weak to regain its feet, utterly confused as to where it was and what had happened to it, the animal dragged itself into the cover of the underbrush. It lay panting, sniffed the woods for scent of prey or running water, and died.

The thing at the bottom of the lake took into its memory the scents of the two young girls and the fleet-footed boy, the shape and character of the charm uttered by the woman, and most importantly, the thrum and feel of the world when that one little she received the gift of true-sight. It filled the boulder with these memories then withdrew the way a spider withdraws, completely attuned to the trap of its web, ready to lunge and deliver a lethal bite.

Alexandra woke to find the living room evenly lit by the next day's light, the two dogs still curled in their respective chairs. She listened to the sounds of her aunt already or perhaps still puttering about in the kitchen. She rose and crossed to the doorway and peaked in. Her aunt was nursing a pot of coffee and frying bacon. An open carton of eggs sat on the counter. Sensing someone behind her, Mrs. Dwyer turned and smiled at her niece.

"I know I said I'd wake you, but you were so completely asleep. Your uncle called when they got to the ER and again when he knew more. She's fine and she's going to be fine. A rib that got broken or re-broken punctured a lung, but they've taken care of that and cleared the lung out, and she's breathing much better," she spoke all of this while placing her coffee mug on the counter and crossing toward her niece who, before she heard all the news, found herself wrapped in her aunt's arms.

As one large tear slid from each eye, Alexandra wished she were in the arms of her own mother. She wanted to go home now, this minute, to see her dad and hear him singing, to see her mom and step dad and be in the kitchen with them as they made breakfast, but she knew that wasn't going to happen. With her next breath, however, she realized how soon in fact these reunions were going to happen, the day after or the next day, and that idea sent her heart pounding. *What was she going to tell her mom and dad? What were they going to say?*

"Can we go see her?" Alexandra asked trying to push back any thought of having to lie to another group of adults about how she injured Becca.

"After breakfast and only for a short visit. Can you mind the bacon while I go and wake Josh and fill him in?"

Alexandra nodded.

❖

As they pulled into the hospital's parking lot, Alexandra spotted her Uncle Bob waiting for them outside the Emergency Room entrance. He greeted them with good news and reassurances that Becca was doing well.

"She's sleeping off some of the anesthesia and pain medication," he explained. "And for now, only immediate family is allowed in the room with her."

"What about me?" interrupted Alexandra.

"She should be moving out of the ER this morning to a regular room and then you can see her. I know it's not what you want to hear, but there's a nice waiting room for families with a TV, there's a coffee shop and cafeteria, they might even be getting her room ready now,..." his voice trailed off as he turned to lead them into the hospital and speak with muted tones to his wife.

Alexandra spent her morning watching whatever it was the other people in the waiting room wanted to watch and trying not to stare at each new accident that walked through the door. When she successfully blocked out thoughts of all the little daily disasters that surrounded her and the strange mix of catastrophe and comedy that seemed to fill daytime television, Alexandra found herself worrying about whether or all her lies were holding firm. *Had Becca even heard her take responsibility for the accident? Had she maybe said something in the last few hours, uttered some other version of the truth? Why had Aunt Sue looked at her so strangely this morning in the kitchen? Did she already know what had really happened? Having lied about hurting Becca, would anyone believe her about how she had been able to save her?* By the time her Uncle Bob reemerged, Alexandra was queasy from the combination of worry and either seeing or overhearing about a foot that had slid under a mower, a finger nearly severed off by a knife, a fall down concrete stairs, two twisted ankles from the same soccer game, and several attacks of allergies and asthma. When her uncle beckoned for her to follow, Alexandra almost gave in to the impulse to let the full story spill out just to be rid of it and the nearly nauseating pressure of keeping it in.

Yet before she had the chance to speak, Josh appeared from behind his father, gave her shoulder a playful punch, and said, "Nice job. Did you body slam her or what?"

"Josh," scolded his dad. Alexandra started to apologize again but her uncle was having none of it, "It happened. She's fine. We're done talking about it. They're moving her to a regular room, and your aunt stayed up with her to help settle her into the new digs. We came down," he continued grabbing Josh playfully behind the neck, "to take you and get a snack while all that's being done."

"When can I see her?"

"Soon. Let's get something to eat. Then we'll head up to her new floor, find her room, and see if she's up to a visit, which I'm sure she will be."

The cafeteria was still serving breakfast, and after having only picked at her Aunt Sue's earlier offering, Alexandra found she was starving. She polished off a plate of pancakes and two cartons of milk in no time. While Josh sat playing a game on his dad's cell phone, Alexandra's uncle quietly broke the news that she'd be headed home this afternoon. The news hit her like a wave. Her stomach rolled and for a moment she thought she was going to be sick. Her uncle must have seen the change in her and quickly leaned in to explain that it was only a few days earlier than she was scheduled to leave anyway, and that with Becca in the hospital it just made more sense to see if her dad could make the trip up. Once it was late enough in the morning, he made the call and arranged it. Alexandra found herself nodding in agreement. What could she say? This was how it was with parents. They called the shots. She was used to it. Ever since she was three and her parents split up, she'd had her schedule dictated to her. This Christmas there. This Thanksgiving here. Whatever suited that mix of parents and their plans. Now this trip home today because it suited this mix of parents.

When it was time to clean up, she gathered her things and carried her tray to the stainless steel rimmed window that opened into the kitchen. As they waited for the elevator to take them up to the floor where Becca had been moved, she felt completely like a child again. In the woods, she led. She and her gift-vision

186

led. But now her summer was done, just like that, no more woods, no more tracking. She wanted to protest but what could she say? Everyone thought she did this to Becca, first in the woods pushing her into a rock so that she cracked a rib, then last night somehow breaking that rib and puncturing her lung. Even her dad, she realized, would be thinking she did this to her cousin, and he would have called her mom. They always talked to each other when something serious happened, so *they'd be on the same page* when dealing with her. Explaining to her dad was going to be bad enough. Trying to explain to her mother how she'd been careless enough to send her cousin to the hospital, that was going to be pure delight. The lies had taken over. Her lies and the adults were making all the decisions for her. *If she had only told them the truth, then they'd probably be letting her stay, they'd probably insist on it. No*, she told herself, *that was another lie. They wouldn't believe the real version of it. Who would?* Half the time she barely believed it herself. She followed her uncle along another tiled and brightly lit hallway trying to imagine how she could come clean, trying to imagine what that first sentence would sound like as she corrected everyone's misconceptions about what happened this past week, but no first sentence that she tested proved up to the task.

They turned a corner and caught sight of Mrs. Dwyer standing by an open doorway talking quietly with a nurse. Alexandra's aunt seemed much less tense now that she had seen her daughter. She smiled and waved her niece in then blocked her son from following.

"We'll be down just past where you got off the elevator in the visitor's lounge. But not too long. She needs to rest."

Alexandra nodded and entered.

"Did you stick to the story?" were the first whispered words out of her cousin's mouth.

Alexandra could only laugh. For the first time since watching Becca being driven away in the middle of the night, she remembered exactly why she'd agreed to take the blame for the injury. There were no half measures with Becca, no backing down. She was a rock, a rock with a punctured lung but a rock nevertheless.

"Yes," confirmed Alexandra, "But I thought I was going to spill it, I don't know how many times."

For the next few minutes the two girls caught the other up on what they had said and what they had done. Becca remembered very little about getting to the hospital. She remembered that whenever asked she just kept repeating that her cousin did this to her.

"You're such a jerk," chuckled Alexandra. "You know their sending me home."

"When?"

"Today."

"What!" Becca exclaimed then winced from the jolt to her body.

"Easy, are you okay?" Alexandra stepped to her cousin's side. "They called sometime this morning. My dad's on the way already. Easy. Try and catch your breath."

Becca's face did not falter. She continued to look utterly surprised. Then Alexandra realized that she was looking past her and turned to find Will standing in the doorway. Before either of the girls could think of what to say, he walked into the room hands raised as if in surrender.

"Don't pop a stitch. My aunt's got three or four friends who work here and the story that she and I are telling is that one of them knew the connection between you and me and called her this morning and she told me because she knew I'd want to know and we decided to drop by as we were out running errands anyway. Alright? Alright." Will took a deep breath before starting again, "Now, I'm to send Alexandra back out because I'm not supposed to stay long and your mom doesn't want the two of us in here getting you all worked up. Okay? Okay."

He dropped his hands and took another deep breath. Both girls laughed. Becca waving her hand to ward off the pain.

"So your aunt knows?" asked Alexandra.

"You need to scoot or her mom's going to come in here, but *yeah*, she was up for some reason when I wandered back in, so she's knows I was out. She figured it was you," he explained pointing to Becca, "even though I told her otherwise." Will decided before he came in the room to keep the story of his ordeal to himself, not only because he figured Becca had been through enough but because he'd been asked to hold his tongue for now by both his aunt and uncle. "Really," he turned to Alexandra and insisted, "you need to go, or we're both going to get pulled out of here."

"Alright, I'm going."

"Don't leave for good without seeing me again," cried Becca softly.

"I won't," Alexandra assured her.

Alexandra stepped outside the door of Becca's room, got her bearings, and walked back down the hallway toward the elevators. Will crossed to Becca's bedside and slipped his hand into hers. She gave it a quick squeeze and then reveled in the pressure she felt him return.

"What the hell," she said quietly.

"Exactly," he agreed with his heart pounding in his chest.

Alexandra continued down hall in somewhat of daze. Her cousin was lying in a hospital bed but recovering. The lies of how it all happened were safe or, for the most part, seemed to be. Will was there by Becca's side, and in a matter of hours, she would be sitting by her father heading home to face the rest of her family. What else could possibly happen?

She turned into the entrance of the visitor's lounge and sitting beside her uncle was a woman wearing the shawl that Alexandra first saw several nights earlier being worn by a wavering, storm-riding apparition.

❧ 23 ❧

The Shawl Speaks

Alexandra had no time to hide her reaction. She felt as if she'd gone pale then flushed with embarrassment. There was no doubt in her mind that this was the shawl she had seen the night of the storm and equally no doubt that this was not the woman she'd seen wearing it. This woman was younger, though something about her, something around the eyes, maybe the set of her nose, seemed familiar. Alexandra worked to regain her sense of composure, certain that everyone in the room had seen her initial shock and that a wave of reaction would follow, but none of the adults reacted, and Josh's attention stayed turned toward the television. Her Uncle Bob jumped up, both to introduce Will's aunt and to half-offer half-insist that Alexandra take the seat beside her.

"This is Will's aunt, White Feather Woman," he spoke her name as a kind of question, unsure if he was repeating it correctly.

Will's aunt nodded to Alexandra. If her uncle picked up any reluctance on her part to be thrust into conversation with this new person, he didn't seem to care. As he guided Alexandra toward the open chair, he begged off with the excuse that he and his wife had things to discuss. Will's aunt nodded politely and reassured him that Will's visit would be brief. Alexandra thought the older woman sat ramrod straight like royalty. As she moved toward her seat she noticed how the woman's silver-gray hair shimmered against the dark shawl. Sitting, she fully expected the next few minutes to take one of three directions. Will's mysterious aunt or not, Alexandra expected that this woman would speak to her like child three years younger than she was, or she would launch into an interview process intended to identify grade level, favorite subject, sport or instrument played, or she would use the opportunity to turn the conversation immediately back on herself, make it a teaching moment in which she would share the great wealth of her experience.

"How is your cousin?"

The interview, thought Alexandra relaxing – she found this to be the least onerous of the adult-speak options. "She's fine. She was glad to see Will," Alexandra answered. Then as she listened to White Feather Woman's response, Alexandra leaned back so she could examine the shawl more closely. It looked more worn now that she was seeing it well lit.

"I have a good friend, family actually, who works here in the ER. She knows that Will and this girl are friends. Called with the news," explained Will's aunt then paused. White Feather Woman felt no need to offer more, to let this girl know how she had been pulled from her sleep to stand outside her house in order to summon a protective charm strong enough to save her nephew from whatever darkness chased.

In the brief silence, Alexandra thought with her heart sinking, *Oh God, the teaching moment.* She dreaded this option the most and really disliked adults who feigned one way then went the other.

"How is it...," the older woman began flatly, staring straight ahead as if she were looking out of the waiting room window, "... you have seen this shawl before?"

Alexandra froze. Usually this was the conversation she preferred, the adult who spoke with you as if you actually had ideas of your own, but of all the options she expected, Alexandra was least prepared for this one, and she stumbled in her response, in the end offering little more than stunned silence.

Sensing the girl's confusion or reluctance, perhaps her desire to keep the story of Becca's injuries safe, White Feather Woman filled the silence with a further explanation delivered in a calm and gentle tone, "Your surprise was not directed at me, you'd never seen me before, but the shawl, seeing it again... that tripped you up." She paused as if weighing exactly what next to say, "Let me start us off. Until late last night... or rather early this morning, I have not worn this cloth since before you were born." She paused again and Alexandra waited hoping to hear more before she offered up her story, but Will's aunt seemed willing now to wait.

"The other night before the storm. I was out back of the house," Alexandra began quietly, desperate not to be heard by anyone other than Will's aunt, "and I saw an old woman wearing it." Then realizing how that might have sounded, she quickly added, "Not you, an old woman."

White Feather Woman smiled to herself then continued quietly, either out of respect for Alexandra's subdued tone or because she also didn't wish to have their conversation overheard by others, "In this dream, was the old woman…"

But before Will's aunt could finish her thought, and without really thinking it through herself, Alexandra interrupted, "It wasn't a dream."

Now White Feather Woman froze. A look of concern replaced her smile. She quickly looked around the room to be sure that no others besides Becca's family were still present. She saw Becca's mother check her watch and then speak quietly to her husband. Drawing the shawl more securely around her, she spoke again trying to control her voice so its urgency would not cause the girl to overreact, "When do you return to your home?"

"Today," Alexandra answered sensing the older woman's agitation.

"I see. I wish that wasn't the case, but…" her voice trailed off as she watched Becca's father take a seat beside his son and speak quietly. White Feather Woman knew she didn't have much time. The family was getting ready to leave, taking this remarkable girl with them. Her sentences came short and to the point.

"Choose carefully who you tell about that night. And about your sight." Alexandra snapped her head toward the older woman. "I pressed my nephew to speak of it. He did not break your confidence easily." She paused to reconsider what she needed most to say and to hear, "Tell me how it feels when you gain this greater vision."

Alexandra too was aware that the Dwyer's were growing restless. She needed to pack and she wanted to say good-bye again to Becca, but she also wanted to hear what this woman had to say. She answered as best as she could, "Like a wave or a pulse."

"Do you summon it?"

"Yes. No, it's… it's more like I ask for it."

White Feather Woman sat up a little, turned, and while still gripping the ends of the shawl with either hand reached out toward Alexandra. The girl offered up her hand almost as a reflex and as soon as she came into contact with the shawl the image of the old woman she had seen flashed like a projection over the face of Will's aunt. Alexandra's hands tingle softly as with the tail-end pins and needles of a limb that fell asleep. White Feather Woman felt the weight of the shawl dissipate and grow lighter as if someone were lifting it free of her shoulders. She looked hard at the girl and saw that the child was staring equally hard right back at her. White Feather Woman felt the weight of the shawl return and curiosity seep into the girl's face.

"This gift is a doorway, not to be entered but to be known, to be… acknowledged. If you sense guidance, let it be your guide. Do not talk about it casually or carelessly. And when you come to visit your cousin again, we will need to talk more."

Alexandra's aunt appeared beside them.

"We have to get you packed."

"Can I see her just to say good-bye?" Alexandra asked.

"Of course," she answered then turned to White Feather Woman, "Thank you for visiting."

Will's aunt nodded slightly as Alexandra rose from her chair. The girl was struck by the sudden coolness in her Aunt Sue's tone. Just before they exited the room, Alexandra shot a glance back toward White Feather Woman. She was sitting again much as she had been when Alexandra first walked into the room, self-contained, face relaxed, and her eyes focused on the world outside the windows.

Once they were out of ear shot, Mrs. Dwyer leaned toward Alexandra, "I find it odd that they came so quickly. I don't like the idea of one of the staff here calling friends and family based on who they see come through the emergency room. There must have been some kind of breach of confidentiality."

Alexandra had never been so grateful to meet an unexpected stranger as she had Will's aunt and quickly looked to diffuse her own aunt's anger, "I think it's just that Will and Becca really like each other."

"I know that," her aunt responded somewhat defensively.

"But he must have talked about her at home. How many boys do that?" Alexandra explained still hoping to cool her aunt down before they turned into the room, maybe to find Will and Becca holding hands or worse.

Her aunt looked over at her niece, "Not many."

"You didn't see him when he came in. He was really worried."

"He seems sweet," her aunt conceded as the continued down the hall.

"He is," Alexandra confirmed sensing the change in the tone and intensity of
her aunt's voice.

"Just promise me that when you come next summer," her aunt started as they neared the door to Becca's room, "you won't put your cousin back in the hospital."

"I'll try not to," agreed Alexandra.

Her aunt pulled up short, "Yeah, I don't think that's good enough."

"Okay, okay," laughed Alexandra, "I promise, no hospitals."

They found Becca asleep and Will sitting in the chair flipping through the TV channels with the sound muted. He sprang out of his seat the moment he saw Becca's mom.

"She's been in and out of it since I came."

"She's got a lot of chemicals still in her system, from the anesthesia to the pain killers to stuff to ward off infection, but I want to thank you and your aunt for coming. I know she was glad to see you."

"I met your aunt," added Alexandra.

"Did you talk?" asked Will quickly.

"A little."

Will started to form another question, but Mrs. Dwyer cut him off and ushered him out of the room with another bit of thanks for coming but not before he shot Alexandra a glance ripe with both curiosity and concern.

"Let's not wake her. I'll tell her you said good-bye," Alexandra's aunt half-insisted half-offered.

Alexandra looked down at her cousin. She looked frail and tired. She had a tube pumping oxygen enriched air strapped to her nose. Alexandra couldn't remember if it had been there all along. *It must have been*, she thought, *I just wasn't paying attention*, she added to herself somewhat reproachfully. She let herself be led from the room back to the waiting area to gather Josh. A new family had settled into a number of the seats, the station on the television had been changed, and Will and his aunt had disappeared. Mr. Dwyer was to stay behind and to be with his daughter through the morning visiting hours. He gave Alexandra an extra-long hug trying to convince her that he was not upset with her in the least, and she was thankful for the comfort.

As she drove her son and her niece home, Susan Dwyer fought to keep her fatigue at bay. The last week had taken its toll. From the moment her daughter woke with the bruised ribs after her picnic at the river, she had been worried and confused. In her gut, she assumed Becca carried much of the responsibility for her injuries. *She was an instigator, not malicious, more reckless than anything. But the punctured lung. What had gotten into Alexandra?* she wondered. *What should I say to Cy?* From the corner of her eye, she watched the girl riding beside her, and again, her anger and concern faded. *There's something else going on here*, she conceded, just as she had done time and again over the last week. *I can't put my finger on it, but these girls didn't hurt each other. Not like this.*

For the most part, their ride back to the Dwyer's home was quiet. Josh asked whether plans he had made to see a movie with friends needed to be changed, and when the answer came back, "No, you can still go," he settled into his own thoughts. Alexandra found it hard to read her aunt. She wasn't sure if she was still mistrustful of her now that she had seen her daughter laid out with tubes running here and there or if she was just concerned and tired. In truth, Alexandra didn't really want to know. She was tired as well and wanted to find herself alone so that she could think back to what Will's aunt had said to her and what she might have meant by what she said.

At the house, Josh disappeared into his room. Gruff and Muffin made their appearance to sniff each returning person and gauge their level of tension. They seemed satisfied that whatever had upset the house earlier was under control and drifted back to their favorite lounging places. Alexandra made herself busy, gathering the damp clothes from the tent and packing her things up as quickly as possible. Soon her little pile sat on the porch by the front steps, a suitcase, plastic garbage bag filled with dirty laundry, and her backpack with her books and the notebook in which she had begun to catalog her experiences with her gift-sight. What she really wanted to do was to retrieve the book and add as much as she could remember from the night before through her visit with White Feather Woman, but she sensed that her Aunt Sue would rather have her continue to busy herself. She offered to break down the tent and get it back into the barn. As she unsnapped the poles, shook out and folded the tent as best she could, Alexandra used her time alone to revisit what she remembered so that when she had the chance to write it down, she wouldn't forget anything. Though not a perfect job, she finally managed to shove all the pieces for the tent back into its carry-case and crossed toward the barn. As she entered the half-light and breathed in the musty air, she recalled two things above all else – the idea of this other sight being a doorway and also being a guide. These were hard images to combine into the same thing, and as she played around with variations of these metaphors, she suddenly felt her hands tingle the way they had when she touched the shawl. She hoisted the tent up onto the shelf where it had been and felt the pulse of her gift-sight descend, but this time it was only the pulse, no new light broke into view, the barn and its shadows remained dark. Without warning, tears rolled across her cheeks, and she broke into a sobbing fit, pressing her face into her hands. She had nearly lost Audrey, she had nearly lost Becca, she had lied to her dad and to her aunt and uncle, *What kind of summer vacation was this?*, she asked herself. The thrum rose through her again delivering an odd sensation of comfort, *But you didn't lose them and these lies will not*

196

hold, she heard herself think at the same time realizing that these were not her words, that the phrasing was formal and foreign. *But how would I think someone else's thoughts?* she asserted clearly in her own words.   Yet before she could consider the weirdness of what just happened, the very real voice of her Aunt Sue rang out from beyond the barn announcing that her father was less than an hour away.

↣ 24 ↢

The Pull of Stone

Suddenly the only thing Alexandra wanted to do was visit the woods one last time before she took the ride back to normal. *Back to normal*, she thought and laughed to herself. She emerged from the dusty dim of the barn and called to the house.

"I'm going to take a walk!"

"Don't go far!" came her aunt's voice.

Alexandra looked to the kitchen windows and thought she could make out a silhouette.

"Okay!" she agreed even as she thought that *not far* could be interpreted to mean almost any distance.

She stood at the edge of the mown lawn and studied the contour of the distant tree line as she had done the night of the storm but in the sharp daylight no apparitions appeared. *The short loop*, she thought, but as soon as she stepped into the taller grass of the field leading up to the familiar forest entrance, she turned and headed north, cutting diagonally across the field as if to follow the tree line toward the path leading to Will's house. She held her hands out from her sides with palms turned slightly forward so that the tips of the grasses and wild flowers brushed her fingertips. *A doorway and a guide*, she thought, and with an odd comfort, Alexandra felt the pulse as the quiet light rose within her. The field's colors shifted, muted by the light within. The light had never swept into her so full and easy. Alexandra's stride grew long. She breathed deeply and cut a straight line through the tall grasses, calm and swift, like a ship in full sail.

Stretched between rock and lake, Matchi Manitou itched and thrummed. He felt the little she-thing toying with the quiet light. Then he felt the great gift-sight descend and the pulse of it moving toward where the bit of him lingered in the fabric of the stone. Only briefly did he wish for the body of the coyote back, for to wish this thing was also to concede the miscalculation in the scheme for his triumph, and the great Manitou did not easily concede errors in his thinking. The coyote was gone, discarded. Indeed the scent of its carcass already drew the slow circling climb and descent of buzzards.

As they neared their home on the way back from the hospital, the sight of the same buzzards unsettled White Feather Woman. And the fact that such a common sight disturbed her only confused her more. She let her foot sink down on the gas pedal.

"Okay, Aunt Pat," Will offered almost immediately, "We in a race I don't know about?"

"Maybe," responded White Feather Woman flatly.

Will sat up a little straighter and gripped the arm rest of his door a little tighter. The car skidded slightly as they lurched through the turn onto their driveway.

"Jeez!" exclaimed Will.

"My shawl is over the back of the chair in front of my mirror."

"Okay?"

"Bring it to me."

"Back to the car?"

"I'll be cutting toward the path to the far fields," she explained calmly even as the car slid to a halt, the tires cutting shallow ruts into the soft gravel of the driveway.

White Feather Woman stepped out of the car leaving her door wide open and began walking as quickly as she could around the house. She looked up to locate the entrance to the forest path then made a bee line in that direction. Will slammed shut his door, loped up the front stairs, and disappeared into the house. He found the shawl exactly where his aunt said it would be then cut through the kitchen and out the back door. His aunt was nearly half way through the field.

"Aunt Pat!" he yelled. He watched to see if she had heard him. Without turning, her arm shot out and beckoned for him to come. "What the hell," he whispered to himself as he broke into a run.

He caught up with her as she neared the path into the forest. She stopped and snatched the shawl from his outstretched hands.

"Thank you, boy. Now go and find your uncle and stay with him," she demanded. Will began to speak but she cut him off, "Find him and stay with him!" Before he could muster a thought of protest, she turned and continued toward the trees.

Over a decade of living in this house, Will knew better than to argue. He watched the woman moving more steadily and quickly than he had ever seen her move. Suddenly his stomach knotted and he remembered the darkness that had chased him home only a few nights before. He turned and looked at the house and broke into a full run back to find his uncle.

Stretched between rock and lake, Matchi Manitou itched and thrummed. The little two-legger continued to draw near but now he felt the needling will of the first people hag as well. *Stay clear!* he screamed into the silence of the rock and lake. *I will crush your medicine and you with it! Wipe you both from the face of this earth!* But buried by stone and water, the threat held no measure. The great Manitou felt the weak medicine plodding ever nearer.

With the instinct of the imprisoned, Matchi Manitou rallied his thoughts deep within him until he could piece together the story he needed to avoid losing himself in his anger. He remembered back just after the beginning of time when he and his meek brother first roamed free naming the creatures they brought forth, claiming new portions of their world, dreaming up new spells to test, and scheming how to out maneuver the other brother. *Meek Gitche*, chided the Manitou, *Mother's little favorite, sun-child, stream-wader, always singing at the birds and chuffing at bears, charmed by the two-leggers and their frantic need for a sense of place and dignity beyond their measure.* Matchi's thoughts swirled in this eddy of ancient grievance almost to the point of slipping completely back into the living tomb of the icy lake bed, but in the instant his grip and purchase in the rock began to slip, he snapped himself back from ancient into the present. He focused and reclaimed more of the boulder where Becca and Will had sat oblivious to Alexandra's spying eyes. At the same time, he recalled and brought forth a split spell designed to both thwart the approach of the meddling old medicine woman and to spur on the two-legger to deliver the quiet light to a more appropriate host.

Both White Feather Woman and Alexandra felt the effects of the spell almost immediately.

For White Feather Woman, the spell poured along the forest trail like an invisible rising tide of water. Suddenly each step became more laborious. She found herself straining as if wading waste deep against a slow but persistent current. She struggle blindly. *Come on legs*, she complained to herself. *So old so quick sometimes. Always old going uphill… a little old coming down too.* As she trudged along the spell crept into her mind and muddled her intent. *What's the point of this little stroll*, she thought absently. *Should turn around, ice tea, another chapter in that novel.* She stopped walking and let the current of the spell slide past her legs like a cool breeze urging her to turn about and head home.

For Alexandra the spell came as a voice similar enough to the one she had just heard in the darkness of the barn that she mistook it for the same. *More swiftly*, she thought with the voice of another, *Time is of consequence and light is of essence and too much for my frame. To release it would be best, relinquish and be free, relinquish and be free.* Marveling at the folding light within the fields, the odd majesty of the twice lit forest, and with the voice spurring her on, Alexandra began to lengthen her stride until she found herself running up the last hill desperate to see the kissing rock come into view.

Matchi Manitou trembled with delight at the ease of the trap. He simultaneously felt the old woman stall and the two-legger's eager approach. Alexandra crested the hill and her heart jumped strangely at the sight of the boulder. Matchi's will leapt as he felt her eyes strike the surface of the rock where he lay in wait. For an instant, to cement the triumph and snap the trap closed, his split spell grew imbalanced. Much more of his attention spun out toward the weak-minded two-legger and wavered slightly in its pinning down of the old medicine woman.

Alexandra gasped and bolted toward the stone. White Feather Woman felt the current pushing against her grow chill and falter and she reached to pull the shawl she wore more tightly around her shoulders. When she touched its fabric, for an instant her eyes cleared, and she looked at the pin point of light that was the end of the trail and beginning of the back fields.

Alexandra drew up and faced the boulder. She stood working to catch her breath, mesmerized by the light of it, and seeking to hear a guiding voice direct her thoughts. Matchi Manitou leapt at the chance. *Touch!* cried Alexandra to herself. She froze. *What are you?* she asked herself. *This is not the voice from before.* The light within the rock began to change. Like the inverse of the night sky, the stern bright gray dotted by pinholes of utter black slowly began to turn, miniature constellations inverted and hypnotic. *Relinquish and be free. Relinquish and be free,* Alexandra thought to herself. Part of her calmed under the strange comfort of this other voice. Part of her resisted. But all of her watched the slow swirl of the quiet light as it seemed to turn the stone into putty. *Touch,* she thought again and half of her wanted scoop a handful of that light right out of the rock. *Touch,* she thought again more urgently and half of her sensed a lie within the desire. *Cannot hold light,* she thought defensively. *TOUCH!* she commanded and felt her hand rise and reach. Her heart swelled with joy at the contact. She watched her fingers dip ever so slightly into the stone. The dark pin points of void moved about her fingers like water past five small pebbles. *Touching light,* she thought with great satisfaction. *Touching light,* she thought greedily. *Cannot touch light,* she wavered. Then the pins and needles set came. Alexandra felt as if her hand were falling asleep. The numbness glued her fingers to the rock. Suddenly she wanted the light to cease. She tried to wish it away but to no avail. *Mine, you speck of tottering waste,* she told herself, and her mind clamped shut with panic. *No...mine,* she thought with her own voice. Matchi recoiled and raged at the resistance. Alexandra felt her fingers burn. She tried to pull free of the rock but looked to find her finger tips encircled by tiny dark rings with more and more black pin points of nothingness drifting toward them. The numbness began to spread slowly toward her first knuckles, and even as she fought the urge Alexandra shuffled closer to the stone. Something in her desperately wanted her to lay her body fully against the rock. Alexandra tried pushing back but instead felt the sensation of sinking her hand further into the putty of the boulder. *Mine*, she again told herself in the voice that was not hers. *I am lost*, she cried. *No little thing, you've just been found*, she chided herself in her madness.

Then the softest most gentle and reassuring sensation spread around Alexandra's shoulders. Her eyes cleared and she saw the rock for what it was. *I cannot hold light*, she said calmly and firmly told herself, *and should not try*, a milder, deeper voice affirmed. *Relinquish and be free*, she told herself in her own small voice even as she heard them echoed by the deeper voice. And with what seemed like both a great effort and no effort at all, she slid her fingers free of the stone. The burning ceased and the quiet light reclaimed its true form. Alexandra looked down at her shoulders to find herself wearing the shawl which in its shimmering state seemed to float around her. She turned to see Will's aunt flustered and blushing, trying her best to look collected as she struggled to catch her breath. But in spite of this outward appearance of nearly utter fatigue, the light blazing within this woman astounded Alexandra.

"Step back, child! For goodness sake, just take a step back!" White Feather Woman gasped.

Alexandra obeyed and felt the pull of the stone dissipate further. She turned and watched the swirl of dark pinpoints slowly sink back into the general gray mish-mash of the stone's coloring.

White Feather Woman stared at the surface of the boulder where the girl's hand had rested. For an instant it seemed to waver as if liquid. Then like a mirage that disappears under closer inspection, the wavering surface of the stone snapped back to solid granite. White Feather Woman suddenly felt she needed the touch of her shawl in order to regain her composure, but when reached to retrieve it, she found that it too had changed in appearance. For an instant, it looked as if its pattern floated on a material made of light, a light which seemed to shine through from the girl herself.

Alexandra turned to face White Feather Woman. Behind the look of wonder, she saw a woman near collapse. *Her shawl,* she thought, and in one simple, fluid motion, Alexandra pulled the cloth free of her shoulders and draped it onto White Feather Woman. In that moment of connection, with the shawl acting as a kind of conduit, each saw what the other saw and heard what the other thought. Alexandra saw herself through White Feather Woman's eyes and glimpsed the magnitude of the danger in which she had been. She also sensed the need to keep her experience of the quiet light a secret for now. White Feather Woman saw that she had blazed with the inner light and felt the raw mixture of fear and resolve at play within the child. She also heard the distant whisper of the powerful voices at play within Alexandra's mind. The shawl dropped onto White Feather Woman's shoulders and the connection faded.

"You understand the need to keep this to yourself a little longer?" White Feather Woman asked.

"I do. But you're going to help me?"

"Oh yes, child, you are not alone in this anymore."

White Feather Woman watched Alexandra struggle to put her next thought into words. Her brow knitted as she tapped her front teeth together lightly.

"I sometimes don't think in my own voice," she finally said flatly.

After a long pause, White Feather Woman admitted, "I know... and that can be a wonder and a horror... but I also know this, that you are stronger already than you can imagine. You held off a power that would have overwhelmed anyone else I can think of. Follow your gut... and follow any voice that you hear from your gut."

A breeze worked its way up along the fields to whisper the woods. Alexandra looked back toward her aunt's house.

"You're dad's already there, so you should go."

"Thank you..." Alexandra began seeking for how to finish her thought, "for lending me your shawl."

White Feather Woman's eyes sparkled, "Doesn't really go with your outfit though."

Alexandra laughed and turned toward home. The woman accompanied her to the top of the first rise then let Alexandra drift away on her own. As she crossed toward the next hill top, Alexandra looked back several times. Each time reassured to see White Feather Woman still marking her progress. When she reached the hill that dipped down toward her aunt's farmhouse, she turned and waved. She watched the dot of an old woman raise a hand in farewell. Alexandra smiled and turned, glad for the thought of her father.

Matchi Manitou's rage rumbled like muted thunder through the dense cold water along the lake bottom. For an instant he thrust the focus of that rage through the vein of him that had escaped sending it into the center of the boulder. At the same time White Feather Woman stood looking down toward the Dwyer house and raised her hand in response to Alexandra's wave, a deep unnatural pop like a quick clap of a distant gunshot sounded within the stone and a starting beneath where the boulder sank into the earth and running along the side turned toward the woods a crack formed. Nothing emerged.

The First-people have forgotten! That witch-woman will wish she had never interfered! I had the she-thing! I had the light! I had it! I had it. Could have seen my way free. Through this brother-cursed darkness.

Matchi wrapped the tendril of himself around and around the center of the stone then retreated to console his rage with dreams of escape, retribution and revenge.

On her way back toward the cut-through path leading to her own house, White Feather Woman began to give the boulder a wide berth, but something she thought she had seen demanded a quick examination of the boulder's surface. As she neared the rock, she pulled the shawl more tightly about her shoulders and let her eyes scan the mottled gray.

Nothing, she told herself as she slowly passed by. Then she froze. From straight on the boulder's surface yielded only the random shades of gray and the generally rough and dimpled skin of every other piece of abandoned ice aged granite. But just as she turned to seek the gap in the trees that would lead her home, five distinct little dimples caught the light. *There!* she gasped and held her right hand out as if she were going to press it against the stone. *Her thumb and four fingers. She's left her mark on the stone. It was going to eat her,* she thought and snapped her hand back down. *But that child resisted. That child pushed free. That child left finger prints in stone,* she thought. White Feather Woman's knees buckled and she turned her eyes away from the sight. She stumbled toward the woods. When she reached the entrance to the forest path, she pulled the shawl up over her head looking only at the ground and the steady progress of her feet. It wasn't until the passed the half-way rock that she heard their calls and raised her eyes up to see the welcomed sight of her husband and nephew coming toward her.

☙ 25 ❧

Homes Sweet Homes

Shock can be a gift. It can create a buffer between an experience and being overwhelmed by that experience. As she made her way down the hill toward the wonderfully familiar sight of her aunt's house, Alexandra walked in a bubble of shock. She remembered the rock pulling her in, remembered the competing wills speaking out within her thoughts, the feel of the shawl, her resistance, and now, even through the buffer of her shock, a joy in that resistance. Outside of her thoughts, she saw that she was almost to the edge of the mown lawn. *I'm leaving the woods behind. But not the quiet light,* she nearly whispered out loud. Then in a deep, rich voice, another part of her mind reassured her, *No, you will always carry the light within.* Her heart swelled and she stopped at the edge of the field, surrounded by the tall grass and fern. She started to turn to look one more time at the tree line but instead closed her eyes and saw it clearly in her mind. She imagined some new knowledge hovering just beyond her ability to pull it forward, like the flash of something in a lake bottom seen from the corner of her eye. Then it was gone and she stepped onto the short, mown scruff of the Dwyer's backyard.

In the seeming safety of familiar surroundings, as a sense of normalcy returned, she thought back to the moment when she pulled her fingers free of the rock and let the pride swell in her chest. But when she saw her father emerge from the kitchen doorway, all her bravado melted away and Alexandra's emotions got the better of her. Before she knew what hit her, she ended up in his arms sobbing. For all her strength and resilience over the last couple of weeks as simple outings had turned into trials of endurance, for all the friendship and love she had discovered among her pack of pals as they faced and overcame each new challenge, all her wonder at her gift-sight and the admiration it seemed to bring from others, her unexpected strength in the face of forces she had yet to understand, she was exhausted. Seeing her dad let her become a little girl again. She held onto him and let the adults talk their condescending nonsense, yes and no it wasn't about feeling guilty about Becca, yes and no it wasn't about not getting much sleep the night before, yes and no it was about being away from home for so long for the first time. They all knew less than half of what she did, and she felt that she knew less than half of what she needed to. So she hung onto her dad and indulged in a good cry. As her breathing finally grew less ragged, her father loosened his grip and rubbed her back.

"I want to thank you," he began, "because you know I don't have a dry shirt to change into."

Alexandra laughed in spite of herself and slapped his chest. "Well, that cleared the pipes," she admitted. She very much just wanted to get in the car and leave.

Mr. Stepp sensed his daughter's fatigue beyond her emotions. He begged off the offers of lunch or even a snack as he helped toss her things into the backseat of their car. Alexandra gave her aunt a rather perfunctory hug which she regretted before she even made it back to the car, so she turned and gave her Aunt Sue a genuine embrace. She felt her aunt kiss the top of her head, and when Alexandra started to let go, she felt herself pulled back in for another quick squeeze. Alexandra watched her dad speak with his sister knowing they were still commiserating and reassuring themselves and each other with only bits of the story pieced together with incomplete facts.

For the first forty-five minutes of the trip, they traveled in silence, Mr. Stepp assuming that his daughter would speak up when she was ready to talk. Alexandra gazed out the window watching the mountains rise and fall and the forests advance and recede. She was conflicted by her sense of escape from any further demands on her new vision and her sense of loss in leaving those demands behind as they had come to define her as gifted and important. She thought back to those moments in the semi-darkness of the Dwyer's barn when she felt what she thought was the pulse of her vision-shift only to remain in the dark, yet it was a darkness replete with an odd sense of comfort and foreign thoughts. Part of her was glad to be leaving behind the fact of her cousin lying in a hospital bed, though the idea of it remained cemented in her mind. In contrast, part of her was sorry to be leaving behind the reality of the woods and the mountains, whose contour and silhouette she so desperately tried to memorize, the place where her gift-sight filled her with purpose and competence. *A girl divided*, she thought, *that's nothing new. Two houses, two homes, one of me for each. Now two sets of eyes, one North, one South, one for the woods, one for pavement.* She laughed a little to herself and at herself. *So very dramatic*, she concluded as she turned to her father.

"So how's Boxy," she asked, her voice sounding odd after so much strained silence.

"Ahhh," began her father.

Alexandra dropped her head back against the head rest and closed her eyes. She had heard this particularly brand of *Ahhh* for years. It was her dad's 'here comes a load of nonsense' *Ahhh*. She took in a deep breath ready and willing for a few moments of complete idiocy.

"There was a circus in town," continued her father.

"Dad," she said flatly.

"So I sold her as a back-up elephant."

"Dad, she's not fat."

"Shaved her, sculpted a couple of duct tape ears… a little duct tape trunk."

"Dad," complained Alexandra through her giggles.

"Ringmaster was very impressed."

"You did not sell my cat to the circus."

"No, I didn't," admitted Mr. Stepp, then added after a beat, "Damn cat couldn't pick up a peanut to save her life."

Alexandra squealed with laughter and indignation. She swung her hand out slapping her father's arm.

"Hey, I'm driving here."

The ice broken, they chatted about all sorts of inconsequential things – favorite dinners, movies seen and not seen, what else she had done besides try to kill her cousin, and what else he had done besides try to pass off her shaved cat as an elephant. To her relief, his report on Audrey was glowing – she was fully recovered and back at ballet camp. Her mother and step dad were excited to see her and, of course, still a little concerned about all these mysterious injuries, though her father reassured Alexandra that he'd already gotten them to agree that a return visit next summer was both reasonable and expected.

"This is our time together, you know… this drive down. Since you were with me before you left, I'm to take you right to their house." He paused and when he sensed no response was coming, he added, "I'll see you on Wednesday as usual, and we'll be back into the routine.

Alexandra listened to the schedule stoically as she had from when she was three years old. Gone was the time at one house playing at family with an older sister and a younger brother. She was back to her regular commute.

"Shag is coming back to the Burrito Rojo," he added hoping for some kind of reaction. He knew she loved the little Mexican place. Since he had wandered onto it the past fall, they'd made it in there about twice a month, free music of all stripes and her favorite avocado tacos.

"This week?" she asked with more than a spark of interest.

"Thursday night."

"Can we stay for the whole set?"

"You're still on vacation, so I don't see why not," he agreed still searching for some sense of normalcy to what little time they had left in the car.

Alexandra accepted the bribe – she was used to that as well, pushing each house for whatever prizes and concessions she could get. She leaned up and switched on the radio scanning for stations. The music let her avoid further conversation and at the same time masked her continued desire to keep to her own thoughts. The car bounced over a small dip in the highway, but at their speed it felt a lot like it did when her gift-sight descended, and Alexandra's mind was swept back to the night she and Will had rescued Becca from whatever it was that treed her. The thumb of one of her hands rolled itself over her fingers as she remembered the feel of that wasted, dusty soil cutting what looked like a perfect circle around the truck of the tree where they found her cousin. She thought back on all the scatter of the last few weeks, from the randomness of the near disaster on the river and how Audrey fell in at a time when the rain swell was peaking and the river's course shifting, to the nature of the wavering light she could see within her gift-sight, to how the dull impressions of each thing's touch differed. Among all this scatter and happenstance, the incongruity of the near perfect geometry scribed by that circle of dead powder still sent a flutter of fear through her stomach even as she rolled farther and farther away. Although she lacked the words to explain the return of this ball of fear, she regretted not having mentioned it to Will's aunt. Again her body felt a lurch, but this time it wasn't the car on the highway, it was the thrum within her. The pit in her stomach dissolved as she realized or was guided to realize that Will himself would certainly mention the circle to his aunt and uncle. After all, he had marked the spot, and he wasn't one to forget. *Leave it for now*, she told herself and as the station on the radio began to give way to more and more static, she leaned up and switched it off.

Ten or so minutes later, her dad quietly spoke up, "I wrote you a new song."

"Oh, God," Alexandra half-laughed half-sighed.

"Would you like to hear it?"

"No."

"Here it is then…
I tried to bend my cousin just a little,
But she ended up breaking in the middle.
Busted rib, busted lung,
Poppin' eyes and swollen tongue
What in the world has that girl done?
Just wanted a bit of fun,
When she tried to bend her cousin just a little.

"That's just great, Dad," offered the girl sarcastically. Then as she heard her father take in another deep breath, covered her face with her hands.
Now my auntie doesn't seem too pleased
Having to listen to her own daughter wheeze.
Busted lung, busted rib,
Laid out and needs a bib,

Told the truth when she could have fibbed,
All this fuss, all this muss, all this tattle, all this tittle,
Curse the cousin who won't bend just a little.
Yes, curse all cousins prone to break in their middles.
"Are you done?" she asked flatly.

"Actually, I have seventeen more verses."

"Liar."

"You know, that kind of attitude is not appreciated by the management," Mr. Dwyer whined. He leaned over and squeezed the knee he could reach saying, "We'll talk when you want. You don't have to carry all this on your own."

"I know," she said glad for the gesture, even as she knew how much she would be holding back whenever they sat down to their little heart to heart.

They pulled off the highway for a quick, late lunch, and as they sat across from each other, Alexandra's head suddenly filled with thoughts of Will and his aunt, then of how when she reached to touch the shawl she had seen the old woman's face from before the storm floating on White Feather Woman's face like a translucent mask.

"How much Native American blood is in our family?" Alexandra blurted out to her dad.

"Are cantaloupes cheaper in Maine or Michigan?"

"What?"

"I thought we were trying to see who could ask the most random question."

"Seriously, Dad."

"I have no honest idea. All I know is what I've told you before, that on your grandmother's side someone came back from the north with an Indian wife. So we've got it but not much of it. Why?" He waited out the silence for a short time the offered, "All that running around in the woods make you want a little more?"

After thinking of how convoluted the full answer would be, Alexandra offered a simple, "Yeah."

After what seemed like too little time, Alexandra began to recognize the sights along the highway and the names of the towns listed on the exits. Sooner than she expected they were pulling into the driveway of her mom and step dad's house. Her mother circled around the back of the house to meet them before the car even came to a stop. Suddenly, all Alexandra wanted to do was be with her mom. She was out of the car and in her arms like a shot listening to the familiar coo of her voice and breathing in the familiar perfume of her hair.

"Can we make dinner here," she asked.

"Already started," she said as she pushed her back and held Alexandra at arm's length. "Have you grown?" she asked as if offended.

"You know I'm going to be taller than you," the girl teased gazing into the eyes that almost matched her. People always remarked on how much she looked like her mom. She didn't always see it herself, but at this moment, she hoped it was true.

Alexandra listened to her parents exchange pleasantries and news of the trip and the inevitable update on how Becca and her parents were fairing. Soon she was giving her father another quick hug before he turned the car back toward her other home. Just as he shifted the car into reverse, she remembered her notebook. She gave a shout and waved frantically. He unlocked the doors and watched with a bemused look on his face as she rooted through her backpack until she found the familiar binding of the notebook she wanted.

"Love you," she barked.

"Your cat is fat," he said happily.

"Love you less," she yelled back through the open car windows.

Cy watched the glimmer of confusion on his ex-wife's face. She never liked that kind of teasing. Then he watched his daughter turn her back on his leaving, thinking, *She learned that from me, make the departure seem less present, less real.*

Alexandra found the kitchen full of warmth and the smell of spices. She got a quick kiss on the forehead from her step dad and was put to work dicing scallions for the salad. She repeated the parts of the story that she already practiced on her dad. After dinner her mom made a call to Becca's mom to check in for herself and to let them know that Alexandra was home safe and

213

sound. She reported that all was well, that Becca had maybe another two days in the hospital, and that they expected her to come up again next summer... older and wiser – Alexandra was pretty sure that last remark was her mother's addition. Full and happy from dinner, she helped with the dishes then wandered out onto their back deck to sit and look at the stars. She missed the woods again. The farmland here seemed too flat and the mountains she could see along the Holyoke range were distant and small.

Next summer, she thought then laughed, I don't even want to think about what that will look like.

The thing at the bottom of a lake hundreds of miles north of where a young girl sat on her back deck just beginning to imagine her future wrapped itself in the cold deep water like a cocoon in which to dream a more certain future, one that would enfold all the little two-leggers that had grown so bold. As Matchi Manitou moved back toward its thinking-sleep, it directed its dreams toward the fragment of its spirit left abroad, nestled in a boulder and inured a few specific memories – first and foremost the quality of the pulse which that one little two-legger should never have felt. Sleeping, thinking, dreaming, the thing set these memories across the surface of that boulder, set them like tumblers in a lock waiting to be tickled and aligned, releasing the future it dreamt into being.

Alexandra felt the wear of the past few weeks sink into her body as she watched the details of her familiar world fade into the night. She dozed and snapped awake. Something moved across her backyard. She almost asked for her gift-sight but remembered where she was, remembered White Feather Woman's words to be wise in the use of her vision, remembered the shape of the old possum that crossed their backyard nearly every night as it trekked to forage in the discard left in the fields by the reapers and the migrant farm hands. She decided to wander back inside to find her notebook and add as much to it as she could before falling asleep, but her body was comfortable outside in the night air. Forgetting where she was, one of the adults switched off the kitchen light and immersed Alexandra in near total darkness. She closed her eyes, tilted her head back, and opened them to the great dome of stars. *So little*, Alexandra thought, first of the stars, then of herself.